I0644589

ARAB AMERICAN BLUES

A NOVEL BY PAUL AZIZ ZAROU

Interlink Books
An imprint of Interlink Publishing Group, Inc.
Northampton, Massachusetts

This edition first published in 2026 by

INTERLINK BOOKS
an imprint of Interlink Publishing Group, Inc.
46 Crosby Street
Northampton, MA 01060
www.interlinkbooks.com

Copyright © Paul Aziz Zarou, 2026

Library of Congress Cataloging-in-Publication Data available
ISBN 978-1-62371-563-2

Printed and bound in the United States of America

10 9 8 7 6 5 4 3 2 1

For Mom

Paul Zarou illuminates a rough and tumble neighborhood in Queens in the late 1960s with precision, clarity, and compassion . . . echoes of Philip Roth.

—Steven Schlesser, author of *The Soldier, the Builder & the Diplomat*

Zarou's characters are familiar faces from the old neighborhood: first crushes, overprotective fathers, the bully-gang, mother hens overseeing the block. At the center of a rich tapestry of multi-generational America is Michael Haddad, the son of Palestinian immigrants. His coming-of-age story, set against the turbulent 1960s, widens to encompass the ordinary lives of people we've all known, those who've loved and taught us, those who've gathered us in their folds, and those who've made us suffer. Ultimately, Zarou reminds us of the boundless power of family and friends as we discover who we are.

—Sahar Mustafah, author of *The Beauty of Your Face*

Arab American Blues is an involving, well-told, multi-layered tale of Palestinian immigrants deepening their way into American life. They move from safe, Palestinian Brooklyn to a Queens neighborhood with more opportunity. We see Michael Haddad mature from a fifteen-year-old working in the family grocery store to manhood as an NYU freshman—toughened against neighborhood prejudice, sweetened by a passionate, highly sexual affair with a slightly older woman.

Set in the Vietnam War era, the novel portrays a working-class neighborhood that nurtured young men like Michael but also did its best to hang onto them. Michael does not triumph. Yet, in the end, he manages to break free.

—Frederic Hunter, author of *Kivu: Travels in Eastern Congo 1963–1965*

This is a sensitively-written and heartfelt book about an Arab family pursuing the American Dream in the late 1960s. It's an important story, and I learned a great deal from their travails—both about the complexities of Arab-American identity and about the issues facing all immigrants to this country. In that sense, it's a very timely novel about a subject that needs this kind of in-depth exploration.

—Stephen Fife, author, *The 13th Boy: A Memoir of Education and Abuse*

One

IT WAS A BRICK, STILL LAYERED WITH THE PITTED CRUST OF MORTAR and chipped on one corner. Thrown with reckless anger, the brick hit dead center, collapsing the grocery's large picture window. The shattering glass startled Michael awake some time after 2:00 am. He had been in the middle of a dream, which allowed him to imagine—if for only a couple of fleeting seconds—that he was still back in the comfort of his old bedroom in Brooklyn. Michael's torso tensed and he jerked upright. A sour knot formed in the pit of his stomach at the disquieting realization that the crash that had woken him was the storefront window—the window directly beneath his bedroom. Michael heard muffled hoots and shouts, followed by the sound of skidding tires as a car sped away.

During an oppressive mid-June heat wave, and a week after the Six-Day War, Michael's father had taken ownership of the grocery in Queens Village and moved his family from their Brooklyn neighborhood, where their native Arabic was spoken and everyone was in some way related to each other—if not by blood, then by heritage and community. Palestine, the country that Michael's parents had emigrated from several years before his birth, was now occupied. And in his upstairs apartment bedroom, Michael was just starting to get comfortable in his new surroundings—just beginning to learn how to sleep again.

Michael's father, thick black hair disheveled, jumped out of bed and into his pants and flew down the stairs. Michael trailed after him, but as he took his first step out of their apartment door, his mother—who had hesitated at first—grabbed his arm for balance. As they carefully navigated the narrow staircase, her firm grip tugged on Michael, slowing him, holding him back, as if she didn't want to let him go.

Michael's mother had never spoken about her reluctance to embrace what her husband considered his stake in their future. But Michael, an only child, intuitively knew his mother's emotional undercurrents. He often understood his mother's position on things not by what she said, which was very little on most topics, but by the subtle shades of quiet she slipped into. By measuring the depth and weight of her introspection, he would know when to be concerned.

When his father had announced his purchase of the store, Michael felt her unspoken reluctance by her immediate retreat. But he couldn't discern whether it stemmed from general caution or regret over their savings being sunk into a new business. Perhaps she had received an unsolicited warning from her aunt who read prognostications from the intricate swirls at the bottom of her Arabic coffee cup—which Michael believed his mother wouldn't heed anyway. But as time progressed, whatever it was that was causing her reticence seemed to dissolve, and she moved forward with a renewed acceptance. After all, how could she argue with a husband whose goal was to better their lives?

Michael had forgotten her initial reaction until this moment. As they neared the bottom of the stairs, he turned to look up at her. Her eyes widened and she gave him a slight nod, her best effort at reassuring him. But her small hand nervously clutched his arm, speaking to the contrary. She remained stoic so as not to betray how she really felt. But at fifteen, her son knew better.

The Schaefer light, which hung in the window by two thin wires, was still swinging, unbroken by the impact. The shattered window, jagged edges glistening under the swaying of the fluorescent light, reinforced Michael's sense of exposure. He stood frozen, staring at the black gaping hole, until his father called out, "Come help."

While Michael busied himself sweeping up shards of glass from behind the counter, he spotted a large piece wedged under the worn butcher block that held the cash register. He knelt down awkwardly, and as he stretched an unsteady hand out to reach for it, he caught the sharp edge and sliced his index finger open. Blood oozed to the surface in a thick line that defined the length of the gash. As he stood up and moved his hand to examine the damage, a bright red drop spilled onto the floor and was swallowed up by the porous wood. Michael stuck his finger in his mouth the warm blood tasted sweet as he gently wrapped his tongue around the cut. And as he took that moment to nurse his finger, his nerves let go and he suddenly felt tired, faint. This feeling lasted as long as it took for his mother to splash alcohol over the cut and examine it for slivers of glass.

The 1967 Plymouth police cruiser eased up to the curb across from Haddad's Grocery as if stopping for a routine dinner break. Sergeant Neal McClusky stepped out of the patrol car, followed by a young rookie officer, Phillip Bosco, who lagged several steps behind. McClusky walked right in, but Phillip stayed outside and surveyed the broken window and then, with the beam of his flashlight leading the way, walked the perimeter of the building. When Phillip returned, he hung back and studied the family as intently as he had the broken window.

"Do you have any idea who'd do something like this?" Sergeant McClusky asked.

In his mid-thirties, Sergeant McClusky was fit and had tight, pasty skin that appeared translucent over his sharp features, features that reflected his earnest professional demeanor.

"No," Mr. Haddad said.

McClusky shook his head. "It's unusual. Not something that happens here. It's a good neighborhood."

"What does that mean?"

McClusky, caught a little off guard by the pointed response, stammered a bit and then said, "Uh . . . it's probably just some kids horsing around."

Mr. Haddad didn't appreciate the vandalism to his store being dismissed as "horsing around," but just shook his head.

"We'll keep an eye out," McClusky assured him.

As if suddenly remembering something that he should not have forgotten, Mr. Haddad asked, "Can I get you coffee? From upstairs?" He gestured toward the deli case. "Or a sandwich?"

They politely, and somewhat awkwardly, declined both offers.

"It's no trouble."

Phillip stepped up to the counter. "Can I get a pack of Winstons?" he asked, digging into his uniform pocket to fish out the 39 cents.

Mr. Haddad handed him the cigarettes and then waved him off. "It's okay."

"You sure?" Phillip asked with exaggerated earnestness, trying to assuage an immediate pang of regret. Maybe he shouldn't have asked for the cigarettes. He'd become accustomed to businesses readily handing over a pack of cigarettes or a sandwich or coffee and refusing payment, but he lived in this neighborhood. It was his home. And these were new owners. Despite being in uniform, on official business, walking into this store reminded him of the countless times he'd been there to pick up groceries for his mother. Somehow it didn't feel right to accept Mr. Haddad's gesture, or at least as comfortable as it had with the others.

"Yes. Please, take the cigarettes," Mr. Haddad insisted, nodding reassuringly.

Phillip, still uncertain, held his hand out for a bit longer, cupping the change. Then he slowly stuck his hand back into his pocket and felt the change slip through his fingers and settle at the bottom, next to his extra handcuff key. "Thanks."

McClusky was jotting down some notes on a small pad, and without looking up he asked, "Haddad, would you spell your first name for me?"

"Aziz, A-Z-I-Z."

"Got it." McClusky flipped his pad closed and assured Aziz once again that they'd keep an eye out.

Michael watched as the two officers drove away with more haste than they'd arrived with. Then Michael and his father found a couple of sheets of plywood in the basement and boarded up the window.

Back in his small bedroom, Michael sat down hard on his bed, feeling an uncharacteristic weariness in his young body. He surveyed his small room through the haze of yellow light cast by an old gooseneck lamp on his nightstand. It crossed his mind that maybe he should get up and brush his teeth, but he decided that since he hadn't eaten anything while they were downstairs cleaning up—the few drops of blood from his finger didn't count—and since he had brushed before he went to bed the first time, he didn't need to. Sleep wasn't possible, so Michael reached under his bed and slid out a small cardboard box he still hadn't finished unpacking. He sifted through the various books and keepsakes until he found his worn copy of *Casino Royale.* Michael wished to escape into the world of clear-cut bad guys and a cool good guy who always wins—and beautiful women, of course. But despite his infatuation with James Bond, the words written on the page were out of focus. After rereading the same page three times, he gave up, shut off the light, and just lay there staring at the murky shadows splashed on his gray ceiling until fatigue carried him past the throbbing in his finger and the gnawing in his stomach and he drifted into a fitful sleep.

Aziz Haddad's face was outlined by the dim amber glow of his burning cigarette as he sat in his car, watching over the store for hours into the night. Despite his vigilance, it had happened again. And again. And Michael had received his share of splinters from the plywood they'd used in the late morning hours to secure the broken windows.

Michael's anxiety tempered a little each time they had to clean up glass, and he wasn't sure why this was. Did each subsequent violation make it easier? Maybe he'd grown used to the routine or maybe, at least for the moment, picking up some broken glass was the worst of it.

After the third incident, whoever was breaking their windows finally grew bored and stopped. But for Michael what remained was an underlying foreboding, which would fade with time but never completely leave. Michael had accepted that their lives had changed, but he couldn't foresee the extent to which their lives would become entangled in their new store and the surrounding neighborhood. Michael wanted to believe as his father did, that it was all for the better. But whenever he thought about that night, he could still feel his mother's anxious grip squeezing his arm.

Two

MARY CONTE'S KNIFE HIT THE CUTTING BOARD with experienced rhythm as she chopped away at the green pepper. She was becoming more and more incensed while she shouted in her heavily accented English at her husband, Vinny. "What the hell's wrong with Tony? He's gone dumb! He has no business. No business! He doesn't know what the hell he's doing!" Mary's round, weathered face tightened with indignation as each consecutive slam of the knife hit the cutting board harder than the one before.

"Albert's going sick in his head. Going pazzo! It must be. Otherwise, this'd never happen. Selling to those people . . . Phooey on him!" She feigned spitting on the floor.

Vinny was sitting at the other end of the kitchen table and, accustomed to these tirades, was trying his best not to be sucked into another of his wife's no-win arguments. He held the pages of the Daily News high, blocking himself from her, as if somehow the thin sheets of paper with their black streaky ink could shield him. Vinny felt his face flush and knew he wouldn't be able to help himself. She wouldn't stop until he responded, but responding only made things worse. He lowered the paper just enough for his head to peek out and barked, "Whatdayawant, huh? What? It's not *your* business, it's his. He can do whatever the hell he wants with it! He can burn it down if he wants!"

Mary stopped cold and pointed the sharp knife at him with the same resolute expression she used to discipline her children. "No! He has an obligation to keep it with his own people!"

Vinny stood and raised his voice to match hers. "You don't know what the hell you're talking about! It's his business. He can burn it down if he wants."

"Better! Better he should do that than sell to those people."

Their daughter entered through the side door and stepped into the kitchen. A few months shy of her seventeenth birthday, Maria Conte was an excellent student, so bright that she'd skipped a grade in elementary school. And even back then she'd known better than to get into it with her mother. "Sometimes you too smart for your own good," her mother would say. Maria had overheard what her parents were shouting about as she was coming up the sidewalk—and sided with her father. But while the argument was one she could have enjoyed making, she wanted no part of it.

Maria gave her mother a respectful greeting and started upstairs to her bedroom.

"Hey you! Wait one minute, you!" Mary pulled an envelope out of her smock pocket and thrust it in Maria's face. "What's this—this letter? From this school, this Columbia?" She shook the letter in Maria's face. "What's this nonsense? This college?"

Maria dropped the library books she was carrying and in a single swift motion grabbed the letter from her mother—who was so startled by the aggressive gesture that she allowed the envelope to slip out of her hand without the tug-of-war that would have torn it in half.

"That was addressed to me! You had no business opening my mail!"

Maria surprised herself. Sure, she'd argued with her mother, but never before had she made such a forceful move. Lashing out at someone who deserved it felt good, but it also unnerved her. Even though she knew the stand she was taking was right, she still couldn't help feeling like defying her mother was wrong. Maria had simply given up discussing anything with her mother that she was opposed to, which included most things Maria cared about. Fortunately, Maria had successfully intercepted the previous letters from Columbia, and her acceptance for the fall was assured.

When Mary recovered from her shock, she said, "This is my house, you will not tell me my business. Vincent! Vinny, come here. Talk to your daughter." Vinny looked sheepishly at Maria and got up from the table.

Fifteen years earlier the Contes and their two children, Louie and Maria, had moved into the neighborhood. They were followed by two of Vinny's brothers and their families, Mary's widowed mother (now deceased), and Mary's single sister (who rented someone's basement apartment). It took Vinny's cousin Annette a year to persuade her husband Mario, a union butcher, to join them, but they eventually followed. Though only after Annette's sister Sarafina and her husband Frank Perone moved there with their three children.

It was around this time that Albert opened the grocery store. After ten good years he passed the store on to his oldest son, Tony, so he could retire to Florida, where he had a winter home. But Tony hated the grocery. He didn't have the patience for the long hours and tedious detail. Small grocers didn't have a formal inventory system; they intuitively knew what was needed and how much to order. But Tony never caught on. He would either order too little or order too much, like the time he ordered eight dozen mousetraps. Most of his customers wouldn't buy a mousetrap from him anyway, even if they needed one, for fear that someone in the neighborhood would think they had mice. But most of all, Tony didn't like dealing with the neighborhood people and their small lives. Tony dreamed of making big money. He thought the store was beneath him. So when he'd been approached by Aziz Haddad, he knew it was the perfect opportunity to get out.

Three

When you stepped into Haddad's Grocery, there was a slight incline that caused delivery men to hold on tight to their loaded dollies as they rolled through. To the immediate left was a small freezer that housed ice cream, popsicles, and frozen pastas. And on top of that sat the Daily News, stacked high for easy access by the customers. Where the freezer ended, a counter began, creating an L shape with a slight gap at the corner for easy exit from behind the counter area. This was the checkout counter where shoppers stacked their groceries and the Victor adding machine totaled the items and spit out receipts. The deli case stood where the checkout counter ended, proudly displaying Boar's Head cold cuts—ham, salami, bologna, prosciutto, liverwurst, lean roast beef; Swiss and American cheese; Polly-O mozzarella; and ricotta. Also chilling were pans of green and black olives, and homemade macaroni and potato salads.

Michael waited on customers, stocked shelves, restocked the cooler with beer and soft drinks, swept the floor, sliced cold cuts and made sandwiches for customers, made sure the windows (when not broken) were spotless, wiped down the refrigerators and deli case, cleaned, and then cleaned some more. And at the end of the day, Michael was *tired.* But it was a tired he hadn't felt before his father bought the store, one that brought him a sense of accomplishment, a sense of pride. As summer rolled along, his fear and discomfort over the move were dissolving with each day's routine, and at night he didn't lie awake very long anymore before falling into a deep sleep.

The neighborhood kids, many of them teenagers—bored, angry, with too little to occupy them—wandered in and out aimlessly throughout the summer days. They'd pick up a nickel candy bar or a Coke or some forgotten grocery item: a loaf of bread or quart of milk that their mothers, happy to have them out of the house, had sent them to purchase. Michael would eye them and wonder which ones were involved in breaking the windows.

On one of those humid days where your clothing clung to you like another layer of skin, a few of these kids drifted in and spread out around the store. Michael had just stepped out of the back room and was heading toward the counter where his father was sorting receipts. "Walk around, see what's going on," his father said to him in Arabic.

Michael thought nothing of that. These kids were familiar to him by their daily shopping routine. He recognized customers by what groceries they bought, what cigarettes they smoked, what beer they drank. If asked to pick a face out of a crowd, he could immediately tell you what ends up in a their grocery bag (a half a pound of Genoa salami along with their Italian bread, a quart of Tropicana orange juice, and two packs of Kools) before he could tell you what color hair they had.

Michael walked by the narrow aisle toward the fully stocked white grocery shelves at the opposite end of the store. Joey was the first one Michael encountered as he rounded the aisle, now out of his father's view. Joey was waiting, palming a can of Campbell's soup, his head tilted down on the pretext that he was studying the label. At seventeen years old, Joey Fino was a big boy. He was already six foot three and weighed in at 253 pounds. Everything about him was sloppy, from his greasy brown hair to the way his flabby stomach stuck out from under his shirt and hung over his belt. Joey lifted his head and stuck the can into Michael's face. "See this? I can crush this into your face and there ain't a fucking thing you can do about it."

Michael's throat went dry and his stomach tightened, but he tried to remain calm. He heard himself ask, "What're you looking for?" Seconds after the squeaky words left his mouth, he realized how lame they sounded.

Joey opened his hand and let the can drop, and when Michael's eyes followed the falling can, Joey slammed Michael into the shelves, throwing him off balance and knocking a half-dozen cans of garbanzo beans to the floor. Michael tried pushing back. Joey's thick body didn't budge, but Michael was at least able to keep him at arm's length.

Michael was surprised by his strength. He even *felt* strong. Adrenaline? Fear? He had no idea. He'd always done whatever he could to avoid a fight of any kind, and outside of his imagination, the thought of hitting someone made him feel weak. Since working in the store, though, he'd been getting stronger. The work was developing muscles on his lean frame, and he was able to carry a few cases of beer at a time instead of only one. Now that his world had changed, his body was starting to adapt to the physical demands required of it. It wasn't quite prepared for this large, sweaty man-boy, though.

Joey stuck his face close to Michael's and cocked a fist, readying his punch. When he snarled at Michael, his warm breath was the first assault—it smelled like month-old sour milk and was as off-putting as his threatening fist. "Fuckin' camel jockey."

As soon as those words left Joey's mouth, Billy O'Neil, who was at least a foot shorter than Joey, came up behind them and snapped, "Leave him alone!" Like a trained dog, Joey dropped his fist.

From behind the front counter, Michael's father called out to him in Arabic, "What's going on?"

"Nothing!" Michael shouted back in English.

Joey continued to glower at Michael. And just before he turned to follow Billy out of the store, he muttered "asshole" under his breath and gave Michael a halfhearted shove. A couple of other kids moved to the front of the store and followed them out. It took several moments for Michael to compose himself. He scooped up the cans that were on the floor and lined them up neatly, hiding the dented can of soup in the back of the shelf. His stomach was tight and his hands were shaky. He stuck them in his pockets and walked up to the front.

"What's happened? What was that?" Michael's father asked, now in English.

"Nothing! It was nothing," Michael said as he made his way to the cooler. He slid the window open, took a bottle of Yoo-hoo out and shook it, then reached in his pocket for his bottle opener and popped the cap. The long drink of sugary chocolate calmed him a bit. His father kept eyeing Michael until he was distracted by a customer.

Roy Orbison's "Oh, Pretty Woman" was playing on the small clock radio that sat behind the counter on the shelf next to the Bayer Aspirin. Michael forced himself not to listen. He liked this song. He didn't want it associated with this incident. He didn't want it to be a reminder of the weakness he felt.

"I'm going to fill the box," Michael announced and thundered down the basement stairs. Musty and dank, the small basement was a cool dark place where Michael could retreat to collect his thoughts, or just isolate himself. He sat on a stack of beer and finished his Yoo-hoo, fighting off tears, confused by the overwhelming frustration and fear that welled up and choked him. "Stupid, fat fuck," Michael mumbled under his breath. "He doesn't scare me."

Four

"You look like a girl," Michael's father snapped at him in Arabic as Michael kneeled in front of the cooler, replacing six-packs of Rheingold beer. He had been stretching the time between haircuts, wanting to look more like his peers than someone fresh out of boot camp. Short and regular. That was the haircut Michael was always told to get. And before the British Invasion, he'd thought nothing of this. But now his thick hair had become a symbol of potency, of independence, of expression. He already felt self-conscious and out of step, and short hair exacerbated those feelings. Michael needed to hold on to every inch of hair as much as President Johnson needed to figure out how to win the war in Vietnam.

It was a dividing point between him and his father. Johnson had much better odds. And after continued harassment, Michael agreed to get a trim.

Vinny the barber worked out of his basement a couple of blocks away from the store. Michael's unenthusiastic pace eventually brought him to the front of a large two-story house whose street number matched the one scribbled on the scrap of adding machine paper. He knocked on the front door, and Maria Conte slid it open, her large brown eyes landing on Michael with surprise. "Yeah?"

Michael locked eyes with her and lost his ability to speak. He couldn't seem to put the right words together to explain why he'd knocked on her door, but Maria came to his rescue. "Oh. You want my dad." She pointed to the side of the house. "Over there. You'll find the basement door."

Michael nodded and mumbled, "Thanks," under his breath and backed off the stoop. As he made his way to the basement, the image of Maria stuck in his head. He always noticed her when she came into the store to shop. She was probably at least a year older than he was, and she was clearly different than the other girls in the neighborhood, more serious. She was attractive in a subtle but intriguing way, her light, creamy complexion offset by thick, short black hair. And whenever Michael saw her, he couldn't help noticing her breasts—not just how they seemed out of place on her slight frame, but the way they curved softly upward—even though she tried to hide them under dark, loose-fitting tops.

The barber chair sat in the middle of the room, directly across from a wide round mirror and a credenza that held Vinny's bottles of hair elixirs. A few worn chairs were lined up against the paneled wall, and next to them some dog-eared magazines were piled high on a small table.

Vinny was a slight, frail man with a full shock of white hair and slow, deliberate movements, all of which made him appear older than his age, and his cigar habit had stained the middle portion of his white mustache a dirty brown. Michael sat down in the barber chair, and Vinny wrapped thin tissue paper around his neck, draped a smock over his shoulders, and clipped it on—all while dangling a smelly, crooked cheroot out of his mouth. With nowhere else to go, the smoke hovered in the room, forming a gray cloud just below the ceiling.

"This wasn't my idea, so just a trim, okay?" Michael said and then added, "Don't take a lot off." And then, without a moment's hesitation, Vinny took the trimmer to Michael's hair as if he were an Army barber shearing the head of a new recruit. Michael couldn't believe what he was witnessing in the mirror; he felt like he'd entered the *Twilight Zone*. He turned to face Vinny, desperate to say something, but his mouth went dry and nothing came out. Vinny firmly twisted Michael's head back, as if Michael were a petulant, fidgety child that wouldn't allow him to do his work. Michael turned again, causing Vinny to stop abruptly. "What? Whatdayawant?"

But Michael couldn't speak. He just stared in the mirror at his half-shaven head as the overwhelming feeling of having lost something—something irretrievable—sank in. His Sunday school lesson about Samson and Delilah came to mind. A burning sensation traveled from his nasal passages to his eyes, filling them with tears that he desperately worked to hold back.

When Vinny finished, Michael felt like a little boy. It wouldn't have surprised him if Vinny handed him a lollypop.

Michael's hair would eventually grow back to a length that made him feel a little more like he belonged to his generation, but from that point on, he never looked at a haircut the same way. When forced to get a cut, he'd visit the barbershop in the Village. It was less convenient, but the barbers had better hearing.

Five

"TREAT THEM LIKE SHIT—like you don't give a fuck about em'—and they'll keep coming back," Billy said.

"Why the hell would they keep coming back?" Michael asked.

"They just do. Treat em' nice and they fuck you over."

"That doesn't make any sense."

"It's true. It's the way it is," Billy said.

Michael was skeptical, but Billy remained steadfast about his theory. Michael knew that Billy had much more experience than he did, but this one he just wasn't buying.

Billy O'Neil was the neighborhood boys' unspoken leader, which is why he'd been able to stop Joey from hitting Michael. Billy had just turned nineteen, passed his civil service test, and been hired by the Post Office. He often stopped by the store after finishing his route and bought beer for his younger friends, for a fee of course, and the fee was a two for one—they paid for two six-packs and he kept one. He'd share his street-savvy logic with them, steering them in the ways of petty crime, often to do his bidding. (In fact, Michael thought that Billy was probably one of the kids "horsing around" who had broken their windows earlier that summer.) One of those younger boys was Billy's brother Andy, or Jelly as he was known. Jelly was a year and a half younger and barely making it through high school. Although lean now, as a little boy he'd had a weight problem that manifested in a big (jelly) belly. That—combined with his love of jelly sandwiches (where more jelly ended up on his face than in his mouth)—garnered him the nickname, which stuck.

Billy liked to linger and try to engage Michael in conversation, talk that ultimately focused on sex. Billy would boast of his latest conquests, and if they were alone, he'd share the details—which girls in the neighborhood he'd "fucked," and which ones gave blowjobs. And more important, how he would get them to do whatever he wanted.

Michael's father was polite to Billy, but when he was alone with Michael, he labeled Billy a "bullshitter."

"You'll run into many people like Billy in your life," Michael's father advised him. "They're good-for-nothings. They're full of talk, but do nothing. Don't believe anything he tells you." His father would use Billy and others as examples to educate Michael about people. Every chance he could, he'd define for Michael the differences between those who had ambition and those who did not. His father was determined to teach Michael that he belonged to a different world, a world with higher expectations. It was often subtle, but always calculated to put pressure on Michael to perform—which it did. His father wasn't always long on explanations, but his comments would hang in the air the way contrails remained in the sky long after the aircraft had flown by. Comments that provoked Michael to think. Like the time a well-dressed businessman had stopped in for a pack of cigarettes: his father had asked Michael if he'd noticed how clean the man's hands were. The question came after the customer had already left, but it prompted Michael to look at his own hands, which were dirty from having been downstairs cleaning the basement.

But despite his father's warnings, Michael found Billy engaging. To Michael he seemed credible, at least most of the time. And when he lied, it was entertaining, like the one about how he beat the draft. He had broken his left elbow pretty badly, almost lost his arm. Billy's version of events was that it had happened when he was playing football. As he had extended his arms to make a catch, two players had tackled him, and as they slammed him to the ground, his arm was bent the wrong way and his elbow snapped. Ever since that injury, he hadn't been able to stretch his arm out all the way. And that was how, he would proudly exclaim, he'd received his medical deferment from the draft.

It wasn't clear to Michael whether Billy fabricated those stories to polish his image or to hide the truth. Maybe it was both. His father had busted his arm. Bernard O'Neil drank, and when he did, he'd use his family as punching bags. He'd perfected his brutal style, using an open hand when hitting their faces, but a tight fist when pounding their bodies. As Billy and Jelly grew older, the beatings stopped, but only because Billy could now stand up to Bernard, giving better than he got. To which his father would comment, "At least I made a man out of you, not like that weak, sissy-ass, momma's-boy brother of yours."

Billy and Jelly's mother, Lucy (an Americanization for Lucia), was an Italian girl from the neighborhood. Billy looked like his dad: wiry and fair, dirty-blond hair worn short, and watery blue eyes that would dance when he became animated. He often came into the store wired, talking a mile a minute, and Michael would notice his glazed eyes bouncing all over like those cheap rubber balls kids would smack against the brick wall of the store. Slightly darker, Jelly had his mother's olive complexion, light brown hair, and green eyes. Jelly was a quiet kid, compliant. He faded into the background and always followed his brother's lead.

Martha Filomina arrived every morning at 10:00 am to purchase her large bottle of Rheingold, every day except Sunday. On Saturday morning, Martha bought two bottles to avoid the blue laws that would have forced her to wait until noon on Sunday.

She was in her early sixties and had stooped shoulders and a tired face, but she was feisty. Her grandson, Jack Jr.—"affectionately" known as J.J.—lived with Martha, along with his parents and sister, which only added to her crankiness. At seven, J.J. was a scruffy little juvenile-delinquent-in-training who would run into the store on a dare, grab something off an accessible shelf—a bag of Wise potato chips, a Devil Dog—and run out the door screaming obscenities like, "Fuck you, fuck you, fuck you!" or his favorite refrain, "Camel jockey assholes, go back to the desert!" The first time this happened, Michael just stood there in shock, watching as this child spewed his hateful diatribe. Once Michael snapped out of it, he chased J.J. out into the street. But his father called out for Michael to stop, and he put the brakes on just short of nabbing the little thief. "What are you going to do after you catch him?" his father asked. It was a good question—even though Michael wanted to smack the kid around, he knew better.

So they would just tell J.J.'s grandmother what the damages were, and she'd apologize, pay for whatever he took, and then add, shaking her head, "They can't do a thing with that boy. I'll tell his dad. He'll take care of him." From the bruises J.J. sometimes had when he came in, his father tried. But it didn't seem to make much difference.

It was J.J. who gave John Harris his first introduction to the neighborhood. On one of his grab-and-run attacks, J.J. ran right smack into John as the man was about to step into the store. John picked J.J. up by the shirt and dragged him back in.

"Now, put it on the counter," John commanded, while Michael and his father watched. J.J. glared at John, who still had a grip on his shirt, and said, "Fuck you," and tried to squirm away. He appeared fearless against this big stranger. John lifted J.J. up, face-to-face this time, and said again, very sternly, "Put it on the counter."

With all the defiance his seven-year-old body could muster, J.J. squeezed the stolen Devil Dog, and then let it drop on the counter. John lowered J.J. back down. The kid's head barely reached the counter.

"Okay, now apologize," John said.

"Fuck you."

John bent down to meet J.J. eye to eye. "Now listen, son, if you want to get out of here without me calling the police, you'd better apologize."

J.J. gave some thought to this and then belligerently shouted, "Sorry!"

Michael had to stop himself from cracking up.

"Good," John said. J.J. started to take off, but John grabbed him again.

"Wait." John reached into his pocket and pulled out a nickel, which he put on the counter. He picked up the Devil Dog and handed it to J.J. and said, "Here, this is what you came in for." J.J. was stunned. He wasn't quite sure what to do, and he wondered what the catch was. He expected one of the other adults to speak up and say, "No, don't let him have it." But when Michael and his father just stood there and said nothing, he scooped up the Devil Dog, stuck his tongue out at them, and ran out. John shook his head and said, "Tough little bastard—kids today, no respect." Michael's father picked up the nickel and handed it back to John.

"Hold on a second," John said as he walked over to the cold beer and took out a six-pack of Rheingold. "How much more do I need for this?"

John was a New York Transit Authority mechanic, and had just finished moving his wife and young son into the house he'd bought using his VA benefits. He'd paid a little over twenty-one thousand dollars for the three-bedroom house. John was clean-cut and disciplined, and a peek in his toolbox would reveal shiny, clean tools organized neatly in their designated compartments. At one point he'd given serious consideration to making the Army his career, but when his wife became pregnant, he didn't re-enlist. John had a rugged handsomeness to him, but his enjoyment of beer was causing him to sprout an out-of-character but well-defined beer belly. His sandy hair was cropped close, a remnant from his Army days, low maintenance. And when Michael first met him, he couldn't help thinking that John would have no problem with one of Vinny's haircuts.

Six

DISTANT RELATIVES BOUND BY BLOOD or mere geography—men making their way, traveling absent their families—arrived with few resources, at the goodwill of their hosts. At their old apartment, these men (Michael called them "live-in relatives") had slept on the sofa and lived with his family for the time it took them to find jobs, start school, establish themselves, or move on. Michael's mother picked up after them, did their laundry, fed them—and never complained. Cigarettes piled up in ashtrays until she cleaned them. Often the men didn't help her even if they were home all day. Michael watched, harboring an unspoken resentment at their indifferent expectation that his mother was supposed to do these things.

In late August Fareed arrived—or Freddie as he was called—another cousin. Actually, he was the nephew of the wife of one of Michael's father's first cousins. Having just graduated from American University in Beirut with an engineering degree, he enthusiastically arrived in the United States with dreams of working for an auto company. He was headed to Detroit, where he was going to stay with an uncle while he pursued a job. His stopover in New York was something of a holiday for him after five years of school.

Michael realized Freddie was different the first morning of his stay. When Michael got up, Freddie had already neatly folded the sheets and blankets from the sofa where he'd slept. And not only was he dressed and ready, but he'd made the coffee while everyone else was still sleeping. If his ashtray had more than two cigarette butts, he'd empty it. Freddie was mannerly, polite, and not only did he help around the apartment, he was happy to give them a hand in the store as well. Michael's mother engaged Freddie in conversation in ways that Michael hadn't seen her do with the other men that stayed with them, and she prodded Michael to do the same, to speak with him about school and his life in the old country. Michael was convinced his mother was hoping Freddie's behavior would rub off on him.

After they closed the store on Sunday they took Freddie to the City for some sight-seeing. They visited the Empire State Building, Rockefeller Center, Times Square, and they drove past the Statue of Liberty on their way to Brooklyn to have dinner with relatives. Lively discussions about the young girls Freddie should meet ensued. Freddie politely dismissed the idea, but was promptly lectured about the importance of finding a nice girl.

Yvonne, a very attractive distant cousin who Michael knew and liked came to mind, but he didn't say anything. Michael liked Freddie, but resisted the idea of him and Yvonne together—as if by not suggesting it, Yvonne's ultimate destiny would be delayed and she'd somehow be there for him.

After his parents went to bed, Michael and Freddie stayed up and talked.

"Do you play football?" Freddie asked.

"Football?" Michael was surprised by the question, because Freddie didn't look like a football player. Freddie had a slight build, was only about five feet eight, 140 pounds. But he was fit and handsome and had a gentle manner. A pretty boy. His hands impressed

Michael; they were clean and unblemished, well manicured and refined. That was it—Freddie was *refined*. Michael understood why Freddie's parents were proud of him. Michael wondered if he would project that kind of refinement when he was older, but decided that he probably had a long way to go.

"You know. You kick with your feet into the net," Freddie said.

"Oh. Soccer. No, I don't play. It's not very popular here. My dad said he used to play when he was in school. The other football is popular here. You know, where you hold the ball and run, and everyone tries to tackle you."

Michael wanted to talk about girls, so he changed the subject. "Do you have a girlfriend back home?"

"I did in school. Not now."

"What was she like? Your girlfriend."

"Smart. She was very bright. She was fun."

"Was it hard to leave her?"

"Sure, a little. But when it's time, I'll go back and find a nice girl to marry."

Michael knew Freddie said that because he'd grown up in Palestine, but he still couldn't understand why some of his peers who grew up in America felt the same way. Michael wanted to bring up sex, but had a difficult time being so direct, especially because Freddie lacked the crudeness of the guys Michael hung out with around the store.

Finally Michael summoned the nerve and asked Freddie if he'd ever slept with his girlfriend. Freddie grinned shyly and said, "That's something a man doesn't talk about if he respects himself and the girl he's with." Michael was even more impressed, but he still didn't want to introduce him to Yvonne.

For Jamila Haddad, cooking was a creative outlet. She didn't view it as the chore that her sisters sometimes complained about. She'd learned young that a well-prepared meal was a simple gift that she could share with those she cared about. She relished the joy her husband and son took from what she served them. She was bold in her use of spices and had learned that careful preparation was the secret to melding flavors—and the difference between food that tasted flat and thrown together and meals that others savored. But her pleasure also came from feeling the food pass through her hands as she shaped the meat, rice, vegetables—or whatever she was preparing—into their final form of epicurean delight. Michael was a challenge, because even though he enjoyed what she made, he wasn't a big eater. And her husband, who early in their marriage had appreciated her gift, was now so often distracted that he took it for granted. It was only when company was invited over that she had the opportunity to serve an Arabic feast for whatever meal she was preparing.

The morning after Michael's talk with Freddie, his mother prepared breakfast. It was Freddie's last day with the Haddads, and she put out the *za'atar*—a traditional blend of coarsely ground thyme mixed with sesame seeds and other herbs that Freddie had brought them from Ramallah—when she put out the maza. Michael loved the ritual of dipping a piece of pita bread soaked in olive oil into a plate of *za'atar*, and enjoyed the rich, slightly tangy taste. His mother also set out plates of dips and appetizers, including *hummus*, *baba ghannouj*, *ful mudammas*, Arabic cheese, pickled beets, olives, and *labni*—a creamy yogurt spread. She fried the falafel and warmed up the pita bread. And even having made all that, she still offered to prepare them eggs, which everyone declined. So she poured the Arabic coffee and prepared some eggs anyway. Freddie insisted that she sit down and join them at the table. "*Sallim dayki,*" he said, complimenting her for the meal. Freddie then offered to help clean up, but she insisted she'd take care of it, so Michael, his father, and Freddie went downstairs to open the store.

The morning started out a bit slow, but when Joey Fino came in, Michael sensed that it would soon change. Michael's father had left to make a quick run to the bakery to pick up cookies and some loaves of Italian bread they were running short on, and Freddie had stepped into the back room to use the bathroom. Joey passed the counter and mumbled, "Marlboro box."

Whenever Joey suspected that Michael was alone, he'd seize the opportunity to give him a hard time. He seemed to enjoy testing Michael's limits, especially if he had a few friends with him. He'd toss grocery items in the air, posture like he was about to catch them, and then at the last minute step aside, letting them hit the floor. He once did that with a dozen eggs, leaving Michael to clean up the mess. Another time, he'd boldly come around the counter and tried to open the cash register. Michael had shoved him away from the register, pushing as hard as he could and yelling for him to get out, but it wasn't until a customer walked in that Joey stopped taunting Michael and ran out.

Joey appeared especially disgruntled this morning. Unshaven and with his stained and wrinkled shirttail hanging out, he looked like he'd either slept in his clothes or hadn't slept at all. He was sweaty and reeked of last night's alcohol. "What the fuck you looking at?" he barked at Michael as he headed for the beer. Michael knew better than to respond. Joey grabbed a six-pack of Rheingold and ripped a can out of the cardboard, opened it, and started guzzling.

"You can't drink that in here!" Michael shouted.

Joey sauntered back to the counter. "What the fuck are *you* going to do about it?" He took another swallow from his can.

Good question, Michael thought, and put the remaining beer and cigarettes in a bag.

"A dollar ninety-seven," Michael said, hoping Joey would pay and get out.

Joey sneered at Michael and took his time polishing off his beer. Michael could read Joey's simple mind; he was debating whether to pay him or not.

Freddie came in from the back, walked around the counter, and stood next to Joey. Joey was at least five inches taller and a hundred pounds heavier than Freddie, but Freddie was glaring at him, not intimidated.

"What the fuck you looking at?" Joey snarled. Freddie didn't respond, so Joey turned to Michael. "This one of your camel jockey cousins?"

"Just give me the money and leave," Michael said.

Joey ignored Michael and directed his attention to Freddie. "You look like a little faggot. Are you a fag?"

"Pay what you owe and leave," Freddie said in his thick Arab accent.

"A *queer* camel jockey," Joey taunted.

Freddie slid the bag over to Michael and said to Joey, "Just go, we don't want your business." But as Freddie turned to look at Michael, Joey grabbed Freddie and put him in a headlock and shouted, "You little fuck, whatcha gotta say now?"

"Joey! Let him go!" Michael rounded the counter and scooped up a small boning knife that was lying by the slicing machine. He ran up to Joey and waved the knife in the air. "Let him go!"

Joey sneered. "Whatdaya think ya gonna do with that?"

Michael glanced down at the knife and asked himself the same question. His hand was shaking.

"Let him go!" he shouted again in desperation.

"Go ahead. Stick me. I dare you," Joey said.

Freddie was struggling to break free and his face was turning red. Joey squeezed even tighter. Michael wanted to stab him, but he was paralyzed. Just as Michael let go of his fear and was lifting the knife to plunge it into Joey's arm, Martha Filomina opened the front door and screamed, "Joey!"

Her high-pitched squeal caught Joey by surprise, and as he turned to look, he slightly released his hold on Freddie—just enough for Freddie to twist out from under him and knee him in the groin. Joey hit the floor, writhing in pain.

Freddie was gasping for breath and rubbing his sore neck as Martha scurried over to where Joey lay on the floor, moaning. She continued to berate him. "What the hell's the matter with you? Wait till I tell your mother . . . You're nothing but a common hoodlum!"

Michael saw John Harris tie his German shepherd to the mailbox out front and then step inside.

"What happened?" John asked with genuine concern.

Joey got up slowly, clearly still in serious pain. Michael was still clutching the knife.

"Joey's giving us trouble," Michael spit out.

"Fuck all of you," Joey muttered, and stumbled toward the door. He turned, scowled, and then pointed his index figure at Michael. "I'll get you, fucker! Count on it. I'm gonna fuck you up!"

John's jaw tightened—the veins on his neck were popping out. "Get the fuck outta here," he snapped at Joey. "And don't come back. If you do, you'll answer to me." Joey eyeballed John and slithered out the door. When he got outside, John's dog growled at him and barked viciously. While John went out to settle his dog, Martha went over to the beer case to get her two bottles.

Michael could still feel his heart in his throat, pounding rapidly. His hand was clenched so tightly around the knife, his fingers were turning blue. Freddie had already regained his composure and asked for the knife, so Michael relaxed his grip—and as he handed it to Freddie, he could see a clear imprint of the knife's handle on his palm.

Freddie was flying to Detroit that afternoon. Michael's father agreed to drive him to the airport, but not until he asked Jeannie, a young neighborhood housewife who worked for them part time, to work with Michael for the hour he'd be gone. Michael, still raw from the morning's drama, fell into an even deeper gloom after saying goodbye. For a brief time he'd gotten to experience what it would be like to have an older brother. Michael wrestled with that thought, then decided that an older brother like Freddie would have been a hard act to follow. As it was, Michael was pretty sure he wasn't measuring up to his father's expectations. At least Freddie had promised to write and stay in touch.

Phillip Bosco stopped by for some groceries the day after the run-in with Joey, and Michael's father explained what had happened and asked what they should do. Phillip said he'd set Joey straight the next time he saw him, but that they probably wouldn't have to worry about Joey for a long time. Apparently, he'd enlisted in the Navy the day before the incident because he was afraid of being drafted. Michael immediately hoped Joey's ship would sink, but then realized that wouldn't be fair to the other sailors. So he wished someone would push him overboard instead.

Seven

Sarafina Perone called the store and asked if Michael could bring over a few items, including two cans of plum tomatoes, since she was in the middle of preparing dinner and couldn't leave. She was recently widowed, her husband Frank having died the previous year, so Michael agreed, and after that word got out somehow that he was making deliveries to some of their better customers. At first, the idea of running around the neighborhood carrying bags of groceries didn't appeal to Michael. But the tips weren't bad, and he liked earning his own money. Plus, he had to admit that on a long day, getting out was a nice break.

Shuffling back from one of these deliveries, feeling the cracks of the concrete sidewalk under his feet, Michael passed by John Harris's house and was struck by a sight that he had a hard time pushing out of his head. Despite its masculine, polished presence, it wasn't John's bright candy-apple-red 1964 Pontiac GTO coupe that stood like a proud trophy in his driveway that grabbed Michael's attention—Michael had often seen John tucked under the open hood tinkering with his 389 cubic-inch engine. No, it was the child in John's front window. Michael slowed his pace to watch the little boy peering out at him. He looked small standing in the big picture window, a sorrowful expression on his face. Michael realized he didn't know the boy's name, had never even met him. John would occasionally buy candy, but he never brought his son to the store to let him choose for himself like all the other young kids did. Seeing him there made him real to Michael. It touched him, affecting him in a way that he couldn't quite explain.

Later that day, Michael was working with his mother at the store. His father had left to make a quick run to the wholesalers to buy the cigarettes they were out of, including the brand he smoked, L&M.

Michael's mother was straightening out the area behind the counter. Whenever they didn't have customers to wait on she kept herself busy, perhaps to distract herself from being there or to make time pass more quickly. But whatever the reason, she couldn't stand still. The area around the cash register, which sat on an old butcher block in front of the Hobart slicing machine, was a collection point for the paper receipts gathered from the day's deliveries. She sorted through them and carried them to the back room, stuffed them into an envelope, and stuck it into the desk drawer. Then she headed back in with a damp towel to clean the deli case.

"So, Ma, how do you like working the store?" Michael asked. "Does it beat sitting behind a sewing machine all day?"

"There's advantages to both," she replied.

"What could possibly be the advantage of being hunched over a sewing machine all day?"

"That depends."

"Depends . . . on what?" Michael asked. "That's such boring work. At least here you're out, you get to talk to people."

"Remember that blue suit? Last Easter?" she asked casually, as she continued to work.

"I love that suit."

"I made it for you. I enjoyed making it. What do you make here?"

This stopped him for a minute, and he studied her as she was wiping down the front window of the deli case.

"I get it . . . I guess. But there is one thing I get to make."

His mother turned to him. "What?"

"Sandwiches, I get to make all kinds of sandwiches."

She smiled. "You know what your father would say?"

"No. What?"

"Money. That's what *he* gets to make." She gave him a satisfied smirk as she folded her towel. "It's quiet. I'm going. If you need me, call." She made her way to the back door.

"Okay," Michael said. "I really love that suit!" he called after her. And even though she didn't turn to look back at him, he could tell that his comment made her smile by the slight tilt of her head.

A few minutes after his mother left, Angela Russo breezed into the store, accompanied by her aunt, Donna. Seeing her only a couple of feet away stunned the breath out of Michael, and as she walked past him, he was reminded of the first time he saw her.

Michael had been stocking the shelves from a delivery of canned goods from their supplier, Krasdale, and had one last case of corn waiting for him. His fingers were stained dark, an occupational hazard of using the price stamper. If he didn't position the stamper on top of the can evenly and snap down with the right amount of pressure, the price would come out smeared or only a portion of the price would print. An eighty-nine could come out looking like two half-finished zeros, irritating his father to no end.

Michael was pretty fast and could stack a case of canned goods, label facing front, in record time. But that day, Michael was in no hurry. He was enjoying the lyrics of "Can't Buy Me Love" as it played on the radio, and he decided he *liked* how the ink looked on his skin. It reminded him of the faded tattoos some of the men had emblazoned on their arms.

Michael was holding a razor, ready to cut open his last case, when he turned his head in her direction. Her back was toward him. She was facing the counter and her lustrous long black hair hung straight to the middle of her back and swayed as she moved her head. Michael figured she was probably gorgeous, and as she turned to face him, he flushed with all the hormonal energy a sixteen-year-old could produce. She was everything he'd hoped for: light olive skin, chocolate-brown eyes, full lips, a petite frame.

Everything moved in slow motion as Michael shifted into automatic and continued his work. He kneeled and swiftly dragged the razor through the side of the cardboard box, toward himself, and the razor flew off the end of the box, slicing into his leg like a steak knife through a rare filet.

It was at that moment that Michael and Angela first made eye contact. She smiled at him, and Michael felt no pain. Then she'd turned and vanished as the blood surfaced, soaking his pants.

She was just as beautiful as he remembered. It was amazing how well—with only a glance—he had captured her in his mind. He'd seen her aunt come in on a number of occasions. She was one of those customers who did their major shopping at the A&P in the Village but stopped in Haddad's for items she'd run out of or forgotten.

Michael was in a trance; he couldn't stop himself from staring. It was painfully obvious that Angela noticed, and she blushed as she approached the counter with a quart of milk. Her aunt met her there with a pound box of sugar and a five-pound bag of flour. "Angela, are we forgetting anything?"

Angela, though flattered by Michael's attention, was feeling self-conscious, and was glad for the brief distraction of her aunt's question.

"Do we need eggs?" Angela asked, knowing full well that they didn't.

"No, I think we have enough," her aunt replied. She looked at Michael and said, "That's it."

Angela noticed that Michael's fingers fumbled as he punched the numbers into the adding machine. He had to do it twice before he had the correct total.

"A dollar thirty-nine," he said in a tone that was barely audible as he bagged the items.

Angela's aunt handed the money to Michael, suppressing a smile at his obvious shyness. Michael made change and said, in a voice still slightly above a whisper, "Thank you."

After they'd walked several feet outside the door, Angela's aunt turned to her. "He's kinda cute."

Angela shrugged.

"I guess."

Eight

When Maria arrived home for Thanksgiving break, her mother greeted her with, "You no look good. Skinny. You look like you're not getting any sleep." Then she added, "This school, this Columbia, not good for you."

It had taken Maria's older brother many attempts before he finally convinced their mother to let her attend Columbia. Even his offer to help out financially was rebuffed at first. Louie was twelve years older than Maria and a successful real estate developer in New Jersey, and he'd told their mother that she should feel proud that her daughter was smart enough to attend such a prestigious university and that he expected his children to attend college, including his daughter. And while at first she didn't want to hear it, Maria's mother had finally agreed, grudgingly, to let her go.

A "Welcome home, Maria" would have been nice. Most students at Columbia held their parents in contempt for being part of the establishment, but Maria's mother didn't represent that for her. Her mother was just stuck in time, a throwback to a place too long ago to resemble anything like today's repressive establishment.

Maria found Columbia to be mostly what she'd hoped for, but upon her initial plunge into school, her insecurities had surfaced—at times consuming her. As much as she'd desperately wanted out of her mother's house, living under her mother's indefatigable shadow had done little to prepare her for the real world. Maria wasn't as emotionally ready as she'd wanted to believe. Also, she was younger than most of the other students and, at times, felt alienated and inexperienced.

On her first day, as she listened to her humanities professor lecture on Homer, Maria had surveyed the fresh faces of the other students in the large lecture hall and noticed that the clean-cut, khaki-wearing students were outnumbered by the long-haired, jeans-clad hippie students. She'd wondered which ones felt like her—out of place.

But her real education had come a week after she'd settled into the dorm with Susan, her roommate from Mill Valley, California. It was sometime after 1:00 am, and Susan was not in her bed. Maria was experiencing a fitful night and was beginning to wonder if she should worry about Susan—as if somehow she should be responsible for this relative stranger—when the door creaked open and she heard the sloppy whispers of Susan and some skinny guy creeping into the room. Maria froze.

"Is she cool?" the guy whispered.

"Shush. Be quiet and don't wake her," Susan said.

Maria, still a virgin, had to listen to their sexual fumbling: wet kisses, clothing being stripped off, the guy pushing Susan forcefully onto the bed. Susan's bedsprings squeaked loudly several times in rapid succession and the guy made some noises—"Ah . . . oh . . . oh"—and then moaned loudly. "Oh fuck . . . you were fucking amazing," he said.

"Shush. Jesus, be quiet!" Susan said. She pushed him off the bed and his bony body fell to the floor with a thud.

Maria went from feeling embarrassed terror to finding this

whole situation absurdly funny. She couldn't stop herself from giggling out loud, which tickled Susan, who joined Maria in laughing at her indiscretion and subsequent indignation.

"What? What did I do?" the guy asked, still sitting on the floor.

Susan picked his shirt off her bed with two fingers—as if picking up a dirty, wet towel—and flung it at him. "Just leave, okay? Can you at least do *that* quietly?"

He slid his pants on, balled up his shirt in his hand, and slunk to the door. He hesitated before opening it. "Can I see you again?"

"Are you really asking me that? First let's see if you can sneak out of here without getting us kicked out of school."

He stood there a moment, not sure what to make of her answer, and then cracked open the door and slipped out.

"No more freshmen," Susan said, and turned onto her side and went to sleep.

After that Maria had a new best friend. Her determination resurfaced, overriding her fear and discomfort, and she began to settle in and establish a routine. She exercised the discipline required to manage her workload, and when she found that she could compete, her uncertainty slowly evaporated, replaced by a newfound confidence. She and Susan came to an understanding about the guys they could and should invite into their room, and before she knew it, her life had transformed into a world a thousand miles and years away from the one she'd left—although on bad days doubt would still creep in like a spider in the bathtub.

Now that Maria was back at home, she had a hard time sitting still. Even to read, which had been her one reliable way to escape.

The shrill sound of her mother yelling out her name made her nauseous: "Maria, Maria, come now! Maria, I waiting . . . Maria! I show you, you learn. A girl needs to cook or she's no use." Maria took secret pride in burning every dish her mother tried to teach her to make.

At night in bed, Maria would hold her pillow to her face and scream into it with all she had, hoping it would help tire her out so she could fall into the sleep that had eluded her since returning home. And during the day, she took long walks around the neighborhood in the cold weather, lingering at the corner grocery or at the Woolworths in the Village.

Maria had been conspiring with Louie on how they could persuade their parents to move close to him, in Jersey. Then maybe Maria wouldn't be expected to come home so often. But her mother was resistant; she didn't want Vinny to quit working, afraid that having him underfoot would make her crazy, or worse, kill him. To shut her kids up, she'd told them she'd consider it in the summer, saying "Be quiet until then, okay?"

The day before she returned to school, Maria went down to the basement and sat in her father's barber chair, watching him tidy up the bottles of hair elixirs, shears, and razors. Vinny seemed to have aged faster than the few months that she'd been gone. He looked older than she remembered and was moving slower. "You like college?" her father asked.

"Yeah, Pop, I like college a lot."

"Good," he said.

She wished for more conversation, but it just wasn't there.

Nine

Michael's deliveries had become more frequent, and he welcomed the opportunity to get out of the store and walk around the neighborhood. It was interesting to peer inside people's homes, to see how other families lived. Some customers grabbed the grocery bag from Michael at the door, but others welcomed him in and offered him a drink or snack. The homes and families were an assortment, from the calm to the chaotic, and often the members of large extended families lived crowded together in boisterous bedlam, filling their homes with a familial energy.

What was left of the sun's light peaked scarlet and there was a chilly dampness in the air as Michael walked the familiar streets, his mind enjoying the opportunity to wander without distraction. He was making one last quick delivery. He brushed aside a pang of urgency over the algebra test he had the next day—that he still needed to study for—and stepped off the curb. He didn't hear the person running up from behind until it was too late.

Joey Fino slammed into Michael as hard as he could, carried by the momentum of his 250-plus pounds of body weight. It was a brutal hit, backed by pent up fury, by months of replaying his embarrassment and longing for revenge.

Michael, propelled by the force of the attack, hit the ground hard, the bag of groceries collapsing underneath him. A large can of pork and beans tore through the bag and stabbed his chest. His head had been slightly turned to the left, helping him to avoid a broken nose, but the right side of his face bounced off the asphalt, scraping the skin off his cheekbone. The dizzying sensations of his brain sloshing around his skull, his eyes filling with tears, and his mouth flooding with blood slowed his response.

Michael lifted his head and, through the blur, saw Joey's giant outline looming over him. Joey's crew-cut hair glowed like a halo in the glare of the streetlight, and his Navy pea coat flapped open as he swung and slammed his thick black leather boot into Michael's ribs. Michael managed to raise his arms to protect his face and curled into a fetal position.

"You little fucking faggot, howda *you* like it? Fucking camel jockey, go back to the fucking desert where you belong!" Then Joey shouted out in cadence, punctuating each word with one of his vicious kicks. "Where's. Your. Fucking. Asshole. Camel. Jockey. Cousin. *Now*?"

"Stop that!" a woman's voice screamed out. Joey didn't bother to turn and see who belonged to the voice. As if it were a command from a superior officer, he immediately stopped kicking Michael and took off running.

Michael didn't move for several moments. Breathing hurt. The woman approached and carefully tried to help him up. Gathering his strength, Michael slowly sat up and wiped the tears from his eyes. The right side of his face was bloody and raw, and his ribs ached with each breath—no matter how slight—but nothing came close to hurting as much as his pride. He felt humiliated. How he was going to face anyone? What would he tell his father?

Michael recognized Shelly Wilson's bright, sunny blond hair. It was styled like Marilyn Monroe's, and he hadn't been able to take his eyes off of her the first time she'd come into the store for a pack of Salems. But now, as Shelly tried to help him, he thought that same hair looked harsh and brassy with the street light filtering through it. Maybe his pain and humiliation was making everything around him seem ugly.

Shelly Wilson was an attractive, full-figured woman with a petite turned-up nose and blue eyes. A nurse at Queens Hospital, she was a new addition to the neighborhood, having moved into the Perone's basement apartment only three months ago. And no matter how tired she was, she always gave Michael a warm smile. She was divorced with no children, and it was her inability to get pregnant that had broken up her marriage. Her ex had turned mean and abusive, calling her defective, damaged. And then he'd cheated on her and gotten his girlfriend pregnant, as if in triumph over the barren years spent married to Shelly. But even worse, the chickenshit never even told her. One day while she was at work, he packed his things, took most of the money out of their bank account, and left. The sting of failure haunting her, Shelly was desperate to move, to make a change. So when someone suggested Mrs Perone's basement apartment, Shelly moved underground—where she sometimes felt that she belonged.

With Shelly's assistance, Michael slowly stood up. He was trying his best to hold back his tears, but a few leaked out.

"It's okay," Shelly said softly. "Come on, let me help you."

Michael looked down at the wreckage of groceries he was supposed to deliver. The carton of milk had been crushed, spilling all over the other items and making them a total loss. The loaf of Italian bread and the pound of ham he had carefully sliced and wrapped were both soaked, and a bag of flour had split open and blended with the milk, creating a muddy paste. In a burst of rage, Michael scooped up the can of pork and beans and smashed it to the ground, screaming, "Fuck!" Sharp pains shot through his midsection.

"Come on, don't worry about that now. Come with me. Let's get you cleaned up." Shelly lightly took his arm and guided him a block away to her apartment and down the four concrete steps that led to her private entrance. Her apartment was small, tidy, and comfortable; Michael thought everything seemed to fit, to belong. Once in the kitchen, Shelly slid a chair out from under the table and directed Michael to sit. In the warmth of her home, Michael felt weak and small. His nostrils burned and tears streamed out of his eyes and slid down his cheeks, mixing with blood and then dripping onto his coat. The right side of his face was swollen and throbbing. It hurt to breathe. Shelly took a clean dish towel from a drawer, wrapped it around some ice, and instructed him to hold it against the side of his face.

"I'll be right back," she said, slipping out of her coat and hanging it on a hook on the back of the door. She disappeared into her bedroom.

Shelly was wearing her white nurse's uniform, but not her nurse's hat, something she occasionally got criticized for. Nurses were supposed to wear their hats with pride, because the design of the hat indicated which nursing school they'd graduated from. But Shelly was past all that. Her hair was one of her best features, so why cover it up with a silly hat? She was excellent at her job and didn't worry about jealous criticism. It was work that had kept her sane when the rest of her life had fallen apart.

When Shelly returned, she was carrying an assortment of supplies—including an ace bandage. Michael removed his jacket and the pain seemed to amplify throughout his upper body, making him feel exposed.

"It looks like he got you from behind," Shelly said.

"Yeah," was all Michael could manage. He was nagged by the thought that he should call his father, but what would he say?

"Should I call someone?" Shelly asked.

Michael nodded, appreciative that she'd read his mind.

"Let me get you a little cleaned up first." She carefully dabbed the side of his face with astringent-soaked gauze. It stung like hell, causing Michael to flinch, which in turn sent a stabbing pain through his ribs and back. Shelly aimed a reading light at his face and moved closer, her face now a couple of inches from Michael's, looking to see if there was any gravel embedded in his cheek. Michael could smell a faint but delicate fragrance from the shampoo or perfume she'd used much earlier that day. He closed his eyes to hold back burning tears and allowed himself to feel comforted by her caring touch. "You're going to have a shiner," she said.

Shelly then called Michael's father and told him that his son had a slight accident but would be fine. While they waited for his father to arrive, she helped Michael slip off his shirt and checked each of his ribs. As gentle as she was, Michael flinched each time she touched his side. Shelly smiled reassuringly at him before announcing that none of his ribs had been broken and wrapping his upper torso with an ace bandage. Then she poured a glass of water and handed Michael a pill. It was Valium.

"Take this. It'll help you sleep tonight." He did. Even lifting the glass caused him pain.

Michael had rarely seen such concern on his father's face as when he came to pick him up. But once he'd determined that his son was going to be okay, his father turned his attention to Shelly, staring at her awkwardly for what seemed like a long time, clearly unsure what to do or say.

Shelly's blue eyes fixed on his face, steadily returning his gaze.

"We should go," Michael said, breaking the silence.

"Thank you for taking care of him. How much do I owe you, for the supplies?" Michael's father reached into his pocket.

For some reason Michael was embarrassed by his father's question—as if he could be any more self-conscious. That was just how his father was, though: he always felt the need to pay his way.

"Oh, no . . . No, that's not necessary, not at all," Shelly said.

"Are you sure?" his father asked.

"Of course. I'm just glad Michael's okay."

Thanks to Shelly, and Valium, Michael slept that night. He dreamed that he was beating up Joey, pounding and kicking him and making him hurt the way Joey had made *him* suffer. The dream brought Michael the sweet satisfaction of revenge and it brought him some peace, at least for one night.

Michael missed the next two days of school and didn't leave his room. Along with the agonizing pain of a swollen face and bruised ribs, he felt the deep disgrace of having been beaten up without standing up for himself. When he was eight, he'd gotten into a shoving match with a kid who was about his age, right outside their old apartment building. Shoving turned into punching and Michael's mother, instead of immediately coming down to break it up, watched for a time from the window. Michael saw her and wanted her to come and rescue him. He was afraid and hated fighting. "Mikey, hit him hard!" he heard a friend say as he and the other kid were going at it, but he didn't want to. He didn't like hitting anyone. He didn't have the stomach for it. Punches were thrown and punches were landed by both of them—and then it was over.

While his mother was tending to his bruises, she told him that he should never start a fight but that he should always stand up for himself.

"Is that why you didn't stop it?" he asked angrily.

"Yes. It would have been easier for me to come and get you. I wanted to," she said. "But now you understand; it's important to stand up for yourself."

"I don't understand *anything*," he'd shot back.

Michael figured that he hadn't learned his lesson, because he *still* didn't understand fighting. But he swore that he would never let anything like this happen to him again.

His father wanted to tell Joey's parents what happened, but Michael begged him not to. Even worse, his father wanted to call the police. Michael was too ashamed to do anything; he just wanted it to go away. And for whatever reason, his father let him have his way. But he did give Michael a stern lecture about keeping his head out of the clouds when out in the world.

Michael didn't do any deliveries for a few weeks. And when he started back, he became keenly aware of what and who was around him. No longer trusting the streets, he constantly surveyed his surroundings, wary of shadows or anyone approaching too quickly. He also started carrying a knife he bought from Billy, and any time he had a free hand, he'd reach into his pocket and grip it for reassurance and the sense of security it brought.

Ten

MICHAEL SAT IN THE BACKSEAT. He leaned into the door and pressed his right cheek up against the window, feeling the thick, chilly night air whirl past as his father's station wagon barreled east on Southern State Parkway. He was thinking about all the ways he could have avoided going to the party but didn't try. It occurred to him that maybe he was too old to be pressing his face against the window, but he dismissed the thought because at that moment he felt like a little boy, one who'd been forced to join his parents someplace he didn't want to go: a Christmas party organized by his father's club. The men's club was a group of Palestinian men and their families who came from the town of Ramallah, and had been organized to bring the community—related by either blood or heritage—together by extending the traditions of the old country and creating new ones. They'd rented a VFW hall in East Meadow for the party. Michael suddenly realized the real reason he didn't protest—he might get to see Yvonne. And with that he pulled his face off the window and adjusted his posture, sitting up tall.

As his father eased their station wagon into the parking lot, Michael could hear music from an Arabic band seeping through the walls of the hall. And the singer's deep voice, coming through the occasionally crackling amplifier, grew louder when Michael and his parents entered. Michael secretly enjoyed the music he'd grown up with; it belonged to him in much the same way as his mother's cooking. Michael wouldn't admit it out loud, but he heard similarities to the rock and roll he loved so much. Arabic music could be upbeat and smooth all at the same time, and the singers' melodic voices were expressive and evoked deep emotion. One of his uncles had explained to him that they always sang either about love or about country.

Up on the makeshift stage the singer was playing an *oud*, an instrument that Michael thought resembled a pregnant acoustic guitar. The singer's voice was smooth, and he played the instrument well.

Michael searched the room for Yvonne as he trailed behind his parents. He recognized many of the animated faces he saw clustered around his family's table but had no luck finding her. The familiar scene reminded him that as the night moved on—given the mix of male egos and alcohol—voices would grow louder, to emphasize whatever point they were trying to make, and passions would be on display, fueled by the strong need to be heard. The rule seemed to be this: the more forcefully and loudly you spoke, the more value there was in what you were trying to say.

Before Michael had a chance to remove his jacket, David and his younger brother Sammy approached him from behind. "Hey, Cuz, how's it going?" David shouted, grabbing Michael and pulling him close. David kept an eye on Michael's parents as they continued on to their table, and when he deemed it safe, slipped Michael two cans of beer he'd stolen from the kitchen. "Here, quick, stick these in your jacket and go out back, behind the building. Sammy, show him."

Michael followed Sammy out the side door and around the building. The back of the VFW hall faced a sparsely wooded area and a small but steep hill that led to the Meadowbrook Parkway overpass. From where they stood, Michael could hear the cars speeding by. Sammy also had two cans, and the two of them hid their beers behind a tree, where three other cans had already been stashed.

Michael admired David the way you admire someone who seems fearless. David had been suspended from school on a number of occasions for smoking, fighting, and cursing at his teachers. He wasn't afraid of anyone. Sammy was smaller and desperately wanted to be tough like his older brother—but couldn't quite pull it off.

Michael shoved his hands in his coat pockets. "How's it going?"

"Got suspended for a week," Sammy said with pride.

"For what? What'd you do?"

"For fighting. Eric Cunningham, this big, fat fuck, thought he was tough. I wanted to cut him, but I couldn't get my knife out. So I just beat the shit out of him. You should've seen it. I punched him in the nose. He was bleeding all over."

"Wow," Michael said in a patronizing tone.

"Yeah, that fat fuck won't be bothering me again."

"What did your parents do?"

Sammy shrugged. "Nothing. I told them he started it."

"Nothing? Really?"

"Yeah. Nothing," Sammy said firmly.

"It's cold. I'm going back in," Michael said.

Michael entered the VFW hall for the second time. A festive energy filled the space. While his eyes were adjusting to the fluorescent lights, the bright holiday colors of the women's dresses melded together and reminded him of the ornaments on the small

Christmas tree his mother put up each year. Before his vision completely cleared, he felt a tug on his arm, and Yvonne, who had snuck up behind him, was dragging him toward the dance line.

"Come, *habibi*," Yvonne said, flashing a smile. She knew how uncomfortable Michael got on the dance floor.

The line had more women than men. In the *dabka* everyone held hands and moved to the rhythm of the music, dancing together in a semicircle, every other step kicking their legs in the air in the best synchronization they could manage. Michael's face flushed as he felt every pair of eyes on him. There was nothing he wouldn't do for Yvonne, but this was pushing it. As awkward and goofy as he felt, he was stuck; he had to dance until he could break free or the music ended. Yvonne smiled at Michael reassuringly, which did nothing to assuage his discomfort.

Yvonne was Michael's third cousin, or something like that. Michael often got confused about who was related to whom and how—sometimes he even lost whole branches of his extensive family tree—but Yvonne and Michael's father had grown up together in the old country and were close. Michael would tag along with his father whenever he visited her family, hoping Yvonne was home. She usually was. She was a year and half older than Michael, and with anyone else the age difference would have made Michael feel more like a kid brother. But Yvonne treated him like a peer, with a respect that made him feel significant. They'd spent countless hours commiserating, and it hadn't taken Michael long to develop a serious crush on her. Her large dark brown eyes, flawless complexion, and long, straight black hair—not to mention a figure like Raquel Welch—certainly contributed to his desire. But there was more to it. Michael felt they shared a mutual sense of dissatisfaction with their lives.

From a young age, Yvonne had loved to learn. She loved the challenge of solving a difficult math problem or debating some historical event and its impact on current affairs. And her love was not diminished by her father's indifference to her straight-A report cards—or encouraged by her father's endless lectures on the importance of education when haranguing her older brother about his poor grades. For Yvonne, learning wasn't important for the reasons her father laid out for her brother. And it wasn't about being the smart one, either. (She'd learned early on that her intelligence was best left in the background if she didn't want to risk emasculating her brother or any other men who might be in the room.) No, for her it was more essential. The more she learned, the more she wanted to know. She had tried to explain it to Michael once, during one of their long talks. "I'm not sure I can put it into words, but the idea of discovering something new, new to me at least, excites me. You think that maybe you can understand the world better, how we got here, why people do the things they do . . . but what you actually find out is how *complex* it all is. And that just makes me want to understand everything that much more."

"A waste. A waste of money, a waste of time for a girl to go to college," her father had said to her. "Many men—successful men, good men—are interested in you. Why waste your time with school? For what?"

Yvonne had refused to even meet these men. She'd even gone so far as refusing to come out of her room one Sunday when she was ambushed by her father. He had invited some young man over for dinner. A man from a "good family," who was doing his residency in cardiology at some hospital in New Jersey. She knew she would pay for embarrassing her father, and sure enough, right after the young man left, her father had laid into her, shoving his sweaty, round red face within an inch of hers and yelling about how ungrateful and worthless she was. "You know how many girls would be interested in this man, this doctor?" Then he had turned to her mother. "Something's wrong with your daughter!"

After her father had exhausted himself, Yvonne had apologized for embarrassing him and proceeded to negotiate a deal. She would meet some of these men, but only if she could attend Nassau Community College until she found the right man.

Dancing next to Yvonne, Michael tried to relax. But whether it was from nerves or lack of rhythm, he kept messing up which foot to cross over and which to kick in the air. Not the best way to impress a girl you like.

The music stopped. The dance line collapsed, and Michael felt Yvonne's hand slip out of his. He also saw her smile slip away as she was surrounded by several girls vying for her attention.

Michael's father waved at him to come over to the table where he and his mother were seated.

"Did you eat?" his father asked.

"Yeah," Michael said, thinking that he should but that his stomach was too confused for food.

Michael's parents were sitting next to his uncle Elias and his wife, Aunt Suad. A hardworking man, Elias had built a successful carpet business. He wasn't tall or broad, but had a vise-like handshake, the by product of years of lifting heavy rolls of carpet.

"Hi, *Amo*." Michael stretched out his hand to his uncle, tensing in anticipation.

"There he is! How's the big grocery man doing?" Elias asked, grabbing Michael's hand.

Michael suppressed a wince. "I got your pound of baloney in the car."

"Baloney? I ordered salami," Elias said, grinning.

Michael bent down to receive the obligatory kisses on both cheeks from his aunt. "*Habibi*, I saw you dancing," she said.

Even though it had only been minutes before, Michael had let himself forget those awkward moments. His face flushed. "If you can call it that," Michael mumbled under his breath and then forced a smile. "Gotta go!" He patted his father's shoulder as he walked by.

"Eat something," his father said.

As Michael headed off to find David, he turned to look back and felt a twinge of something like pride. His father looked distinguished in his dark blue suit and red tie, his full head of black hair now slightly graying at the temples, and his mother looked quietly elegant. She saw Michael looking and flashed him a shy smile. *She's the best-dressed woman in the place*, Michael thought. She was wearing a long black dress of her own design, accented with white borders around the sleeves and neckline. He remembered that it had been inspired by something she'd seen Jackie Kennedy wear a while back. It always impressed him how she could do that, even when she'd only seen the dress once. His mother was wearing a hint of makeup tonight, something she rarely did, just enough to highlight her features. She was a reserved woman and usually sat quietly at these affairs, observing. Michael knew that even though she enjoyed catching up with extended family occasionally, she still preferred the solitude of her home.

He caught up with David as he was heading out the side door.

"What were you doing in there, jerking off?" David said.

"You know how it is. You gotta stop and kiss everyone."

"Here, take these." David handed Michael another two cans, and they went around back where the other cans of beer were waiting. David eagerly yanked the tab off a can of beer, spilling some in the process, and then took a long drink. Michael peeled back the tab on his own beer and dropped it back into the cans opening. It was something he'd seen John do when he was hanging out at the store and couldn't wait until he got home to pop one open. Michael took a long drink. The beer was bitter tasting, nothing like the sweet sodas he was accustomed to. He'd only tasted beer once before, at another family function—his father had allowed him to have half a glass but he hadn't finished it. This time he persevered and finished the whole can. As David tilted his beer up with the same hand his cigarette was dangling from, Michael watched the glowing tip streak a crescent moon against the dark night. David polished off his second can.

"You getting any pussy at that new school of yours?" David asked.

Michael hesitated, trying to think of a good lie, but his expression told the truth.

"Oh yeah, that's right. What are you, fifteen or something?"

"Sixteen." Michael said.

"That's when I busted my cherry."

"There's a girl I like," Michael said. As his words echoed in his head, he heard how schoolboy they sounded, but before he could add anything else David cut him off.

"Like? Fuck 'em, don't fall in love with 'em."

Michael's head sprang back. "What?"

"Hey, go out, get laid, have fun—but when it's time to settle down, find one of your own."

Even if the effects of the beer hadn't already taken hold, these comments wouldn't have made sense to Michael. He'd heard this before of course, though maybe not stated so *directly*, and he'd come to understand this old-world perspective, the whole arranged marriage thing and why it might be better to marry one of your own—but what he couldn't seem to reconcile was how you could direct your heart. Was he thinking too much like a girl? Should he take David's advice?

Wanting to change subjects, he said, "Hey, I heard Sammy got suspended. Your parents must've been pissed!"

"Yep, a real dumb shit. He got caught bringing a knife to school. Fucking idiot. It fell out of his pocket in class. And get this . . . it was a Boy Scout knife."

Michael shook his head and finished off his second beer. The sounds of the cars zooming by on the parkway up above called to him. He pointed up the hill and said, "Wanna walk up there?"

"What are you fucking nuts? For what?"

"I don't know. I just wanna see what's there."

"Knock yourself out," David said.

"Okay, I'll see you inside," Michael said, waving him off. David glared at Michael for a moment while crushing his cigarette butt under his shoe, then turned and disappeared around the corner. Michael picked up another beer, stuck it in his coat pocket, and started up the hill. It was steeper than he'd expected and he occasionally had to grab a small tree or bush to hang on, and twice he ended up on his hands and knees to avoid sliding down. It got darker as he moved farther away from the VFW hall, and he could now make out the headlights from the passing cars. When he finally reached the top, he parted some bushes. *Meadowbrook Parkway.*

A small strip of grass separated the bushes from the road. Michael crouched down, his left side leaning against the bushes, and faced the oncoming traffic. He opened the beer and sipped it slowly, then looking back through the branches. He could see a halo of light surrounding the VFW building and could just barely hear the filtered music of the band. He now felt far enough away.

Cars sped by Michael intermittently, heading to their various destinations, the strangers inside unaware that Michael sat watching them. He tried to imagine where they were going. Cold gusts blew back his hair and stung his cheeks with each car that flew by. He wondered who was in each one and whether their night was beginning or ending. He imagined hitching a ride and going wherever they would take him. He saw a young couple in a green Ford Mustang and wondered if they were happy, on their way home to make love. Or would something come up to spoil their evening so they'd end it fighting? The beer was empty and his head was spinning. Michael heard his name being called from below, so he parted the bush and saw the dark outline of David, light reflecting from his well-oiled, Brylcreemed hair. It gleamed. Michael carefully made his way down the slope.

"What the hell's up there?" David snapped.

"A parkway," Michael answered, sufficiently buzzed.

David looked at him as if he were crazy. "What the fuck's the matter with you?" He shook his head. "You lose your mind? Come on, let's go. The belly dancer's here."

Michael followed David in. Even though he couldn't really focus on them, Michael knew that his hands needed washing and headed for the bathroom. When he entered the alcove where the bathrooms were, he saw the belly dancer waiting there for her music cue to begin. A light blue silk scarf was wrapped around her face, allowing only her dramatic, elaborately made-up eyes to show.

Michael didn't want to miss her performance, so he hurried past her into the men's room. At the sink he turned the faucet on and stared at the water which seemed to flow in slow motion. He pushed the lever on the soap dispenser and a yellow paste squirted into the sink, missing his hand. He scraped some of it up with his fingers and carefully washed his hands.

Without the cold outside air to keep him alert, Michael's head fogged up, feeling light and spacey, disconnected from the rest of his body. He bent over and splashed some cold water on his face and then realized he had to go. He peed, leaning his head against the wall above the urinal for support, and then, out of habit, washed his hands again.

Michael now had to think about walking, focusing on each individual step. But despite his alcoholic haze, or perhaps because of it, he was confident in his ability to not appear obvious. He exited the men's room and stopped at the end of the alcove, which gave him a view, from a comfortable distance, of the dancer's performance and allowed him to prop himself up against the wall. The belly dancer was exceptional, her moves elegant and sensual. She danced with the rhythm of the music and made eye contact with her audience. Michael took a deep breath, hoping that it might help clear his head, but it didn't. He was grateful he was some distance from the crowd.

"She's beautiful," a familiar voice said. He turned and saw Yvonne standing behind him.

Yvonne moved closer to him and so did the delicate scent of her perfume, a subtle floral fragrance that he would always associate with her. She smelled intoxicating. Without thinking he said, "You're much more beautiful."

Yvonne lit up. "You're so sweet," she said, and then added, "And this coming from the best-looking guy in the place."

"No, I'm serious. You're beautiful," Michael said, not wanting her to dismiss what he was saying. Even though he said it thanks to the false courage of alcohol, he meant it. Yvonne stopped smiling and, almost teary-eyed, gently touched his cheek. She hesitated and then, as if deciding it was okay, brought her face toward his, and he thought—he *hoped*—she was going to kiss him on the lips, but she tenderly kissed his cheek, letting the kiss linger longer than he expected. He immediately flushed with emotion, could feel his heart beating rapidly and his breath shorten.

Yvonne continued to gaze at him affectionately. She took a tissue out of her purse and softly wiped her red lipstick off his cheek. He wanted to say leave it, but didn't. He wanted to kiss her, but couldn't muster the courage. He felt himself straining to break through the paralyzing fear and indecision that wrapped tightly around him, leaving him incapable of action. He continued to stare into her eyes and managed to whisper, "You *are*."

For some reason this upset her. Her eyes filled with tears—which made them sparkle, glisten—and before he could ask why, Yvonne turned and ran back into the ladies' room. He wanted to follow her to find out why she was sad, but he hesitated, believing that all the beer in the world couldn't give him the courage.

Michael's inner debate about going after Yvonne was interrupted by Sammy, who hurried over and said, "Hey, where you been? Your dad's looking for you."

"Go away."

"Fuck you! Your dad told me to find you."

"Okay. Tell him you found me."

"I told him I'd *get* you. Come on!"

It struck Michael that Sammy was doomed to be one of those poor saps who was always in the wrong place at the wrong time. And Michael would definitely remember this moment as one of the times in his life that he should have followed through and didn't. He turned and glanced at the ladies' room door.

"Come on . . ." Sammy whined.

"Fuck, fuck, fuck . . . Okay, okay, fucking Boy Scout Knife, let's go. You lead the way!"

As Michael took his first few steps away from the alcove wall, he was reminded of the fact that he was drunk. So he focused on following Sammy. He was surprised to find that he needed to concentrate in order to maneuver. He tried to act natural, but his exaggeratedly careful movements were probably making his drunken state obvious to anyone who cared to notice.

Michael couldn't remember getting into the back seat of his father's car, lying down no less, but he made it less than mile before bolting upright and shouting, "I'm going to be sick!" As his father pulled over to the curb, Michael shot out of the car before it came to a full stop. His body needed to puke. Unfortunately there wasn't much to throw up, beer mixed with sour bile mostly, followed by bouts of dry heaving. This was Michael's first experience with losing control of himself, with that wretched feeling that comes when your body takes charge, doubling you over to expel the poison you'd introduced to it only hours before. When it was over, he just stood there, breathing deeply, hoping the cold air would help clear his head and settle his stomach.

His father stepped out of the car to check on him.

"It must have been something I ate," Michael said.

A smile crossed his father's face and he slowly shook his head. "Maybe something you drank?"

"Sorry, Dad," Michael said, leaning against the car for balance.

"Learn from this. You have to be careful." And then his father added, "With *everything* you do."

This reaction surprised Michael; he'd been expecting his father to be pissed off. In fact, Michael had been preparing himself for one of his father's lectures, which he probably deserved.

"Nice party," Michael said, trying to fill the quiet.

"You'll know what *nice* feels like tomorrow," his father said.

"Huh?"

"Nothing."

Michael doubled over again, dry heaving, and thought that death would be a comfort.

The next morning Michael suffered through his first hangover, and swore he'd never drink again. His father said nothing more about what happened, but expected Michael to work. And behind his wry smile, perhaps he pushed Michael a little bit harder whenever he saw his son move a little bit slower.

Eleven

LATELY ANGELA HAD BEEN DOING MORE of the grocery shopping for her mother—who didn't understand how someone as bright as Angela could keep "forgetting" an item from the list she'd given her and have to run back to the store. But Angela was flattered by Michael's attention, and was also attracted to him. She hadn't done anything too serious yet, but she knew she was treading on dangerous ground and feared her fantasies and daydreams would get her in trouble. Once when she'd been with her father, he'd made a scene because a man stared at her too long, and would have hit him had her mother not intervened.

Angela had always been obedient, unlike her older sister who'd rebelled and ended up having to get married much too young. But she was beginning to feel smothered and left out of what her friends were allowed to do. Well . . . maybe not *allowed* to do, but certainly got away with. Not being allowed to date until she was eighteen was antiquated. Why should she have to pay for her sister's sins? But one thing she knew for sure, confronting her father head on was not the way to go about it.

Michael stepped into the walk-in refrigerator—located behind the counter, in the far corner of the store—where they kept extra cases of beer and soda. He grabbed a six-pack of Tab for a waiting customer, and when he swung open the thick door to exit, he spotted Angela on the other side of the counter.

Over the past six months, Angela's thick black hair had grown long like Cher's, draping to the small of her back. She was also taller, and her breasts and hips were beginning to develop the curves of a woman; Michael thought she carried herself with a grace beyond her years. And lately each time Angela came into the store, Michael pressured himself into talking to her.

Michael had shot up too, thanks to a recent growth spurt. He was taller than his father now. His peach fuzz had become dark, hard whiskers that required a daily shave, and his face had lost the roundness that used to inspire every aunt to grab and tweak the flesh of his cheeks. Muscles now filled out his lean frame, defining his shoulders, chest, and arms, and giving him more strength and agility as he worked around the store. And his sexual awareness was sometimes all-consuming.

It was becoming easier for Michael to speak with Angela. The pretext was usually helping her to locate a grocery item. While he still had to summon his courage, he was definitely feeling more comfortable. On several occasions he'd even helped her home with her groceries. On these walks, Michael had learned that they were the same age and that Angela attended Maria Regina, a Catholic girls school, which explained why he'd never seen her at his school despite the extensive amount of time he'd spent scouring the halls in search of her. She loved kids and wanted to be an elementary school teacher. Her family was very important to her, and she often baby sat for her older sister's kids.

Angela was holding a grocery list, apparently waiting for Michael. At least he hoped so.

"Hi," he called out in a higher voice than he would have liked.

"Hi," she returned, with a self-conscious smile.

Michael cleared his throat. "Can I help you find something?"

"Oh, no. I, uh, saw you go in and thought I'd say hi."

"Oh!" Michael said, feeling stupid but still excited that she'd been waiting for him. He became aware of the weight of the six-pack of Tab and tightened his grip on the cardboard handle.

"Michael, the Tab?" his father called out.

"Coming!" he shouted back.

After delivering the Tab to the customer, Michael helped Angela find the items on her list and then asked his father if he could help her home with the groceries.

"Go. Don't take all day," his father said with an amused smile.

The cold winter air nipped at their faces as cotton-candy patches of white, wispy clouds swirled around the pale blue sky. Michael carried her grocery bag as they both ambled along, wanting to make the most of the short walk. Michael strained for something interesting to say.

"Did you like the Beatles' last album, *Magical Mystery Tour*?"

"Yeah, it's okay," she admitted. "I like some of their older songs better."

"Do you have a favorite?"

"No. Not really. I like Sonny and Cher, the Supremes. My mom still plays a lot of Elvis."

"He hasn't done much lately."

"Yeah, but she still thinks he's *it*."

After a few steps with neither one of them speaking, Angela said with deliberate casualness, "I'm baby sitting tonight. My sister's going out with my parents. I'll be alone. I'm not supposed to have anyone over, but if *someone*"—she paused, her cheeks turning slightly pink as she peeked sideways at Michael and then quickly looked away—"delivered the quart of milk I forgot, it would only be polite to invite that person in."

Michael could feel his heart racing. "Uh, what time . . . would you need that milk?"

"My sister's kids usually go to bed around eight. Sometimes it takes them a little while to fall asleep. Nine? . . . Yeah, nine should be good."

"Nine. Okay." Michael said, trying not to sound too eager.

Angela stopped several yards before her side door, looking nervous. Michael could see her father through the window, sitting at the kitchen table in a sleeveless T-shirt, smoking a cigarette, hair tousled like he'd just rolled out of bed. Even from this distance, Salvatore Russo's broad, chest and well-defined arms were imposing. A red heart tattoo with a name across it that Michael couldn't make out was emblazoned on his shoulder.

Angela reached for the bag of groceries. "I'll take it from here, thanks," she said. Just then, Angela's father turned and looked out the window in their direction. Michael was pretty sure that Sal couldn't see him from that distance, but he was unnerved anyway and imagined Sal's penetrating, suspicious gaze following him as he stepped away, at least until he was sure that he was well past his line of vision.

On his way back to the store, Michael felt like he was floating. He was overcome with excitement—and fear that he was making more out of this then he should. An electric energy pulsed through him for the rest of the afternoon.

That evening, Michael went upstairs early to get ready. He wanted everything to be perfect, so he tried not to get distracted by imagining what might happen later. But he couldn't even get his sideburns the same length. They were only millimeters apart in difference, but he wanted perfection. After several botched attempts that only made things worse, Michael, in one last frustrated effort, made a quick swipe and pushed down too hard on the razor, slicing deeply into the side of his face. *What an idiot move.* Besides causing him pain and aggravation, it took several minutes to get the bleeding to stop. And then to top it all off, he splashed too much Musk cologne on, accidentally getting it in his cut. It burned like hell. Michael sat on the edge of the tub and tried to slow his breathing. *Now I've done it,* he thought. *I look like a real dork. Okay, stop making a big deal about this. Be cool.* He tried to distract himself by remembering how he'd received the cologne last Christmas from an aunt he didn't like. He disliked her even more now.

After getting himself ready, Michael went downstairs to the store to get the quart of milk he'd bagged and hidden in the walk-in refrigerator. Running out of milk wasn't likely, but he didn't want to take any chances.

Michael's breath shortened with each step he took toward Angela's house, and his heart pounded as he knocked on her door. She greeted him with a smile, displaying her bright, perfect teeth. Michael was too distracted by his own anxiety to notice whether she was nervous too.

"Oh! What happened?" she asked, and touched the side of his cheek. As her fingers lightly brushed his face, it made the hair on the back of his neck stand up and sent a shudder through his body.

Michael was surprised to hear himself say, "I was attacked by a pound of roast beef . . . or was it a can of corn? I'm not sure. It's tough working in a grocery."

Since he hadn't had the courage to make jokes before, it took

Angela several seconds to get his newfound humor. She smiled flirtatiously and said, "I guess you'd better be careful then."

They stood in the kitchen, neither one sure of the next move, new terrain for both of them. Then Angela asked, "Do you want to see something really adorable?" Before Michael could answer, Angela took his hand and led him through the living room to a closed bedroom. There, she put a finger up to her lips and slowly opened the door. Inside were two children asleep, a little boy in a bed and a baby swaddled in a crib.

They tiptoed over to the crib, and Angela whispered, "Isn't she precious?" Michael took in the baby's cherubic face and tiny pouting lips. She looked just like the picture on all those baby food jars that he lined up on their grocery shelves. Until this moment, he'd never looked closely enough at a baby to be able to distinguish one from another. But now, watching her as she slept peacefully, he noticed her soft, delicate innocence, her *newness*. He nodded, fearful of waking the baby. Angela glowed with pride.

They went into the living room and sat on the sofa, and as Angela moved closer to Michael, he was immediately taken by her clean scent. It wasn't perfume, it was the fresh smell of shampoo and soap. She wasn't wearing any makeup. Her parents probably wouldn't let her.

Angela had stacked a few forty-fives on the turntable: "You've Lost that Lovin' Feeling" by the Righteous Brothers, "Stop! In the Name of Love" by the Supremes, and "I Got You Babe" by Sonny and Cher.

"Do your parents get on you about school?" Michael asked after a few minutes.

"No. Not really." Angela responded.

"That's probably because you get straight A's," Michael said. "I'm hopeless when it comes to math."

"I'm sure that's not true," Angela said, and then quickly added, "They get on me about other stuff, though. I'm not allowed to date until I'm eighteen."

Michael was unsure how to respond to that.

"Would you like a Coke?" Angela asked, breaking the silence.

"No. I'm good, thanks," Michael said, despite his throat being dry. He didn't want her to leave. He watched as the light from across the room reflected in her eyes and made them sparkle, like big chocolate marbles. He wasn't sure if he leaned into her or she leaned into him, but somehow they came together and kissed. Michael gently pressed his mouth against hers, his lips partly open, his body flushed with a mix of nervousness and desire. And she returned his kiss. After a moment, he backed off and asked, "Is this okay?"

She slid her face next to his—he could feel her soft cheek brush lightly against him—and whispered, "Yes." All the apprehension and uncertainty that he'd expected to feel dissolved away, and he felt like he was where he belonged. He pulled Angela closer and their kisses deepened. They kissed for a long time, and he willingly followed her lead, not daring to try anything more. Whenever the passion became more than Angela was comfortable with, she would pull away momentarily and compose herself.

Angela asked Michael to leave well before she expected her parents to return, explaining to him that sometimes her father would get into one of his moods and want to come home early. After saying goodbye, Michael walked a couple houses down the block and then turned to look back at Angela's. He didn't know what he was expecting to see, but he was just happy to stare at that small brick house.

Twelve

ROGER GILBERT WAS IN HIS LAST SEMESTER of his senior year at Columbia University and with military service looming, was in no rush to finish. A founding member of the Students for a Democratic Society, he espoused all the virtues of the movement: he railed at the establishment, the war, and authority in general. It made no difference to him that he'd grown up wealthy in a mansion in Connecticut, the son of a successful senior insurance executive. In fact if asked, Roger would deny it. With all that was going on in the country, Roger felt he had every right to reinvent himself.

Maria had decided not to go home for her mother's birthday party, which was planned for the last weekend in January—and if Maria had thrown the plastic-covered living room furniture on the front lawn and set it on fire, her mother probably would have taken it better. Her mother was working overtime to make her feel guilty, but it wasn't working the way it used to.

Maria was going to spend the weekend with Roger instead.

He was her third lover—her previous relationships had been short-lived, and one had even been a one-night stand. Roger was new and exciting, unlike anyone she'd ever known before; he exposed her to a different world, and she wanted to learn whatever he could teach her. Outspoken, he decried the establishment every opportunity he got. "They're lying to us! And our brothers and sisters are being killed for nothing!" Roger would say with a heartfelt conviction that she found extremely attractive.

Maria liked Roger's shoulder-length, dirty-blond hair that resembled frizzy twine. His beard grew like patchwork on his pale face, and he had the habit of running his fingers through his fuzzy chin hair while he expounded on social justice. He always wore the same leather vest over whatever T-shirt he had on, or over no shirt at all if it suited him. Roger played guitar, but he wasn't very talented. Unfortunately he was tone deaf, and the only one who didn't know it. Maria wasn't going to be the one to tell him.

Maria had seen a doctor and was taking the pill. She loved the freedom, but more importantly, couldn't imagine having a baby right now. She was in love with Roger—and he said he loved her—but when she thought about it, there seemed to be something missing. *That just must be how it is*, she'd rationalize, and then push the thought out of her mind.

It was while dating Roger that she decided to change her name, though it was something she'd been thinking about since her junior year of high school. On one hand, she had always disliked her ethnic-sounding name, but on the other hand, she had just started to understand who she was, to feel rooted in the world she came from, and she didn't want to deny that. But now that she was in college, a fresh start was appealing, and she was feeling the need to distance herself from the place she grew up. She liked the sound of "Nancy." It was a simple, clean name, and it satisfied that need. If her mother was upset about her not coming home for her birthday, wait until she found out about her name! She decided her mother didn't need to know yet—why pile it on? She'd wait for an appropriate time, if such a time existed.

When she asked Roger to begin calling her by a different name, she was disappointed with how casually he accepted it. She wanted him to ask her *why*. She wanted him to be curious, interested.

Nancy had some valid reasons for the change, and she very much wanted to share them. But all Roger said was, "That's cool, babe."

Thirteen

FOR MANY PEOPLE CONSUMED by their often demanding lives, there is comfort in the abstraction of world events; these events happen in places that are thousands of miles away and are difficult to reconcile. When it comes to major campaigns, we aggressively vilify our enemies and reduce the world, with all its differences, to stark black-and-white wagers—into good versus evil. We do this in the name of our way of life, our honor, our security. Our fear. And hardworking people—with their busy lives, their families to raise—readily trust their leaders. They *need* to trust them. After all, we're the good guys, fighting the good fight. And unless you've been there or have someone you care about over there, you have no real stake, nothing at risk, no real fear, no real sacrifice. This is the price of democracy.

Michael started to take notice when young men, not much older than he was, were getting killed. But something else was changing in his country: people were starting to wake up, to ask questions, to challenge authority. Michael noticed that too.

Angela was Michael's distraction. But Angela's parents didn't go out that often, and Michael and Angela had only been able to get together at her house two more times. Angela would come to the store and just hang out for as long as she could get away with, and sometimes she'd take her niece for a walk and Michael would join them for a few blocks. Being careful, of course, because the neighborhood had eyes. Michael looked forward to their time together as if every moment with her was a separate treat. When he was with her, he felt heady and distant from everything else. Their intimate relationship never went any further than heavy kissing. Michael wasn't sure that she *wouldn't* go any further—he was just too afraid to ask for anything more, because he thought of her as a "good girl."

Sunday afternoons at the grocery were usually slow, and Michael had no reason to believe this one would be any different. He took a call from Angela's mother: she needed some groceries and asked if he'd mind delivering them. It amounted to one bag, so he packed the items as quickly as he could and dashed over to their house. Angela's mother came to the door absent the smile she usually greeted him with and took the bag inside without asking him in. As she opened the door again to pay him, he peered in and was unable to stop himself from asking, "Is Angela home?" But as soon as the question tumbled out of his mouth, he noticed Angela's dad standing behind his wife, and it hit him what a stupid thing he'd just done. Panicked, he took the money, said "Thanks," and backed off the stoop. He thought he heard Angela's mother say, "Sal, no!" but wasn't about to turn around and check.

Michael had made it only a few yards down the block when he felt Sal's hand on his shoulder. His grip stopped Michael cold and then spun him around. Although Sal was shorter than Michael, his body was wide and thick, and Michael felt completely overshadowed.

"Grocer boy! Whatdaya think you're doin'?" Sal taunted as he stared Michael down. Sal's unshaven stubble and uneven, bushy black mustache—which looked smeared on his sweaty face—made him appear even more menacing. Despite the threat, Michael tightened up, looked him square in the eyes, and didn't answer. This provoked Sal, and he grabbed the front of Michael's shirt with both hands and shoved him hard against the trunk of a large maple tree. Rough bark dug into Michael's back as he was thrown off balance. Trying to hide the fear rising inside him, Michael instinctively grabbed Sal's wrists and fought to break free. But Sal had him pinned against the tree and Michael wasn't able to loosen his grip.

"Ya think you're tough, ya little shit?"

Whether from fear or indignation, Michael dug in.

"Stay the fuck away from my daughter! I won't have some sand nigger sniffin' around her, ya hear me?" He stuck his face into Michael's and snarled, "Ya got that?"

Sal's breath reeked of beer and garlic. Michael clenched his jaw and continued to glare at him, refusing to respond. Sal rammed his fists deeper into Michael's chest, making it difficult for him to breathe and lifting him slightly. Michael could feel the bark scraping the skin off his back.

"Ya hear me, ya little fuck? Why don't you and your fucking family go back to the desert! Just 'cause the Jews kicked your ass out, don't mean you belong *here*!"

Michael tightened his grip on Sal's wrists and eyeballed him defiantly.

Sal's nostrils flared.

"There's something *dirty* about you people."

"Fuck you!" Michael snapped, surprising himself, and catching Sal even more off guard.

"What did you say?" Sal lifted a fist, getting ready to punch Michael in the face. "Say it again . . . go ahead." Someone across the street stopped to see what was happening, and from the corner of his eye, Sal noticed whoever it was and apparently thought better of hitting Michael. Instead, in one quick move, he broke Michael's grip on his wrists and tossed him onto the patch of dead grass next to the tree, as easily as if Michael were a five-pound bag of potatoes.

"If I ever see you near Angela, I'll break your fucking legs!"

Michael sat up and continued to stare at Sal with a defiant expression. Scowling, Sal leaned over and stuck his finger in Michael's face. Michael tilted his head to look past the thick finger.

"Stay away from her! Fucking *sand nigger*." With that parting shot, Sal backed away and swaggered off, Michael staring at the back of his head as if somehow his glare could penetrate and damage him.

"Fuck you," Michael said again, under his breath this time. He remained motionless for the time it took Sal to walk back into his house, then picked himself up. Whoever it was who'd stopped to watch was gone.

In spite of the damage to his back and chest, Michael's mounting rage numbed his pain, and as he headed back to the store, he began to pick up speed until he was sprinting. When he arrived, he rushed past his father at the counter, mumbling something about needing to stock the refrigerator with beer, and headed straight to the basement. He sat down on top of a stack of beer, trying to catch his breath, and then jumped up, infuriated, unable to sit still. He wondered why he was so out of breath, and then realized that his body had been so tense while running that he'd forgotten to breathe. The cool dampness of the basement felt good, familiar, and his body slowly released its tension.

Michael grabbed a large bottle of beer out of its cardboard box and hurled it with everything he had against the wall. It shattered loudly, exploding, splashing the wall with sudsy foam. He stood there for several seconds, watching the beer slowly trickle down the concrete. Then it hit him that *he* was the one that would have to clean up the mess, and for some reason he found that amusing. It made him smile. He heard his father call down from the top of the stairs, "Is everything okay?"

"Yeah, Dad, everything's fine. I broke a bottle. I'm cleaning it up."

Fourteen

THE NEXT TIME MICHAEL SAW SARAFINA PERONE, the woman who had inadvertently started his delivery career, she opened the door wearing all black. Anguish was not only etched on her face, it consumed her entire being. All the vibrancy that used to propel the small woman was gone, and the air around her felt heavy.

Mrs. Perone had three adult children. Her youngest son, Anthony, was in the Army. Michael knew this because a picture of him in uniform was prominently displayed on her mantel. On that first delivery to her, she'd dragged him over to show him the picture. "See? See how handsome my boy is, like you!" she'd said, her eyes shinning with pride. There was something about that picture of Anthony that attracted Michael, and sometimes he'd wander over to peek at it as he waited for her to retrieve her purse to pay him. Anthony *was* handsome. Michael, lacking objectivity about his own appearance, couldn't judge his own looks against Anthony's. But Anthony's dark brown eyes did mirror his own, and that stirred something inside him. Mrs. Perone's two other children, both married and living in the neighborhood, would stop by frequently and bring their kids to visit. For that reason, Mrs.

Perone always had a big pot of tomato sauce—or "gravy," as she called it—constantly simmering. And if Michael made a delivery close to dinner or lunchtime, she'd insist on making him a plate. "Come sit and eat, eat, just a little." And then she'd generously ladle the gravy over a steaming bowl of ziti, grate a pungent hunk of Romano cheese over it, and place it in front of him. *"Mangia! Mangia!"* she'd say. The sweet, spicy sauce, the al dente pasta, and the sharp bite of the cheese combined perfectly, making him feel warm all over.

Michael walked in and placed the groceries on the kitchen table as he had done many times before. The blinds were drawn tight, shutting out the sunlight. The house smelled flat. Instead of the usual spicy aromas of Mrs. Perone's cooking, there was a slight fragrance of gardenias. The air was thick, hard to breathe, and Anthony's picture—the one that used to be on the mantel—was on the dining room table, two candles burning on either side. Mrs. Perone didn't acknowledge Michael, in stark contrast to her usual convivial manner. Michael wanted to say *something* to her but had no idea what he was supposed to say. "I'm sorry," finally came out, and he immediately realized how inadequate the words were.

One evening before closing Billy and Jelly stumbled into the store, stoned out of their minds. Billy could barely find his mouth with the end of his cigarette. Jelly was so wasted that his eyes were rolling into the back of his head, and he could barely walk without Billy's support. From what Michael could understand from their drunken ranting, Jelly had enlisted in the Army, his way of getting out of his father's house. Billy was pissed that his brother did something so fucking dumb, but since it was too late to do anything about it and Jelly had to report to his recruiting office the next morning to leave for boot camp, throwing Jelly a party was what Billy thought was called for.

Billy was clutching a medicine bottle. Codeine. He took a swig of the red liquid and held the bottle up to Michael. "Want some?"

"No! Put it away," Michael said, annoyed.

Michael's father was out making his own delivery, something he'd started to do more and more frequently—and it always included a carton of Salems. From past experience, Michael knew he'd be gone at least an hour. His father never said where he was going. And though Michael was pretty sure he knew where, he had decided he probably shouldn't ask. He didn't want to confirm his suspicions. Or maybe he didn't want to be lied to. In any case, Billy and Jelly were lucky he wasn't there; he'd have thrown them out the second he saw them.

"What do you guys want?" Michael asked.

"Beer," Billy slurred. Jelly had propped himself up on the counter and laid his head down. He looked like he was asleep.

Irritated because he knew better than to leave the counter, Michael said, "Okay, wait here. Don't move!" and ran over to the cooler to grab a six-pack of Rheingold. On his way back he heard a loud thud and then the clank and clatter of several items falling off the counter. Jelly had hit the floor, taking with him several boxes of candy and the wire basket that was filled with hero and kaiser rolls.

"Damn it, Billy, look what he did. Pick him up!" Michael scowled. "How did you guys get here?" He was hoping they'd driven, so he could drag Jelly into their car and be done with them.

"Eddie dropped us off," Billy said. His slurring was getting worse. Michael quickly picked up the bread and candy and placed them back on the counter as if they'd never been disturbed. Then he lifted Jelly's torso up and yelled at Billy, who'd just joined

Jelly on the floor and was starting to nod off himself, "Billy! . . . Billy, grab his feet and help me carry him outside!"

Billy picked himself up, and he and Michael shuffled Jelly outside, laying him down by the side of the store. Billy collapsed next to his brother. "Wait here, and I'll help you home," Michael said. He ran back into the store and called to his mother upstairs. He told her that he needed to make a quick delivery and asked if she could please watch the store for ten minutes. She reluctantly agreed, and Michael went outside and shook Billy awake. Together they lifted Jelly, each putting one of his arms around their shoulders, and slowly dragged him, stumbling, the several blocks to their house.

Above the stoop a single bulb, having long ago lost its covering, was casting harsh yellow light onto the dirty white trim of the doorway. The screen door was missing, and the hinges were twisted as if it had been torn off. When they went inside, Michael tried not to stare, but he couldn't help himself. Billy and Jelly's father was sitting in an old, beat-up chair several feet from the television, which was loud enough to be heard a block away. He was sweaty, wearing a dingy T-shirt and boxer shorts, and had a cigarette in one hand. Next to him, on a precarious metal tray, rested a beer can and a butt-filled ashtray.

Bernard O'Neil was a small man with thinning gray hair and a small beach ball of a beer belly resting on his lap. His bloodshot blue eyes, swimming in watery fluid, were offset by a bulbous red nose with spidery broken veins that flagged his years of alcohol abuse. Michael rarely saw him in the store, but thought he looked older than he remembered.

Bernard didn't acknowledge them as they passed; he was engrossed in an episode of *Gunsmoke.* He didn't even look up. *Okay,* Michael thought, *just a few more steps to their bedroom. I'll drop him on the bed, run back to the store, and I'm done.*

Billy and Jelly's room had a stale, ripe odor, and barely had room for the unmade twin beds that occupied it. Michael and Billy laid Jelly on his bed, and as Michael turned to leave, he heard their old man's whiny voice coming from the living room.

"It's a good goddamn thing that sissy boy is going. It'll make a man outta his sissy ass." His voice was getting closer. Michael could hear him fumbling down the hall toward the bedroom.

Billy yelled back, "Shut the fuck up and go back to your fucking TV!"

Michael didn't want to get in the middle of this. "I gotta go," he said to Billy.

"Didn't hurt me one bit! It'll make a man outta him . . . Ya hear me?" bellowed Bernard, getting closer.

Billy's father appeared in the doorway. He was blocking the hallway, which connected the rooms. Billy, in an angry outburst, shoved his father in the middle of his concave chest and sent him flying several feet down the hall.

"Shut the fuck up, you old bastard!"

Bernard hit the floor with a thud, and the beer can he was still clutching emptied pee-colored fluid onto the already-stained hardwood floor. Billy was about to go at his father again, when his mother came rushing out of another bedroom.

"Billy, stop it," she begged. "Please, stop it."

Bernard pushed himself up to a seated position and called out, "Come on you pussy! Let's see how tough you are!"

"Don't, Billy, *please*. Please don't do this." Lucy O'Neil looked tired and worn in her faded housecoat. Her stringy hair was more gray than brown and her deeply wrinkled face betrayed a hard life.

It was as if Michael weren't even there, as if he were watching a bad TV drama. Cautiously hugging the hallway wall, he eased his way past Bernard, who had picked up the can of beer and was now attempting to drink what was left in it. Michael ran through the living room and out the front door, which he didn't bother to close. As he scrambled past the front lawn, he could still hear Lucy pleading with Billy, but he didn't want to listen to any more.

After Michael made it several houses down the block, he slowed his pace and replayed the scene that had just taken place. Blood rushed to his face. He was embarrassed, he felt naïve, and despite the reality of what he'd just witnessed, he found it inconceivable that a family would behave like that.

As Michael approached the store, he could see through the window that his father had returned. He stopped and peered in, studying his parents as they stood behind the counter talking, preparing to close for the night. He couldn't hear what they were saying, but could tell their discussion was casual, of no real importance. *They fit well togethe*r, he thought. They'd somehow found a rhythm, an understanding of their roles and responsibilities that worked for them. It seemed to keep things simple.

His father spotted Michael and waved for him to come in. As he did, his father said, "Come on, it's time to close." His mother went up stairs to get their dinner ready.

Fifteen

HALFWAY THROUGH ONE OF HIS "short and regular" haircuts, Vinny Conte dropped his shears, clutched his chest, and fell to the floor, dead. Mary, who had suffered from hypertension herself for many years, was filled with a consuming anguish, and several days later her grief manifested as a debilitating stroke that left her paralyzed and semiconscious. Nancy, formerly Maria, had already taken the week off from school to help with her father's funeral, but now faced the difficult decision of what to do with her mother.

Louie couldn't take care of her; he had young children and didn't want to burden his wife. He argued that the right thing would be to put their mother in a nursing home. She needed around-the-clock care, and Louie didn't think Nancy should have to take on that burden anymore than he should. He told her to go back to school and get on with her life, and he'd find the best possible home for their mother.

But as much as Nancy had resented her mother, she still felt compelled to care for her. Was it guilt?—Nancy immediately dismissed that idea—or the shock of seeing this woman who had always been in perpetual motion stopped cold? Her mother was virtually unrecognizable to her. Whatever the reason, Nancy needed to try. She was Nancy now, not Maria, and despite her brother Louie's protests, she convinced him to let her try. Louie provided the money to turn the master bedroom into a hospital room, complete with hospital bed and accessories, and the doctor came in twice a week to check her mother's progress and was on call for emergencies.

Since starting college, Nancy's life had been filled with new experiences and constant demands. Sometimes it felt like being on a racetrack, driving at full speed with few stops. A break could be useful, give her time to think things through, to think about what she wanted to do next with her life—something the intensity of school hadn't left much room for.

Nancy's mother—paralyzed, bedridden, and barely conscious—was in no position to grouse at her anymore. So even though she was leaving school, Nancy refused to abandon her life completely.

Roger thought it was cool that he could come by the house and crash with her. He called it his "off-campus respite," but still complained sometimes about how *far* off campus it was. Now that Nancy was away from their routine at school, she had the opportunity to see Roger in a different setting. And despite her affection for him she came to realize that, with the repetitive anti-establishment mantra he continually espoused, he was rather one-dimensional. And while Roger could recite all the ills plaguing our government, he was insensitive—maybe even indifferent—to the fact that Nancy's mother was lingering between this world and the next. He never asked about her, as if by not acknowledging her presence, she didn't exist.

Nancy wrung the washcloth over the white basin, gauging the water's temperature against her skin to ensure that it was still warm and squeezing the right amount of soapy liquid from the soft white cloth. She'd learned from the nurse how to give her mother a sponge bath: turn the temperature in the room up, wash one section of her body at a time, keep the rest of her covered, keep the cloth warm, wash with one cloth and rinse with another. Nancy never expected to be feeding and bathing her mother in the same way her mother had once done for her. And as she tended to Mary, she found herself talking to her. Talking to her like she never could before.

"Pretty sure, Mom, you'd freak out if you met Roger. One look, you'd hate him," Nancy said in a matter-of-fact tone as she finished washing the right side of her mother's torso and moved down to her leg. "Funny thing is . . . there are times when I'm pretty sure that *I* don't even like him very much." She sighed. "You want to hear something else, Mom? I was so hell bent on getting out of here that I didn't have time to be intimidated by where I was going. Then I got there. And oh-my-God! I looked around . . . and wasn't sure I belonged there." Nancy stopped to check her mother's expression, given that taking God's name in vain would normally have elicited an immediate severe rebuke. But there was no rebuke this time, no change in her quiet, flat expression. "You know what, Mom? I dug in. I wouldn't let some feeling take control of me. And I did . . . I did belong there, just as much as anyone else. And I was thinking about that and then it hit me . . . I got that from you. The stubborn, hard-headed side of you."

The water needed changing. Nancy stood and pulled up the sheet, checking that each side was even and that her mother was fully covered. She took a deep breath and exhaled slowly as she let her eyes fall onto her mother's face, examining her for some evidence that her words were getting through. She hoped so, but it didn't matter. "I know, Mom, what it was like for you . . . Aunt Rosa had no problem talking about it, in fact she *wanted* to talk about it, unlike you. You'd never admit it, would you? I don't get it. Is there some backward tradition, some honor in holding onto family secrets? Your sister told me how terrible it was, how your dad used to beat all of you, how you, the oldest, got the worst of it and how, according to Aunt Rosa, the harder he was on you, the more defiant you became . . . I don't know what makes me sadder, thinking about what you went through or thinking about how you couldn't tell me . . . And here we are, Mom." Nancy carried the basin over to the bathroom.

The only way for Nancy to tell that she was making a difference was an instinctive feeling that would come over her as her mother peacefully fell asleep. Once in a while Nancy caught a small glimpse of what she believed to be recognition in her mother's eyes. But maybe it was just wishful thinking. Other times Nancy would just sit there watching her sleep. And in those serene moments, Nancy came to some understanding of her mother. Mary never allowed the quiet because it would give the past an opening, force her to reflect on all that had gone by. And it was not only the abuse, it was the poverty. Nancy knew that many of her mother's childhood experiences had been brutal, that this was why her mom lived her life in forward drive, fussing, grousing with the strength of someone who *will* and *can* push past or toward whatever it is she needs or wants, leaving no room for thought or discussion about where she came from or what she endured. And this was how she ran her family.

When Nancy needed a few things, she called Haddad's and asked for them to be delivered. She always tipped Michael well. But she also stopped in sometimes. Michael would watch her as she walked the aisles deliberately, leisurely examining the items on the shelves. She radiated confidence, independence, and an individuality that separated her from the other women who came in the store. Most of those women, young or old, seemed to fall in line. But wherever the line was, Nancy wanted to cross it. The neighborhood cronies labeled her a hippie, but Michael thought she defied that stereotype; her dress wasn't outrageous, it was subdued and understated. She appeared to study everything around her—as if on a perpetual search—and Michael found this intriguing.

"What's the country you're from like?" Michael heard her ask his father.

"It's beautiful. The weather in the summer is like no place else," he answered.

"No, what are the people like?"

"The people . . . they are the kind of people that no matter how crowded their dinner table, they make room for you." He paused. "But it's not good there, not since the war." He paused again and then concluded with, "You know, they are people like everywhere, most of them good, honest. A few are not."

Michael was standing in the aisle behind Nancy and couldn't resist making a comment. "The opposite of this place, where a few are nice, but most are assholes." His father shook his head and frowned in disapproval. Surprised to hear a voice behind her, Nancy turned to look at Michael.

"A little young to be so cynical, aren't you?" she shot back, catching Michael by surprise and embarrassing him. Lately,

Michael had gotten into the habit of making smart-ass comments for no real purpose other than to entertain himself. Maybe it was his way of fighting back.

Michael shrugged. "Just how I see things, I guess."

"Interesting," she said, with a smirk.

Michael *had* become a little cynical, it was true. And a restlessness had begun to rattle in him. He wasn't sure why or what to do with it. He wanted more, but wasn't sure what *more* meant exactly. Ever since the incident with Angela's father, he'd felt an overwhelming sense of discontent with his life and a strong desire to *do* something about it, but at a complete loss where to start.

Sixteen

When Michael tried on his tux, it fit perfectly. And it made him feel cool, very debonair—like James Bond. It was Michael's first wedding as a groomsman, and it had sort of been sprung on him. He'd known they had met and were writing to one another—Yvonne had told him—but somehow she'd conveniently forgotten to tell Michael that she and Freddie were getting serious. He'd had no idea until Freddie called a month ago and asked him to be a member of the wedding party.

After arriving in Detroit, Freddie had been unsuccessful in finding the engineering job he so badly wanted, so he'd started working in his uncle's grocery store. Freddie rationalized that despite his education, he was better off owning his own business than working for some corporation. It would be more rewarding financially and would give him a sense of independence. At least that's how Freddie had explained it to Michael. But Michael remembered their discussions when Freddie first arrived, how important that job was to him, and thought maybe Freddie was selling out. What

Michael didn't know then was that Freddie had met Yvonne last summer, the week before he came to stay with the Haddads.

After getting engaged, Freddie, with his family's support and financial help, started looking to purchase a store somewhere on Long Island. So Yvonne could stay close to her family.

A few days before the wedding, Michael and his father had dinner at a restaurant with Freddie and his parents, Samir and Miriam—who had arrived the week before from Ramallah.

"The tanks, the soldiers, they're all around," Samir said, tears welling up. "They treat us like shit. Like animals in a cage. They don't let us leave for days. I can't work. My business, it's nothing now. We can't leave our homes, we can't move from one street to another." He turned to Freddie. "You remember Nader, younger than you, in college now. They came, took him from his house, to jail. No one knows why or where or what to do. His father came crying to me. He's a student, for God's sake! He did nothing! No one can help!"

"I cry all day," Miriam added. "I can't stop. I just want to sleep. I have no will to do anything." She shook her head. "It's no life."

"Don't go back. I'll find a lawyer. He'll fix it so you can stay," Freddie said, and then turned to Michael's father. "Aziz, tell them, tell them not to go back."

"He's right. Stay. Stay with us until Freddie and Yvonne are back from their honeymoon."

"I'm not leaving my home, Aziz! That's what they want. It's my home. I'm not leaving," Samir said with rising anger. "Why would I live here? This country . . . this country that supports the people who have taken over, that have occupied my home? Tell me. Tell me that!"

Aziz struggled with this question, and not for the first time. It swelled up in him the way acid in his stomach would rise and burn intolerably after eating too much spicy food. It caused a great conflict of interest and loyalty—sometimes making him feel like a traitor to his own beliefs, and other times making him feel betrayed, much like how you'd feel after being lied to by your one true love. He *loved* his adopted country. How was he to reconcile this? Sometimes he rationalized—almost convincing himself—that the opportunity here was too great, and that good and bad existed wherever you lived. Aziz particularly hated being asked questions like this directly, because he knew that he didn't have an answer.

"How long can it last?" he said to Samir. "They have to get out. Soon, hopefully. *Inshallah*." Aziz invoked God's will and tried to offer hope, but in his heart he suspected that it *wasn't* going to be soon, that it would take longer to settle than it should. And what would be left of their homeland when it was finally over?

"It's my home . . . *our* home," Samir reiterated, wiping a tear off his cheek.

Michael wondered if Yvonne was happy. Now that she was marrying Freddie, she wouldn't get to start community college. He knew how important that was to her, that she wanted more. Michael liked Freddie and thought he was a decent guy, but he wasn't convinced that Yvonne was ready for this.

When he used to accompany his father to Yvonne's house and their fathers would speak of business or politics, he and Yvonne would find a private place for their own discussions. She couldn't date, so when he came over, she'd seize the opportunity to get out, and they'd go to the diner for coffee. They would talk for hours on a variety of subjects and she always showed interest in his ideas. Yvonne talked about what she wanted out of life and about the world as someplace bigger than the four walls they lived in, and as Michael got swept up in her ambition, his attraction to her grew. She often teased him about being handsome. "A guy like you will have lots of girlfriends, just wait and see." He was flattered but dismissed her compliments, figuring it was just her way of being kind.

She was the only person he'd confided in about Angela—although he never told her about his "run-in" with Sal—and he couldn't help but wonder why she didn't tell him about Freddie.

The vinyl booths, white Formica tabletops, and stainless steel of the diner had become their place.

"I know I should go to school, but sometimes it's so hard to pay attention. I want to be out there *doing* something, not stuck in some classroom."

"You're not listening, Michael," Yvonne said.

"Yes, I am."

"No, not to me. I mean you're not listening to what's right there, what's in front of you. Paying attention can lead you to something exciting, can open up your world. Your impatience is getting in your way."

"How does learning some algebra problem do that for me?"

"You're not listening," Yvonne said again with a sly smile.

"What do you want?"

She looked introspective, almost sad. "It doesn't matter what I want."

"Why? Why doesn't it?"

"Because I will end up someone's wife and raise a family."

"We're not in the old country! You're free to do what you want. Women have rights."

"If I have a daughter, I'll make sure she knows that."

The waitress came over to their booth and topped off their coffee. "You guys okay?"

"We're good. Thanks," Michael said.

"Michael, *habibi*, listen . . . the more I learn, the more I realize how much I don't know. I know you know that feeling."

"Okay, I do, I get it. But you're free to do what you want."

"You don't understand."

"What's there to understand?" he asked impatiently.

"You *can't* understand. You're a man."

"A man can't understand how a woman feels?"

"Most can't. If anyone could, you might. But it's about my family. I could never hurt them."

"Even if not hurting them means giving up what you want? Giving up your dream?"

Yvonne didn't want to answer that question. It assaulted her. She didn't blame Michael for asking it, though. She'd understood that this was where they were headed and could have steered the discussion in a different direction, but it was as if she needed to test herself, to see if the resentment she felt over this reality was sufficiently stuffed away. It wasn't.

Instead she said, "But, I hope I marry someone like you," and after she let this slip out, she turned away, embarrassed.

Hearing that had left Michael speechless. And even though he'd understood the context in which she'd said it, he had still felt like he was floating several feet off the ground.

But now, Michael wished she *hadn't* said it, because she was about to get married to Freddie.

On March 17 at St. Johns Arab Orthodox Church in Brooklyn, with her family and friends gathered, Yvonne gracefully walked down the aisle on her father's arm while the groomsmen and bridesmaids stood waiting, flanking the altar where the priest and Freddie were standing. Yvonne was a radiant bride, with perfectly coifed hair and a delicate lace veil that didn't conceal her expressive brown eyes accentuated by black eyeliner and a hint of eye shadow. Yvonne's white satin wedding gown outlined the contours of her shapely figure and contrasted with her dark complexion, and her glistening red lips separated smoothly when she smiled.

The priest placed the gold crowns, which were connected by a white ribbon, on the heads of the bride and the groom, and then switched them from one head to another and back again. The swinging brass censer filled the air with a sweet, spicy scent. Yvonne and Freddie were carefully guided by the priest around the altar three times—signifying the Father, the Son, and the Holy Spirit—and they both made eye contact with Michael as they circled, Freddie winking at him. Finally the crowns were removed, and the traditional vows spoken and acknowledged, and Freddie and Yvonne kissed and turned to face the congregation as the priest introduced them as man and wife.

Freddie, at Yvonne's request, had hired both an American and Arab band for the reception, and the two bands would switch off. When the wedding party walked onto the dance floor, the American band's singer introduced each of them to the guests. And then with great fanfare, the singer introduced Yvonne and Freddie as "Mr. and Mrs. Habeeb," and the band started to play, signaling the newly married couple to begin their first dance. The rest of the wedding party was supposed to join in.

The idea of dancing in front of so many wedding guests made Michael break out in a sweat, and he was beginning to think that Yvonne was secretly forcing him to deal with his fears. Even his cool tux couldn't keep his underarms from growing wet and his pleated shirt from clinging to his body.

The band's singer was doing his best rendition of Dean Martin singing "In the Chapel in the Moonlight." Michael had been paired with Sonya, one of Yvonne's cousins, a sweet and pretty fifteen-year-old girl with shoulder-length dark brown hair and oval hazel-brown eyes centered over a prominent nose—her father's, he imagined. She was as shy as Michael, which made their dancing clumsy, the self-conscious shuffle of four feet moving hesitantly, often in opposite directions but occasionally colliding, unsure of their next step. But the two of them did their best to avoid stepping on each other as they maneuvered across the dance floor. Michael glanced at his father; Aziz was watching him, cigarette in hand, wearing a proud grin. Michael wasn't sure whether his dad was smiling because his son was growing up, or whether it was because of the way Michael was dancing—if you could call it that. He suspected it was both.

When the dance ended, Michael saw Yvonne making her way back to the table and decided to follow. He wanted to steal a few minutes with her. But Michael heard his name being called and turned to see Freddie frantically waving him back to the dance floor. Freddie was sitting on a chair, and several intoxicated groomsmen were about to lift him up over their shoulders for the traditional groom's dance. Freddie's eyes widened and his voice cracked as he called to Michael.

As Michael rushed to Freddie's aid, he glanced over and noticed that Sonya and Yvonne had their heads together, chatting away. And he could feel their eyes following him as he scurried over to the dance floor. He got there just in time to grab onto one side of the chair as Freddie, visibly shaken, was being bobbled by the groomsmen while they attempted to raise him into the air. Michael positioned himself at the back to provide the most leverage in case anyone faltered. Freddie craned his face toward Michael, his brow furrowed, and shouted above the loud Arabic music, "You got me?"

"I got you!" Michael assured him, nodding his head. He wasn't sure if Freddie could hear him, but Freddie gave him an appreciative but weak smile. The groomsmen managed to dance around the floor several times to the beat of the rhythmic music with Freddie high in the air, and the closest they came to disaster was when they were presenting him to his new bride. One of the groomsmen slipped and let go, tilting Freddie to one side and coming close to dumping him onto Yvonne, who jumped up in fear for her new husband and stretched out her arms. Fortunately, Michael was able to pick up the slack and even out the chair, preventing disaster.

After Freddie was safely on the ground, he grabbed Michael and gave him a hug, saying "I'm going to go find a chair that isn't moving!"

Michael went over to the bar and asked for two Cokes. But when he got back to the table, Sonya was gone. Yvonne stood up and smiled. "You haven't danced with me yet, Michael." Michael put the Cokes down and Yvonne took his hand and led him to the dance floor where, to Michael's relief, the band was playing a slow song. He did his best—though Yvonne may have led more than he did—and at least he was able to get a few moments with her, which helped him to forget what a bad dancer he was.

"You look happy," Michael said.

"Isn't a girl supposed to be happy on her wedding day?"

"Freddie's the luckiest guy in the world," Michael said under his breath.

"What? What did you say?"

"How lucky Freddie is."

She hugged him closer, and he felt her soft cheek press against his. When the dance was over, she didn't look him in the eyes like she usually did, but instead kissed him sweetly on the cheek and drifted away.

Seventeen

Having been told by Nancy several times to just bring the groceries she ordered into the house, Michael now found it routine to open her front door and walk in. When he let himself in this time, however, Roger was standing there stark naked—with the exception of a dark brown floppy leather hat. Michael took a couple of steps back.

"Hey, how's it hanging?" Roger said.

Michael was speechless and not sure where to lay his eyes; it was difficult to keep them off Roger's penis since Roger repeatedly adjusted or fondled it. Outside of the school gym shower, which he preferred to rush through, Michael had never seen another man standing around so naked—and so casual about it.

Clearly enjoying Michael's discomfort, Roger wore his smug grin as proudly as his dangling penis. He moved closer to Michael and looked into the grocery bag, then called upstairs to Nancy, "Did you get the cigarettes?" He grabbed a pack of Marlboros from the bag and said, "Good girl!"

Nancy bounced down the stairs—fully dressed—and when she saw them she snapped at Roger, "Put some clothes on!"

"Why? It's nothing he hasn't seen before." Roger cocked his

head, looked Michael up and down, and said, "Well, maybe not," and then went into the living room, where he stepped into his bell bottom jeans and sat down on the couch and lit a cigarette. Roger huddled over the coffee table, and from where Michael was standing, he appeared to be sifting his fingers through oregano or some other green spice that was in an upside-down shoebox lid.

Roger called out, "Hey babe, bring me a beer. Shy-boy *did* bring beer, didn't he?"

"Just ignore him," Nancy said to Michael. And then she added, "Come in the kitchen with me and I'll pay you."

"How's your mother doing?" Michael asked as they stepped into the kitchen. Nancy paused to think for a moment before answering.

"I'm not sure I know. She sleeps a lot. Thanks for asking though." Nancy handed him the money and took a six-pack of Rheingold out of the bag. "You in a hurry? Would you like to have a beer with us?" Michael hesitated, thinking of all the things he still had to do—cleaning, stocking shelves, helping customers—but it didn't matter. He was staying.

"Sure," Michael said.

Nancy smiled. "Good." She handed him a beer and a large bag of Wise potato chips, grabbed two more cans, and led the way to the living room.

When Michael got closer to the coffee table, he could see that the green spice was definitely *not* something they sold in their store. Roger was rolling a joint. Since this was the first time Michael had ever seen this done, he watched intently. Roger placed a precise amount of pot on the paper, rolled it carefully, licked it, twisted one end slightly, and stuck it in his mouth. Noticing Michael's admiration of his dexterity, Roger decided to educate him on the process. He pointed to the table. The pot was spread out on the shoebox lid, and next to it was an ashtray full of seeds. "See this? It's important to first pick out all the seeds."

From the Zenith phonograph stereo, with its walnut finish and sliding doors, came the tin-band, pounding rhythm of Bob Dylan's "Rainy Day Women #12 & 35." Nancy sank into the sofa—now absent its plastic covering—next to Roger. Michael sat in the stuffed chair across from them and opened a beer. The chair was positioned in front of the table, across from the sofa, and Roger's guitar sat on the floor next to it. Michael imagined Roger sitting in this chair performing for Nancy, strumming away as she listened attentively, encouraging him.

Roger lit the joint. He drew the smoke deep into his lungs and held on tight, his cheeks billowing out like a frog. He held it in for several moments until starved for oxygen, and then he tilted his head upward and released the smoke. Then he held the joint out and said to Michael, "You want to talk about moral hypocrisy? Our government will send me to jail for years for smoking this, but they'll happily send me halfway around the world to kill people in some rice paddy. And for that, they'll give me a medal." Roger passed the joint to Nancy, who took a drag and held onto the smoke in the same way, but with less dramatic flair. She then passed it to Michael. He took the joint and attempted to mimic what he'd seen. But the smoke seared his lungs, choking him, bringing tears to his eyes. He couldn't hold onto the smoke for even a second. Roger laughed and even Nancy smiled. "A virgin," Roger said.

"It's okay," Nancy said. "It's like that the first time. It gets easier. Just take smaller tokes. Trust me, it'll get better and better." She took the joint from Michael—"Here let me show you"—and demonstrated taking in smaller amounts of smoke, not inhaling it so deeply.

Michael tried again, and it still burned, but Nancy was right.

It *did* become a little easier. But something else happened too: Michael's tense posture dissolved, and an overwhelming lightheaded feeling came over him. His face had no feeling, or was it that his mind had let go and no longer had that tight grip on everything? His mouth dried up. The beer got warm, but it didn't matter.

Roger started laughing and Michael wasn't sure what he was laughing at. Whatever Roger found funny he was keeping to himself. Nancy lay back, enjoying the feeling and freedom that the high gave her. Roger picked up his guitar and started to strum it and sing along with Dylan in a much higher voice than Michael believed even Dylan would have sung in.

"The Times They Are A-Changin'" played over and over, and Dylan's breathy harmonica and his expressive, pleading voice would sing in Michael's head for days, reminding him of that first high long after it was gone. And for a long time after that, every time Michael would hear Dylan he would travel back to Nancy's living room.

As Michael walked back to the store, a great fear began to take hold. He was certain that the minute he walked into the store his father would know exactly what he'd been doing. His anxiety magnified with each step he took. Fortunately, his father had gone off somewhere—Michael didn't know or care where. Maybe he was making a special delivery of Salems.

"Hi Mom," Michael said, a little too happy to see her.

"Where've you been? Your father said you wouldn't be long, and that was an hour ago," she said, clearly upset.

"I made a delivery and then stayed to talk to that girl, you know, the one who's taking care of her mother. She had a stroke."

Michael was impressed that he actually thought of something to say.

"Like your father," he heard his mother mutter under her breath. There were no customers in the store, so Michael straightened the shelves to keep busy. He didn't want his mother looking him in the eyes. Even though he didn't believe she'd catch on like his father, he didn't want to take any chances.

"I'm going upstairs," his mother said as she stepped into the back room. He heard the door close behind her.

Michael was hungry. No, he was *ravenous.* Strange food combinations were suddenly appetizing. He started with a Devil Dog and washed it down with a Coke. Then liverwurst in the deli case called out to him—so he went for it. Rather than risk the slicing machine, he cut off a jagged hunk and spread it on a kaiser roll with mustard, polishing it off with a bag of Wise potato chips. Normally Michael was somewhat indifferent to food. Now it was as if he'd discovered his sense of taste, his ability to savor different flavors as they melted in his mouth. For dessert, he decided to have a Hershey bar with almonds and a Yoo-hoo.

By the time his father returned, Michael had pretty much come down. "You tired? Your eyes are red," his father said.

"Yeah, maybe a little. I was up late studying."

Michael's mother came down to get a lemon and asked if he was hungry—she had made one of his favorites, *malfouf*, stuffed cabbage. "Yeah, Ma. I can eat."

As his father passed the deli case, he came to a sudden stop. Then he pointed into it and asked, "What happened? Why is the liverwurst all chopped up like that?"

Eighteen

MICHAEL WAS WOKEN BY THE SOUND of the phone ringing. He opened his eyes to the sight of a still-dark ceiling. A ray of dim streetlight was peeking through an aberrant slat in his Venetian blind, creating a creased, smoky gray shadow that traversed the ceiling before splashing onto the far wall. Michael didn't move. He assumed that it was some relative calling—possibly from overseas—with bad news. That was the general rule when it came to late-night calls. Michael's door cracked open and his father's silhouette appeared. The bright yellow light behind him outlined his body, framing his tousled hair with a harsh halo. His father just stood there for several seconds before he said, "It's for you."

Who would be calling *him* at this hour? Michael sat up, shook the sleep off, and headed to the kitchen, where their black phone hung on the wall. His father was already there. He lit a cigarette and watched as Michael picked up the phone. "Michael?" It was Nancy. Michael glanced at the clock. The night had just crossed over from a late Monday to a new Tuesday.

Nancy spoke in a quiet, controlled voice, much different than her usual vibrant tone. "I need your help. I told your dad that I need help with my mom. Can you please convince him to let you come over?"

"Okay." Michael heard himself say.

He hung up and turned to his father, uncertain of how he was going to ask him. His father was already halfway through his cigarette, and before Michael could frame his request, he said, "Go," smoke streaming out of his nostrils.

Michael hesitated for only a second before going to his room to quickly dress, splash cold water on his face, and brush his teeth. Before he opened the door to leave, he stopped, wanting to say something to his father, who was sitting on a chair in the dark living room. Michael could tell his father was looking at him, and he could see the red glow resting between his fingers. His father slowly brought the cigarette to his lips and the tip sparked a bright reddish orange, burning the tobacco down as he inhaled deeply.

"Thanks," was all Michael could come up with.

"Be careful," his father said.

Michael closed the door behind him quietly, not quite sure why his father had allowed him to go. Maybe Nancy had convinced him that it was an emergency? Michael knew his father believed experience was the best teacher. Even though his embedded traditions called for men to dominate, and he behaved accordingly, Michael's father still possessed a keen awareness of the needs of others—regardless of who they were. And even though he was sometimes indifferent to his wife's feelings, he worked to make her as comfortable as he could. With Michael, he didn't dictate behavior—outside of a drive for him to be educated—instead allowing him to travel his own path. This challenged Michael's judgment and sometimes created in him a state of emotional uncertainty. Yet once he got past whatever trial he was facing, it helped him to feel a little more sure of himself.

Surprisingly, Michael's father seemed comfortable with him spending time with Nancy, and appeared to genuinely like her. He thought she was smart, and a good daughter for taking care of her mother. He'd met Roger on several occasions and had voiced to Michael, "She could do better." He even seemed to think that Nancy could be a positive influence on Michael. Probably in part because she was attending a good college. She was always respectful when she came into the store, and when she'd heard Michael complaining about his struggles with math, she had offered to help. This had given Michael an excuse to spend time with her. And although he always brought his math book when he walked over to her house, it was never opened.

If Roger was there, they would smoke pot, listen to music, and talk about how the government was lying to them, how the war was wrong. At first, Michael just watched and eagerly listened. It seemed to him that Roger's enthusiasm didn't leave much room for debate. At times Roger sounded intelligent and knowledgeable, but on other occasions he'd get heated and take off on a tirade about all the wrongs being foisted on their generation. On these occasions, Nancy would sneak Michael a look—with a little shake of her head or roll of her eyes—as if to say, "he's going overboard again." And sometimes she'd even taunt Roger about his dramatic tendencies. That pissed him off so much he'd attack her and say she was ignorant, lived in a sheltered world, didn't know the truth—and that her apathetic ways, along with those of all the other spoiled students out there, were the reason the government was winning.

When Roger was out, at school or at a meeting, Michael got to enjoy time alone with Nancy, and he noticed immediately how different she was. When Roger was there, she competed with him, like she needed to prove she was as smart as he was. She'd get impatient with him for no good reason other than she said he made too much noise. But there was calm about the place in Roger's absence.

At first Michael thought that Nancy hung out with him because she was bored and lonely, and he was safe and had no expectations. But as he spent more time with her, he realized that he should give himself more credit than that. She probably thought he was okay company. Their conversations often led to discussions of literature and the different authors they'd read, everything from Austen to Friedan. When he shared that Hemingway was one of his favorite authors, they got into a debate about why he killed himself. Michael thought he wanted to go out on his own terms; she believed it was because he couldn't work anymore, and without his work, he didn't want to live. They even discussed *Valley of The Dolls,* which she admitted liking and he admitted reading. Michael felt as comfortable talking to her as he had with Yvonne, and even shared his concerns and indecision over his future.

"Yeah I get it," Nancy said. "It's hard to figure out. There's this constant battle between what you *should* be doing and what you *want* to do, but you don't have to have it all figured out right now." She smiled reassuringly and then added, "All I knew was that I wanted out of here."

And there was always music. Nancy had a great album collection: Dylan, Hendrix, the Stones, Cream, and of course, the Beatles. They debated the current political environment, how Johnson screwed up, the challenges women and minorities faced, and they had discussed in heartfelt detail their mutual shock and sadness when Martin Luther King Jr. was assassinated. With Roger gone, they had the space to share their beliefs without being assaulted by righteous rantings that suffocated discourse.

And when Nancy had mused to Michael about how she'd

never expected to come back, and yet here she was, Michael had jumped to her defense, saying "But you had to help your mother!"

"There was a time when I think I could've easily abandoned her," she'd said.

When Michael arrived at Nancy's, he opened the front door and softly called out to her. Light from upstairs invited him up to the open door of the bedroom. Nancy's mother lay in bed, asleep, neatly tucked under a fresh white blanket and sheet, her chest rising and sinking gently. Her face was framed by neatly brushed gray hair and was centered on a large pillow that made her look small. The room—with its sterile fixtures and glass medicine bottles lined up neatly on a white porcelain cabinet—resembled a hospital. And while the rest of the house was sometimes unkempt, the compulsive tidiness of this room gave Michael the illusory sensation that it was someplace far away, removed, unconnected to this home.

Nancy was standing next to the bed, watching her mother intently as if she were counting each breath. She didn't move when Michael walked in, but continued her vigil. After a few moments and without turning his way Nancy said in a somber voice, "I gave her an extra sleeping pill. She should be okay." She bent over and adjusted the blanket. "I *hope* she'll be okay," she added, an anxious crack in her voice. Then she turned and quickly walked out the door. "Let's go."

"Okay," Michael said, though he was uncertain what he was agreeing to.

Nancy didn't like driving. If there was too much traffic, she'd lose patience with how much time it was taking her to get where she had to go, and if the road was wide open, she'd daydream and wouldn't pay attention to where she was going. But most of all she hated driving in the narrow neighborhood streets where any minute some idiot kid could come running out in front of her car. She handed Michael the key and asked him to drive.

Michael clutched the key in his hand, feeling its weight. So far he'd only driven in large parking lots and side streets, with his father in the car. The Conte's '62 Chevy Impala rarely saw the road—the tires needed air, and it took Michael several cranks of the ignition before the car would start. With Nancy giving instructions from the passenger seat, he maneuvered onto the near-empty Long Island Expressway and then merged onto the Grand Central Parkway, which they stayed on until they crossed the Triborough Bridge.

With each mile, Michael's grip on the steering wheel tightened. He kept telling himself that it didn't matter that he was driving without a license in the middle of the night heading to places he'd never been before. He was there to help Nancy. After all, millions of people travel in and out of the city every day without incident.

In a jumpy, distracted manner Nancy said, "Haven't you heard?"

"Heard what?"

"What's been going on at school. It's been all over the news."

He *had* heard about some protest, but hadn't thought much of it. "I guess I did hear something," he said.

"I was finally able to reach Susan, my old roommate. Some students have taken over a few buildings on campus. Roger is with them." She took a long, deep breath. "And in the middle of all this, my mother's had two seizures. I shouldn't be leaving her."

"Will she be okay?"

"I don't know."

"Do you know which building Roger is in?"

"I don't know that either," she said in a resigned tone, and then added, "Well, I heard there's a chance he's in Low. The dean's office."

They drove across East 125th. And then Nancy directed Michael down Amsterdam and past the school so they could see what was happening. The entrance to the school was barricaded by police, and squad cars and wagons surrounded the area. Even from a distance, Michael could see what looked like a parade of officers in blue uniforms, some helmeted, a number of them on horseback. They turned right and cut over to Riverside Drive, then continued north on Riverside, took a right onto Seminary Row, left on Broadway, and right on 123rd, where they parked.

Michael and Nancy walked quickly down Claremont Ave to 116th. Michael could feel his heart beating faster as they approached the entrance, and the sight of all those uniforms made it hard to catch his breath. But to his surprise, they slipped past the throngs of policemen—who appeared to be standing back, waiting.

Inside, crowds of students and protesters were scattered all around. Some had set up camp, planning to sleep on the grounds. But just as Michael and Nancy stepped on campus, chaos erupted. It was like someone had released the bulls of Pamplona, only not as organized. A crush of uniforms swept past Michael and Nancy, knocking them out of the way. Boots clapped in unison as policemen ran up the granite steps of Low Memorial Library. Students camping out on the steps were shoved aside, and even ones who only looked like they would resist were arrested. Nancy tried to follow, but Michael held her back. "I need to find him!" she cried, trying to break his grip.

Michael pointed to Low Memorial Library, which was now a sea of blue uniforms. "Nancy, we can't get in there!"

They could hear students yelling, doors being broken, and echoes of chanting or singing coming from inside the halls. After only a few minutes, police started to bring out students, some bloodied, some restrained—and some carried out. One resisting student was dragged down the stairs by his feet, his head bouncing off the steps.

Michael's adrenaline was pumping and he felt fearful and unsure, with no direction other than a fierce desire to grab Nancy and get out of there. Feeling desperate, he prayed to God to guide them through this while his mother's lectures about his lack of responsibility when it came to church replayed in his head.

Maybe God heard him, or maybe it was just good luck and timing, but Nancy's information was correct. Roger was in the group of protesters being escorted out of Low. They spotted him in a line of students being shuffled into a police van, on their way to the Tombs. Nancy ran toward Roger, shouting out his name, Michael right behind her. But lines of police officers blocked her from getting near. Roger called out to her, "I'm okay! I'll call you as soon as I get out," and yelled to Michael, "Hey, man, thanks for bringing her! You guys should've been there!" He was then herded into the paddy wagon along with the others. The door slammed shut and the wagon sped off. Now all Michael and Nancy had to do was get out of there.

They had just stepped outside the campus when the police formed a line, a blue human chain, surrounding everyone. As the police started moving in to make arrests, fighting broke out between the protesters and police, breaking up the neat chain and turning it into a full-blown riot. And Michael and Nancy were caught in the middle. Michael's prayers took on more urgency. He was making all kinds of promises: *I swear I'll never lie again. I'll be nicer to my parents. I'll even start going to church. Just, please, God, get us out of here!*

A skirmish broke out right next to them, and Michael was momentarily separated from Nancy. He saw a large policeman grab hold of her arm, and he pushed his way past the protesters, trying to reach her. But it was too late; the officer had begun to drag her away, clutching his flashlight in his other hand and swinging it to create space in the crowd. Nancy was struggling to break free, and Michael ran up to the officer. In his head he thought he'd just explain everything to him, that this was all just a horrible mistake, but the adrenaline coursing through him must have temporarily caused him to lose his mind, because instead of explaining anything, he grabbed Nancy and shoved the policeman hard, yelling, "She has nothing to do with this!"

Michael felt the bitter sting of the policeman's flashlight as it smacked the side of his head, just above his left ear. It rocked his brain, slapping it against his skull, causing tears to well up. His body lost its ability to stand. His knees gave way like the spring-loaded hinge of a hangman's trap door, and he hit the ground, disoriented. Everything felt like a hazy bad dream.

The swinging momentum of hitting Michael had caused the policeman's grip on Nancy to loosen—enough for her to break free. Nancy pushed away just as a few protesters jumped into the middle of a small group of students that were putting up a tough fight. The melee distracted the officer's attention from Nancy and drew all the police in the immediate area. This gave Nancy a few moments to quickly skirt the crowd and make her way around to where Michael was lying. She bent down and helped him up. He was still in a fog, somewhat dazed.

"You okay?" she asked, sounding panicked.

"I'm fine," Michael heard himself say in an echoing voice he didn't recognize.

"Can you walk?"

"Sure," he said, showing her, stumbling a little.

"Come on, let's get out of here." Nancy put Michael's arm over her shoulder, propping him up as best she could. Her cheek lightly rubbed up against his face and Michael could feel her slight dampness, the warmth of her body. Her sweet, moist scent stirred his senses, renewed his energy. Michael shook off the pain; he was getting his bearings back. He remembered what they needed to do, and when he saw an opening, he summoned his energy and took advantage of it, sidestepping the mini-riot next to them and then hurrying back to the car. When they were far enough away, Michael glanced back. Others were fleeing the school and more squad cars were arriving. Somehow the two of them had managed to get out. He thanked God and then started praying that his head would stop hurting.

Nancy drove home. She was obviously very concerned for Michael, and as they were speeding down the parkway she kept taking her eyes off the road, turning his way to ask how he was doing. "I'm okay. Really, I'm fine," Michael insisted, since each time she did this the car would weave out of its lane. And each time he'd quickly add, "Nancy, the road!"

Michael's head pounded. He wanted to close his eyes, but didn't dare, and it probably wouldn't help anyway.

When they got back, Nancy ran upstairs to check on her mother. She was fine. Nancy came back with some aspirin and an ice bag for Michael, but he was stretched out on the living room sofa, fast asleep.

Michael woke up sometime in the early morning. Nancy was curled up asleep in the chair across from him. His head was still tender to the touch, but his hair was long enough now to hide the welt. At least he hoped so. As he lay there and watched Nancy sleep, he felt hung over with a bitter resentment that settled into resolve, a determination to do something. But then frustration surfaced—what could he actually do?

Nancy had told him that the protest was over the Vietnam War, civil rights, and the school's involvement with classified war research. But the catalyst had been a proposal to build a gymnasium in Morningside Park, which would deprive the Harlem residents of their local park. Roger was just one of over seven hundred students and protesters arrested. When Michael read that number in the newspaper the next day, he was awestruck—he'd had no clue that it was that big a deal. Michael couldn't believe he'd been involved in such an important event, even if his involvement was negligible, peripheral at best. It occurred to him that it was a minor miracle that he and Nancy had managed to get away, and then he remembered the promises he'd made to God. He was flooded with emotions. It was empowering to think that he could participate, be part of, something that made a difference. It felt right, but also far away from his world. Even though he knew that getting involved—trying to change something that was unjust—was the right thing to do, he still wondered if any of it would really make a difference.

Nineteen

When Michael woke up, Nancy said that his father had already called. She told him that Michael had been a big help, the worst had passed, and that Michael had fallen asleep on the couch and would head home as soon as he was awake. While Nancy made coffee and sliced up an Entenmann's coffee cake, she talked about the close call they'd shared as if it had been some great adventure. And while he still suffered from a dull headache, her enthusiasm diminished his pain. She was so animated, so swept up in the emotion as she recounted their mission.

"We showed them! We didn't give up and let those pigs get us! We held out and fought for what we believed in. For what's right."

"Yeah, but what difference will it make?" Michael asked.

"Of course it will make a difference. People have to listen. The establishment can't lie to us any longer. They can't do what they *think* is best for us. We don't live in a communist country, we have a constitutional right to express ourselves! What the school wanted to do was bullshit. And the war is *wrong*. The government is lying to us. We refuse to be like all those submissive clones out there, those minions who buy into the bullshit and go about minding their own business, worrying about their petty lives while people are dying." Nancy waved her finger at Michael, "Guys like you are getting killed! For what? We choose to *do* something about it, to be *heard!*"

As he was leaving, she hugged him at the door—and it wasn't one of those cursory hugs, a polite gesture by someone who is barely aware of your presence. She wrapped her arms tightly around him, her soft cheek brushing against his as she whispered in his ear, "Thanks for being there with me." As their bodies connected, her softness—and that light, sweet scent of hers—filled him with a sensual, dizzying warmth. Her firm breasts pressed into his chest. She did not readily let go, taking her comfort from their closeness as he took his, as if she too needed physical reassurance.

Roger was suspended from school, eleven credits short of completing his degree. His draft deferment was revoked and he was classified 1-A. He was required to report to the draft board immediately. Roger's father refused to fund Roger's "career as professional student" any longer, which meant that if Roger wanted to go back to school, he had to do it on his own. Even though his father felt that five years was enough, and even though he wanted to get Roger away from "bad influences," he also didn't want his son to be drafted. So he offered him an alternative.

With a light grip on the grocery bag and energy in each step, Michael made his way to Nancy's, his mind consumed with the thoughts of that night several weeks ago when he'd almost had his head handed to him, literally. He wondered how he would have explained getting arrested to his father, and again marveled that he and Nancy had been lucky enough to slip away without getting caught. He still remembered the promises he'd made to God, but he hoped He would understand if Michael didn't manage to keep all of them.

When Michael entered the kitchen, Nancy was staring at a letter. She didn't turn to look at him, just spat out, "He didn't even know my address!"

"What?" Michael put the bag down on the counter.

"How many days was he here? Sitting on his bony ass, assaulting that out-of-tune guitar . . . and he didn't even know where he was!" Nancy stuck the letter in Michael's face. "Read it."

He took the letter.

> *We'll show them. The establishment will not win. We must stand up and refuse to go. Refuse to kill innocent people in an undeclared war we have no right to be in—for a country that doesn't even want us there. I will not allow them to make me their pawn. I must continue the cause.*
> *Love, Roger*

"He had to have Susan send that lame excuse of a letter to me," Nancy said. "What does it say?"

Michael wasn't sure what she was asking. "Um . . . I'm not sure," he said.

"It says nothing! If Susan didn't tell me, I'd have no idea that he'd gone, run off to Canada. Of all the chickenshit things—"

"But, you wouldn't want him to be drafted!"

"No, I wouldn't, but that's the difference between him and me, Michael. I *care* about him. What the fuck does he care about?"

Michael wanted to respond in a meaningful way, maybe hug

her, do *something*, but he wasn't sure what the right thing to do was. The only thing he could think of was to just be there. Nancy took the letter from his hand, crumpled it up, and dropped it in the trash.

Nancy's initial anger at Roger's departure turned into disappointment, her feelings of betrayal into sadness. She needed time to reflect on what Roger meant to her—and what she meant to him. It upset her to think that she'd become dependent on him. Even though she'd always known it would end sometime, the physical and emotional demands of taking care of her mother had worn her out, and he'd been a needed distraction. Roger had been present at a time she needed support—even though it had been to satisfy his own needs. Perhaps she'd been selling herself short with him. The truth was, Roger lacked much of what she wanted in a boyfriend. Nancy didn't have much experience with relationships, but she came to realize that, despite those feelings of wanting more from him, she had accepted Roger for who he was and would miss him.

Twenty

THE NEIGHBORHOOD IS AN OUTGROWTH *of families building community. Does it possess a psyche? And what of its psyche, of its collective understanding of who belongs, who doesn't, what's right and what's wrong? And what of those underlying rumblings that seem to shape its character? What of the rumors, innuendo, and witless chatter that fuel fear—and fear change? How do we allow those rumblings to run ahead of us without grounding or validity? How does this community take on its own life? And of course when I speak of community, I could just as readily be referring to a government, a religion, an ethnic group, or even an educational institution like ours. Is this community behavior a given?*

For some reason, this opening from a class lecture by one of Ben's sociology professors popped into his head as he was signing the papers on his new home.

Benjamin Brooks, an only child, had grown up in Roosevelt, Long Island. With his height and impressive physique, and his father's encouragement, he'd played some Little League baseball and high school football. He liked the competition, but the classroom was where he was the most competitive, and whenever there was a debate in history class, he would take over the room. Ben enjoyed being prepared and asking insightful questions. That discipline earned Ben a scholarship to Brown, where he did his undergraduate work in history and met his wife, Janet. After receiving his law degree from NYU, Ben was hired by a prestigious Wall Street brokerage firm at a respectable starting salary that, together with his wife's income as a fifth-grade teacher, easily allowed them to buy their first house.

Ben didn't allow the fact that he was only the second Black man hired in an executive position at his firm to affect him. His father taught him that his work had to be exceptional to be considered equal to his white contemporaries. Ben used his superior intellect—absent a superior attitude—to maneuver his success. He grew to understand the corporate landscape.

The location of the house suited Ben—for now. He liked that the working-class neighborhood felt similar to the one he grew up in, but this was their first house and he had a three-year plan. This house was a stepping stone. He could easily catch the train at the Village or the subway at Jamaica, and his wife had only a short commute to the elementary school in Valley Stream. And the corner grocery two block away assured him that he wouldn't run out of cigarettes. Ben would have preferred to live in the City but didn't want his wife teaching there, and she wanted to continue to work until they had a baby. The house was also only forty minutes from Ben's parents, and he was an attentive son. He fully acknowledged and appreciated his parents' support and generosity, and they were extremely proud of Ben and did everything they could to help him.

Ben believed that you should always take the offensive. It was how he practiced his profession, and it was how he approached his life. To say he made an impression in the neighborhood was an understatement. Three homes went up for sale within four months of Ben and Janet moving in.

The first time Michael saw Ben in the store he thought nothing of it. He figured he was just one of the many transient customers who would stop in if they were in the neighborhood. But when Ben became a regular, Michael grew more and more impressed by him and tried to study him without being caught. Ben was a striking figure: tall and good-looking and well-dressed. His standard uniform was a Brooks Brothers suit, a starched white shirt, and a solid tie with a perfect knot. His hands were always well manicured, and even at the end of the day he still looked sharp, not wilted or worn like so many of the men who stopped by the store after a tough day of labor. Michael thought Ben carried himself with an elegant confidence. If he was out of place, it wasn't because of his color. And if he worked at being refined, it didn't show. Ben carried himself with the quiet demeanor of someone who knew that he made a positive impression.

Occasionally Ben would linger and chat with Michael while enjoying a cigarette and a Coke. To Michael, Ben seemed a model of cool in real life, and talking to him got Michael thinking about how someone developed that level of confidence and poise—like a movie star or a politician. Is it something you're born with, or something you can learn?

That evening, Ben arrived around eight, and as he moved to the cooler to grab his Coke, Michael placed two packs of Pall Malls on the counter.

"You got my number," Ben said. He opened one of the packs of cigarettes, stuck one in his mouth, and lit it with a silver Colibri lighter.

"It's my job. Take care of the customer," Michael said as he opened Ben's Coke. This elicited a sly smile from Ben.

"Last year of school?" Ben asked casually.

"One more," Michael answered.

"Where you going from here? College, then own the next A&P chain?"

"Not sure."

"About which part?"

Michael shrugged. "I'm going . . . I'm going to college, I guess."

"What for? I mean, what do you want to study? Gonna be a businessman like your dad?"

This was a difficult question for Michael. "Yes" would be the easy answer, but not the honest one. The idea of being a businessman bored him to tears. But it was what everyone expected him to say. The trouble was, sometimes it seemed as if *everything* else interested him, and other times he was so intimidated by the thought that he should know what the hell he wanted to do that he was at a complete loss about what interested him. The truth was that Michael didn't know. And didn't want to say he didn't know. So instead he asked Ben, "What do *you* do?"

"I'm an attorney."

Quickly, so Ben couldn't ask him another question he didn't have an answer for, Michael asked: "Do you like it?"

"I love it," Ben said.

"Why?"

Ben took a long drag of his cigarette. He needed the time to think, wanting to give Michael a complete answer, but not a lecture.

"For a number of reasons. One, the law is how we manage our world; it's ownership, responsibility, accountability . . . and how we maneuver successfully around those elements of life. Two, there's good money to be made. And three—and this is what's important—it's what I was meant to do. It suits me. I'm good at it." Ben took a sip of his Coke and then added, "And that's what you need to find, what you're *meant* to do. Never mind what people *think* you should do or should be, or what mold they think you come out of."

Michael immediately wondered why Ben told him this. Was Michael's aimless uncertainty so transparent that it prompted Ben to share these thoughts? Or did Ben share them with any young ears he could get to listen?

As they were talking, Michael caught a glimpse of someone he thought might be John Harris start to walk in. Whoever it was cracked the door open and then quickly shut it, apparently changing their mind.

"But . . . what if you don't know what you want?" Michael asked.

"Educate yourself about the possibilities. Even if you don't know what you like, you at least know what you *don't* like. You probably don't want to be digging ditches for a living, right?"

"Right," Michael said. "I don't want to be digging ditches," he repeated to himself under his breath.

"Hey, I should get home. Janet will be back soon from her parent conference. We'll pick this up later," Ben said, and held out his hand. When Michael took it, Ben's eyes widened with a slight smile. Michael noticed that Ben's hand was dry and soft, and his handshake was firm. Ben picked up his Coke and left.

Michael liked him. But he also felt a twinge of envy. How satisfying it must be to know exactly what you want and to be doing it.

Moments after Ben left, John Harris walked in and headed straight for the beer cooler for his requisite six-pack of Rheingold. He ambled over to the counter and plucked a can out of the cardboard wrapping. He tilted his head back, guzzling down the cold, frothy liquid. Michael whipped out a small bag for him to wrap the can in, but it wasn't necessary, because John finished the entire beer before his head came upright again. From what Michael could tell, it wasn't John's first of the night.

"Where's your dad?" John asked.

Michael knew where his father was—somewhere that involved a delivery and a carton of Salems. He also knew he was never supposed to tell anyone that his father was physically off the premises. But John was safe.

"He's out. I'm closing up soon. It's been slow."

"What did the nigger want?" John asked, then shook his head. "It stinks how they can just move in. Turns everything to shit." And then he grumbled, "Fucking niggers. They should stay where they belong."

Michael was speechless, and a had a sinking feeling in the pit of his stomach. He never expected to hear such malicious comments from John. Michael wasn't naïve and he'd certainly heard things like this before—from kids in school, from other adults, and yes, even directed at himself. But John was someone he thought he knew well, someone he liked and respected—someone he expected more from. Michael peered into John's bloodshot eyes, overwhelmed with disappointment.

"What do I owe you?" John said.

"Dollar thirty-eight," Michael answered automatically.

John paid, picked up the bag, and left without saying another word. Michael started the process of closing. It was a little earlier than he was supposed to, but he didn't care.

Twenty-One

Ever since the wedding, the time between Michael's visits with Freddie had stretched out, longer each time, but Michael didn't think he'd let *that* much time pass since his last visit. Freddie seemed different. Maybe the changes just happened to strike Michael at that moment, and Freddie's evolution had actually been more subtle, more gradual. Or maybe this is who Freddie always was.

Freddie had begun to experience some success with his small grocery store, which motivated him to begin searching for his next store, a larger one in a more lucrative area. And Yvonne was right there working beside him. Michael knew that the traditional next step for an Arab wife—and the expectations of the Arab family—was for her to have children, and that this must create unspoken stress for Yvonne. But despite the pressure from both of their families to produce a grandchild, Freddie appeared to be taking the whole thing in stride. After all, if Yvonne had a baby, he would temporarily lose her from the business. And he liked having her there. "You can't trust outside help. Not like family," Michael had heard him say.

Freddie had become one of the men. One of the honest,

hardworking businessmen who took pride in taking care of their families financially. One of the men who met to play poker, discuss business, and enjoy drinks with the other men in their community. Freddie obviously relished the camaraderie of their informal gatherings, and being accepted by these successful men furthered his sense of accomplishment.

But Michael noticed that Freddie had aged in just a short time. Nothing severe: a slight stoop in his posture, a yellow pallor to his skin, dark circles around his eyes. And like Michael's father, he was never without a cigarette.

Michael disappeared inside his head, thinking about Freddie's transition and the rhythm of their lives. It wasn't that long ago that Freddie had appeared in Michael's life, full of promise, hope, and the dream of a successful career as an automobile engineer. Now he was like a color TV suddenly turned black-and-white—flat, with no distinction. Is this just what happens when life sweeps you along? Do we just react to circumstances out of our control, or do we have real choices? Or is this a myth perpetuated to keep us in line? Michael burned with resentment. This somehow felt like a personal violation—akin to when Angela's father pinned him to a tree and assaulted him. This was not how he wanted to end up—mundane, ordinary, missing out on so much of the excitement the world had to offer. Then sadness washed over him. Not for Freddie, but for Yvonne.

Yvonne's stoic facade hid her deep melancholy and inner turmoil. She both longed for and feared having a baby. She cared very much for the kind man she married and was growing to love, but her initial physical attraction for him had faded, and making love had become a chore—something none of her feminine fantasies had prepared her for. While he was gentle and considerate and never pushed when she expressed a lack of interest, she believed something crucial was missing. Where was the excitement and longing that she'd imagined and expected?

Freddie was a good man—perhaps to a fault. His utter decency left him no edge. And while many considered him handsome, his features were soft, and this softness carried throughout him. Though educated, traveled, and bright, he'd settled into a role that occupied all his energy, that consumed him. All that he once aspired to accomplish had been long forgotten. His mission now was to build a level of financial security that would separate him from the rest.

Yvonne had always wanted what she couldn't have. She knew and accepted this about herself. But what she wanted now—what she dreamed about—was a different life. And this persistent desire was often impossible to ignore like she'd done with so much else. As much as she reasoned that she had a good life and could have done much worse and should be grateful, she couldn't always prevent the tears from breaking loose. And she knew better than to share such self-indulgent feelings with anyone in her circle; they would fervently dismiss them and accuse her of not appreciating what she had, what they themselves envied.

Twenty-Two

JELLY, LIKE MANY OF THE YOUNG SOLDIERS surrounding him, couldn't find Vietnam on a map, let alone understand what they were doing there. They were following orders—and more important, watching their fellow soldier's backs—and that's all that mattered. Some were still convinced that this would make men of them, but most knew the absurdity of that bromide. Many were terrified; they chose to hide behind the bravado that the Army so skillfully indoctrinated, but that didn't change the fear they felt. On patrol they were constantly moving, searching, chasing the enemy—and accepting the hot, sticky, sweat-soaked state that they grew to understand was the least of their concerns—as they both inflicted and evaded death daily.

Jelly had been on an assignment, a routine offensive, a mission like many others before this one. Something went wrong . . . but what? Those people, those *souls*, they weren't what good soldiers were trained to understand as the enemy. But the lessons of war can't really be taught at boot camp, and once in combat, who the enemy is becomes diluted with uncertainty and fear, blurred by the denigration of a people and their culture that's required to rationalize killing. Like most hit-and-run battles, this one happened fast, faster than any of them could make sense of. It was an intense mix, a rush of energy and frightening emotion that left them thanking God that they were still breathing and not leaking blood from anywhere besides the deep scratches from thrashing through the brush and diving to the ground.

After the shooting stopped and the dust cleared, Jelly stood paralyzed by what he saw. The village—mostly women and children—had been mowed down in less time than it took to cut the church lawn. He wanted to cry, but he was frozen by sheer terror. And it wasn't likely he could squeeze a tear out anyway; his eye sockets were so dry they burned in his head like pieces of charcoal at a summer barbecue. *Move on.* That's what they were told to do.

Snapshots from that day would come into focus for him again and again, like being forced to watch Polaroid pictures develop. And the worst one was the little girl's face—she couldn't have been more than three years old, angelic even in death—etched forever in his mind. Jelly would never show this picture to anyone, but instead would chase it away using the only means he knew.

Snorting got the job done—even smoking worked a little—but there was no faster, purer form of instant rush than slowly pushing a plunger through its cylinder, shooting the cloudy, cooked liquid into his bloodstream, releasing him from the memories that had been replaying in his mind ever since that day. Jelly had been in Saigon on a two-day pass when he shot up for the first time. It was much-needed medicine. It provided a state of euphoric bliss, which allowed him to live within himself. It was a finer form of the dragon that he preferred to chase—and more controllable than the one that was chasing him.

Twenty-Three

MICHAEL DIDN'T FEEL RIGHT ABOUT SKIPPING out on his mother. She cooked every night, so if his father was out making one of his special deliveries, at poker night, or visiting relatives, Michael would have dinner with her after closing the store. He'd quickly eat a little of whatever was put in front of him and then head out. On the nights that his father *was* home, Michael could leave early and eat with Nancy.

Dinner with Nancy—who so rebelled against her mother's effort to teach her to cook that she was convinced it was something she hated—was usually pizza, burgers from the diner, or a sandwich they'd whip up together from cold cuts. Sometimes Michael's mother would fill a couple of Tupperware containers with the food she prepared. Michael was surprised that his parents seemed okay with him spending so much time with Nancy, but he figured that this was partly because Nancy was taking care of her mom, like a good daughter should, and partly because her mom being there made it seem like he wasn't really alone with Nancy. Still, he knew better than to push his luck by getting home too late.

Michael was at the kitchen table in the upstairs apartment, concentrating on completing a Chemistry assignment, when his mother, who was cleaning a chicken in the sink, suddenly shut off the water and broke the quiet. "What about this girl? Is she your girlfriend?"

"No, Ma, it's nothing like that. We're just friends."

"She's too old for you," his mother said.

"Mom, I said it's not like that."

"What's it like then?"

"We're just friends," Michael said again.

"Well, what do you do all that time you're over there?"

"I don't know, Ma. We watch TV. We talk. Nancy's smart. Dad's always telling me to hang out with smart people." His tone was borderline sarcastic, and his mother examined his face as though his words were lingering in the air and she was weighing them and considering how to respond. But before she could say what she was thinking, Michael spoke up, contrite.

"Look, Mom, I'm sorry. It's just that she's a friend. I just like spending time with her. That's all there is to it. Really, that's all it is."

His mother wiped her hands on a dish towel and came over to sit next to him. "I know you think it's not like that, but do you know what she thinks? What she wants?"

"Yeah, Mom, I do. She just wants to be friends."

"Uh-huh," she said, nodding her head, "I know you think this, but what I want you to know is that sometimes when you spend a lot of time with someone . . . someone you like, someone you care about . . . it can turn into something more. Your feelings obey no rules. You end up caring much more than you expected. That's all I wanted to say."

Despite his mother's warning, Michael wanted to spend every

opportunity he could with Nancy. He knew his feelings for Nancy were growing—maybe he even loved her. It didn't matter to him that she probably didn't feel the same way. His feelings for her were different than the desire he'd felt for Angela, or even Yvonne. He didn't just admire Nancy, he felt for her, understood her. They connected. And, yes, Nancy excited him, but it wasn't because her beauty had struck him at first sight the way Angela's had. With Nancy the attraction was different: richer, more textured, more complex. Her passion for life both warmed him and challenged him. They'd become so comfortable with each other, and he loved the time they shared together. But he couldn't tell Nancy any of this.

Every once in a while, Michael would fall asleep on Nancy's sofa, and as much as she hated to, she'd have to wake him. She wondered what he was dreaming as she gently rubbed his cheek and whispered in his ear that he needed to wake up. Nancy wished she could just let him sleep there peacefully, but she understood his need to not upset his parents.

In the beginning of her mother's illness, her brother Louie would come over on the weekends and spend a few hours with Nancy, but that was happening less and less. It seemed like he was always too busy to come. But he still called often to check on how their mother was doing and ask if Nancy needed anything. Sometimes friends from school would call, but for some reason Nancy didn't want to invite them over. Now that Roger was gone, the gap between school and the world she was in seemed to widen. And for the moment she was okay with that.

Michael thought her sweet breath felt like velvet as she pressed her face close to his ear, sending a warm sensation through his body—he took his time standing so as not to announce the obvious.

Other than Yvonne and a couple of cousins Michael sometimes did things with, Nancy was his only close friend. Occasionally they'd share a joint, but most of the time they'd watch TV, listen to music, or just talk. Michael didn't want to mess that up.

"Do you ever think of Roger?" Michael asked.

"No." Then, after several seconds she said, "That's a lie. Sometimes I think he was a real shit for leaving the way he did and I don't care that he's gone, and other times I miss him a lot. What are *you* going to do when they call you?"

"I don't know. College deferment for now," Michael said, shrugging.

"And what if that doesn't work, you couldn't get one? What would you do then?"

"I don't know."

"Well, you don't want to go, do you?" she spit out.

"No! I don't want to go! But what choice do I have unless I leave?"

"And what's wrong with that?"

"Well, then I wouldn't be able to come over and watch Cronkite with you. And listen to you complain about everything."

That seemed to lighten the mood for the moment.

But later that night when Michael was in his bed, he wondered what he would do. In a little over a year, he'd turn eighteen. He needed to figure it out. He knew he'd probably attend college, which would delay the inevitable, but what if he didn't have a choice? If he were forced to go, would he run like Roger? He couldn't imagine doing that, but he also knew he didn't want go. He *couldn't* go. He wondered if that's how all the others had felt before they resigned themselves, showed up, and the next thing they knew, found themselves in a boot camp in some faraway, humid Southern town.

Twenty-Four

Mary Conte continued to have seizures, so her doctor ordered a stronger dose of phenobarbital and began to question whether she would be better off in a hospital or a nursing home. Nancy refused to consider it. She couldn't let her mother go, because, despite the mounting challenges of caring for her, Nancy wouldn't know what to do if she weren't there. Not only did she not want to give up taking care of her mother, Nancy would then have to make decisions. She would be forced to examine her own life, to put it back on track, to choose a direction with purpose as she'd done prior to the stroke.

If she had the time to think—not having to push, to maintain that perpetual motion, like the little rabbit blindly racing ahead of the dogs—she might have to question everything she was doing, everything she thought, everything she once wanted. But doubts kept creeping in and cracking her previous resolve, allowing uncertainty to spill over the convictions she once held so firmly. She felt like one of the mud pies she used to make in her mother's garden. After she baked them in the hot summer sun, they would dry solid, firm to the touch. But when she took them out of their containers, they would crumble in her hands, turning back to the loose dirt they were made of.

Michael's father drove him and his mother to an empty lot in Uniondale and announced that this was where their new home would be built—it was time to move his family out of their cramped upstairs apartment. If the contractors met their schedule, Michael's family would be able to move in around Labor Day. This meant that Michael would have to change high schools for his senior year. But, having no allegiance to his current high school, this was the least of Michael's concerns. He was enjoying sharing time with someone he cared about, and he wondered how long it would last, how far it would go, and how he would be able to keep the relationship going if he lived farther away. Of course he knew that Nancy would return to school eventually, but he tried to not dwell on it, tried to distract himself with other thoughts. But some nights he found this impossible and was consumed by questions that disturbed his sleep.

Some time in the early morning hours of June 3, 1968, Mary Conte released her daughter from her bonds of service and left the half-state of life she had been lingering in. She died quietly in her sleep.

Two days later, the country lost an important and prominent political figure. Robert Kennedy was shot dead by a lone gunman who turned out to be an Arab, further reinforcing the American public's negative image of them. Michael heard the taunts at school: "One of your people killed Kennedy, fucking Arab!"

Michael wanted to take pride in his heritage, pride in the accomplishments of his people. It hurt him to know that the evil that sprang from a few could color the whole in darkness. And despite knowing that this evil bore no likeness to those he knew and loved, his foundation was shaken, and his position in the world appeared less defendable. It tainted him.

Twenty-Five

NANCY CALLED MICHAEL BEFORE she called the doctor. She was surprised by how calm she was.

"Could you come over? My mother died."

"I'll be right there."

When Michael arrived, he held her tight. She wanted to be held, to feel his warmth. Even though the thermostat was set to seventy-four degrees, the room felt cold. She didn't cry. She thought she would, but no tears showed up. She allowed herself to sink into the feeling of Michael's arms around her and the rhythm and warmth of his breath on her neck as he held her. She was grateful that he seemed to understand that nothing needed to be said at that moment, that all she needed was what he was giving her. It was an intimacy that she hadn't experienced before. Obviously she was vulnerable right now, but that wasn't the reason for her feelings. The truth was, she'd shared more with Michael than with anyone else. She didn't feel the need to be some person he expected, like she had in every other relationship in her life. And now, she was going to let him comfort her.

"I need to call the doctor," Nancy whispered.

Michael hugged Nancy a little tighter for a few seconds longer before letting her go. After calling the doctor, she called Louie. Nancy didn't want to leave the room until the doctor arrived, so they waited. Even though he'd been to a few funerals, Michael had never been this close to death before. It felt surreal and abstract. He hadn't known Mary Conte; he only knew what she meant to Nancy. Michael looked down at Mary's lifeless body lying in her neat, austere bed. Her face was a pasty ash-gray color.

It was a perfect, tranquil day for Mary Conte's funeral: a clear indigo sky, trees filled with the healthy leaves and blossoms of late spring, seventy-two degrees, and no discernible movement in air that was still indifferent to summer's inevitable humidity. Nancy told Louie she wanted Michael to join them in the limo. He wasn't family, but Louie agreed. His sister was the one who had taken good care of their mother during the worst of it, and he thought Michael was a good guy, not like that loser hippie boyfriend he'd met once. So what was the harm? Who cared if the old cronies talked?

Michael sat close to Nancy as they rode to the funeral, feeling a bit awkward, out of place, once again not sure of what he should say or how to say it. Nancy occasionally glanced his way, but she spent most of the ride staring out the window looking off into the distance. He watched the sunlight reflect off her creamy complexion, outlining her profile. The air around them felt full with her vulnerability, her beauty.

Nancy maintained her strong, calm demeanor throughout the ride, the only expression of her emotions her warm hand holding on tightly to his.

After all the relatives and friends paid their respects, what remained were stacks of dirty plates—remnants of half-eaten casserole and pasta dishes, sandwich crusts stuck against uneaten mounds of potato and macaroni salad—butting up against empty beer and wine bottles.

Some offered to stay and help clean up, but Nancy politely sent them away. If it weren't for her brother Louie, she wouldn't have bothered with such traditional etiquette, might have let the mourners go their separate ways after the grave site. Many of the guests still called her Maria, and Nancy cringed each time she heard the name. But she had neither the motivation nor the energy to correct them.

Michael helped Nancy and Valerie clean up. Louie and Valerie's two children—Bobby, who was seven, and Gina, who was six—helped too. They loved their Aunt Nancy, were very well behaved, and seemed eager to please their mother. Even Louie, who didn't usually do this type of chore, pitched in. Michael suspected Louie's method was one he employed in his construction business: he dragged the heavy, metal garbage can from outside and threw the empty bottles and anything else he deemed worthy of disposal into the can. It was efficient, but Michael was sure Nancy had lost a dish or two.

When everything was put away, Valerie and Louie tried to convince Nancy to come home with them, if only for a couple of nights, insisting that it would be better for her. But Nancy held steadfast; she wanted to stay home. Michael hung back, silent. Part of him wanted to encourage her to go, but he didn't. As Louie and his family were leaving, Nancy promised the kids that she would come and visit soon.

After the door closed, Nancy, still in her black dress, stood for a time—allowing the house to settle back into the familiar quiet after the din of intrusive visitors. She stayed focused on the door, unmoving, as if deciding whether to stay or leave. Michael stood back and waited. Finally, she turned and hugged him. He wrapped his arms around her and held her close. Her cheeks radiated heat, and he could feel the whisper of her warm breath on his neck.

"I can't cry. I want to, but I can't. Is that wrong?"

Michael held her tighter and said, "No," as if he knew the answer.

She went upstairs to change. Michael removed his tie and jacket, kicked off his shoes and sat on the couch, feeling tired. He wondered what the future held.

When Nancy returned dressed in jeans and a T-shirt, Michael offered to spend the night on the sofa. She pulled out a joint and lit it, took a toke and passed it to him, and they quietly smoked and stared at the TV, which emitted shapes and sounds that didn't interest them beyond the soothing, blinking buzz and hum.

After they finished the joint, Michael stretched out on the sofa and Nancy curled up on top of him, resting her head on his chest as he covered her with his arms. He kissed her lightly on the forehead. She closed her eyes and fell asleep. Michael could feel the rhythm of her breathing and her heartbeat as his body blended with hers. He wanted to protect her, to love her. His desire for her was so strong he felt like he was going to explode. Eventually he fell asleep too, and they slept like that until early morning.

Twenty-Six

Having driven under greater pressure than sitting next to an austere, overweight DMV supervisor with thick horn-rimmed glasses and a worn clipboard, Michael passed his driver's test with no problem. A rite of passage, freedom, the pure joy of driving . . . but only after getting permission to borrow his father's car.

Michael offered to make some of the runs to the wholesalers that his father normally did, but his father held tight to them. As the business had grown and became more established, Michael's father had become comfortable spending time away from it, trusting Jeannie and Michael to watch over things. But now he had another mission that took him away—he had begun to search for another grocery store. He even had discussions with Freddie about partnering. This surprised Michael. Freddie had only recently bought his own store, and Michael's father had never had anything good to say about partnerships. But when Michael questioned him about it, his father told him that he'd come to realize that what he wanted could be better leveraged if he partnered. Individually, he and Freddie could both move up, but together they could double what each of them could accomplish alone.

Jeannie continued to come in for her four-hour shift and was always willing to work extra hours if needed, and Michael hired Jimmy, a hardworking kid from the neighborhood, to help with the stocking and cleaning up. Jimmy was only fifteen, too young to get hired anywhere else, so he appreciated the job. And as always, if Michael's mother was needed, she'd come downstairs to help.

Jimmy was the one who took the call. He wrote down a list of groceries and then hung up. "Mrs. Perone, delivery," he said to Michael.

"Bag them up. I'll take it."

"You sure?" Jimmy asked. Michael had been letting Jimmy take on more of the deliveries.

"Yeah, I'm sure."

It had been a few months since Michael had seen Mrs. Perone. Her health had been failing and he hoped she was doing better. Before he could knock, the door swung open, and when she saw Michael, Mrs. Perone's daughter Carmela opened it wider and waved him in. "Hi, Michael, come in," she said. "My mom's in the kitchen."

"How's she doing?" he asked.

She shook her head. "Not good."

He stepped into the house and followed Carmela into the kitchen. Mrs. Perone was seated at the table where she used to serve Michael, where she would dish up a plate of whatever she was cooking and insist that he eat. She appeared frail and lost inside herself.

"Mom, guess who came to see you?"

"Hi, Mrs. Perone," Michael said. "I brought the pignoli

cookies you like." He set the bag on the table, reached in, and placed the package of cookies in front of her. She looked up at him and her eyes searched his face for a few moments. He thought he saw a flicker of recognition, but then it was gone, replaced by a tight, sorrowful expression.

"Michael, please sit, have a cup of coffee with us," Carmela said.

"Yeah. That would be good. You know, your mom was the one that got me to like these cookies. They taste kind of like the ones my mom makes."

Carmela put a cup of coffee in front of Michael and said, "I'm moving back home for a while, to take care of her." Then she opened the bag and stacked the cookies on a plate. As she was sliding the plate in front of Michael and her mom, Mrs. Perone lit up.

"I saw that man Sal try to hit you!" Mrs. Perone said, clearly excited by her lucid moment. "I pointed at him." She lifted her arm and stuck her finger out to demonstrate. "I did! I was going to tell him to stop, but he ran off. I didn't need to say anything, because he stopped. And you were okay. You were okay, Anthony."

Michael sucked in a breath and held it. He was stunned by her outburst—but more for the reminder of his altercation with Sal, something he had put away. It was her! She was the one that spooked Sal and saved Michael from getting punched in the face.

And then it was gone. Mrs. Perone's brief animated outburst, her moment of clarity, was over. She stared at Michael with the same pained yearning from before. He reached for her hand and held it in his.

"Thank you, Mrs. Perone. Thank you for being there. For wanting to tell him to stop," he said, feeling his eyes tear up.

"Michael, what was that about?" Carmela asked.

He shrugged, "Sal was upset about a delivery."

"Right. Sal thought you were after his daughter, didn't he? Don't forget, I have a son a little older than you."

"Yeah. I guess."

"Sal's an idiot. He has no idea what he's in for. Keep a kid away from the candy and all she'll think about is the candy. He would have been lucky to have a guy like you spend time with her."

Michael was flattered by Carmela's words. He could feel his face flush. He jumped up and said, "I should go," and turned to Mrs. Perone again and touched her hunched shoulder. "Thank you again for what you did." Then he followed Carmela to the front door.

As she was about to open it, she said, "One more thing Michael. I don't know what your plans are, but I think you're probably not far from turning eighteen. Don't go. Go to college, do whatever you have to do, but don't go. We've lost so much more than just my brother Anthony to that godforsaken war." And now Carmela started to tear up.

Michael nodded his head, acknowledging what she said.

"Oh, Michael, I forgot. What do we owe you for the groceries?"

"Nothing," Michael said as he slipped out the door.

Twenty-Seven

A VAGUE SENSATION OF THE FUTURE as some hazy, illusive image, too distant to be achievable, clung to Jelly like the rancid smell of napalm long after he landed in-country. But now, with only thirty days left, he could see the end of his tour approaching. He could see himself making it out. Unlike other short-timers who boldly counted down, Jelly was superstitious, dared not whisper it out loud. But he knew he was going to make it home.

But the home where he was most comfortable was the one *outside* of his head, a home made possible by fine white powder cooked in a spoon and injected carefully—or not so carefully—into a vein, providing him that rush, that release, that *vacation* from horrific events in bloody landscapes that his head would otherwise insist on replaying.

Despite his superstition, Jelly wrote his mother to let her know he would be home in early August. Once he had mailed it, though, he agonized over writing such a letter. He knew better, had witnessed other short-timers do the same, had watched as their bodies were sent home soon after their letters. But the letter helped him to put his own marker in time out there, and writing to his mother made it feel real.

Twenty-Eight

SATURDAYS OFTEN GLIDED BY QUICKLY. It was odd how sometimes there seemed to be a rhythm to the customer traffic, busiest mid-morning and late afternoon, while other times there was a constant flow. Either way, balancing the intermittent deliveries—milk, bread, beer, soft drinks—that arrived throughout the day kept Michael moving.

The constant activity made the day fly by, but left him tired. He went upstairs and showered, and just the thought of walking the couple blocks to Nancy's immediately renewed him. Nancy often hung out at the store to kill time, depending on how busy they were of course, but she hadn't stopped by that day.

Nancy's front door was unlocked, which wasn't that unusual. But when he walked in and called out to her, he began to suspect something was wrong. She didn't answer. Michael went upstairs and heard some faint sounds coming from the bathroom. "Nancy?" he called out cautiously. The bathroom door was ajar and he pushed it open.

He was immediately assaulted by the stench of vomit, causing his stomach to tighten and his gag reflex to kick in. Nancy was sitting on the floor next to the toilet, leaning against the wall. Her

T-shirt was stained, and her face was red and streaked with tears and sweat. She was grasping the neck of a nearly empty bottle of vodka and breathing erratically, trying to catch her breath. She opened her glassy, bloodshot eyes and looked at Michael. Then she tilted the bottle to her lips and polished off the last couple ounces of clear liquor. She grimaced as she forced down the harsh, burning liquid. With an outburst of anger, she threw the bottle against the wall. Remarkably, it didn't break; instead it bounced onto the rug that covered the tile floor.

"I thought I was smart!" she yelled, pointing at herself. "I thought I understood a lot about the way things are. But you don't know how fucking stupid you are, how fucking worthless, until you watch—watch someone you love go into uncontrollable fits. And you can't do a goddamn fucking thing about it but watch them helplessly. I never felt so useless in my whole life! It doesn't fucking matter how smart you think you are. It doesn't fucking matter."

Right after the words left her mouth, Nancy retched violently, and before her head could reach the toilet, she puked. She tried catching the vomit in her hand, but it spilled through her fingers. Michael crouched down and held her as she continued to heave.

After she had no more to give, he leaned her up against the tub and said softly, "I'm going to get some towels. I'll be right back, okay? Just hold on for a minute."

Tears streamed down her cheeks as her head bobbed in agreement. Michael left the door open and went down the hall to the linen closet, where he grabbed a couple of towels and washcloths. As he hurried back, he heard the squeaky sound of the bathtub faucets being turned on. Nancy was filling the tub. When Michael walked in, she was standing up and attempting to pull her T-shirt over her head. She began to sway precariously, so he let the towels drop and grabbed her before she fell in the tub.

Once she had regained her balance, Nancy tossed her shirt aside, looked up at Michael, and gave him a warm smile. She stood there half naked, her pale skin shining in the golden tint of the bathroom's light. Her full, round breasts stood firm and nonchalant in their exposure.

"I have to . . . bath." She said, slurring each word.

"Um . . . okay, do you want me to help you?"

Nancy bobbed her head as she unzipped her jeans and pushed them and her underpants down around her legs, nearly tipping herself over again.

"Hold on a minute." Michael said. He closed the toilet lid and sat her down, then got on his knees and slid each pant leg off. As he was doing this, Nancy went limp and fell on top of him.

"Do you think this is a good idea?" Michael asked.

"I'm icky . . . I need bath."

Once she was undressed, she sprawled out on the floor. Michael tried not to stare at her body, preoccupying himself with making sure she was safe, but it was impossible not to glance at her soft, round curves. He found so much beautiful about her. He checked the temperature of the water and then gently picked her up and placed her in the tub. His shirt got wet, so he unbuttoned it and threw it over the towel rack.

Nancy faded in and out of consciousness. When she was awake, she smiled at Michael like a little girl wanting to be taken care of. The rest of the time she'd lie there quietly, occasionally mumbling something under her breath, but he couldn't make out what she was trying to say. With a washcloth and a bar of Ivory soap, he gently washed her face and arms. He took his time on her hands, caressing and soaping them in his, rinsing, and inspecting them. Then he washed her underarms, legs, and smooth tummy, careful to stop at the line where her black, curly hair began, conscious of not touching her where she wouldn't want him to. He'd never felt so close to anyone, so needed; he wanted to take care of her and had no interest in betraying her trust.

"You were there for your mom," Michael said. "That matters. That means something."

With her eyes closed, Nancy shook her head no.

Michael continued to talk to her, explaining what he was doing even though he wasn't sure if he was getting through. Sometimes she seemed to respond, occasionally opening her eyes to look at him before shutting them again.

"I'm going to wash your hair," he told her softly. He used a bottle of Prell shampoo that was sitting on the corner of the tub. He lathered her hair up and used a cup to rinse, watching as the warm water cascaded off her thick black hair, bringing back its dark luster.

After he finished bathing her, he dried her off, wrapped her in a towel, and carried her to her bed. He rummaged through her dresser drawers until he found a nightgown and a pair of underpants. With gentle awkwardness, he slid them on while trying not to imagine taking them off again. Then, helping her to sit up, he was able to put on her nightgown. He tucked her into bed. Her hair was still damp, and a few strands partially covered her face, so he leaned over and gently brushed them off her face and then kissed her gently on the forehead. He took off his shoes and lay down next to her.

As his head sank into the pillow, he took a deep breath and released it gradually, attempting to expel his tension. His thoughts were racing, making it difficult for him to settle down. Then he remembered that he hadn't let his parents know that he needed to stay the night. He slipped out of the room, made the call, and then returned to watch over Nancy. Sometime later, his body finally gave in to the sleep it needed.

Michael woke up to the glare of the sun reflecting off Nancy's dresser mirror, shining in his eyes as he first opened them. As he turned away from the piercing light, he discovered that Nancy's side of the bed was empty. He sat up, groggily trying to shake the sleep away, and went into the bathroom, which still smelled of vomit. Nancy's clothes and the used towels had been removed. He peed, splashed his face with cold water, and brushed his teeth with what he guessed was Nancy's toothbrush. His shirt was still hanging on the towel rack, so he put it on, not bothering to button it up.

As he walked past Nancy's bedroom, heading downstairs, he heard her call out, "Where are you going?" She had returned to bed while he was in the bathroom. "Come back."

When Michael stepped into the room, Nancy patted the side of the bed he'd slept on. "Come back to bed. I had to get up to get some aspirin and something to drink. My head is killing me." She held out a tall glass of orange juice and asked, "You want some?" He climbed back onto the bed and took the glass from her, drank a little, and then handed it back. She placed it on the night table next to her.

"You okay?" he asked, amazed at how much better she looked. "How are you feeling?"

"Not good," she groaned. She reached out her arms and said, "Hold me."

Michael shifted his body closer and pulled her to him. She looked up at him, and her eyes glistened, and then she guided his face down to hers and kissed him, parting her lips. Her tongue met his. She tasted sweet. Michael's heart was beating like it could pound right out of him. Then Nancy pulled away and buried her head in his chest.

"Thanks," she whispered. "Let me rest a little; my head is killing me. Okay?"

Michael held her and tried steadying his breathing as she fell back asleep. Sleep was the furthest thing from his mind. He worked to come up with thoughts distracting enough to allay the yearning that was overwhelming him.

After about thirty minutes, Nancy's head stirred on his bare chest, and he felt her hair lightly sweep across his skin, teasing him. She turned and began kissing him where her head had been resting. She moved down to his stomach, delicately exploring every inch with her soft mouth, starting with small kisses and then opening her mouth, tasting him with the tip of her tongue. Her touch made him hard, took his breath away, made him tingle all over. She unbuckled Michael's pants, continuing to kiss him. She reached in and took him out and before he could blink, she had him in her mouth. Warm, moist passion enveloped him as she moved her head and held him tight. "Oh my God, Nancy, I'm—ah, I'm . . ." Michael's whole body shook as he exploded. Nancy continued to hold him, and when he finished, she looked up and smiled, then slid off the bed and went into the bathroom.

Michael lay speechless, exhilarated. When Nancy came back and sat on the bed next to him, he started to sit up, but she tugged at his shirt and said, "Take this off." He did. She reached for his jeans and, just as he'd done with hers the previous night, slid them down his legs and dropped them on the floor. She lifted her nightgown over her head. She was no longer wearing the underwear he'd put on her last night, and in the daylight he could see each softly sculpted curve, the smooth roundness of her perfectly developed bottom the proud fullness of her breasts.

He took her in his arms, and this time he was the one to initiate the kiss. Feeling her nakedness against his made his blood rush, and his body responded again. He touched and explored each curve, every inch of her amazing body, including where she grew wet with anticipation. He cupped her breasts, eagerly taking them into his mouth, discovering her with his tongue, and then moved his mouth down her body. Michael wanted to give her the same pleasure she'd given him. He felt her soft hair on his face and enjoyed her breathy moans, excited that he could bring her pleasure.

She reached for him, gently guiding him. And as he entered her, she lifted her head to meet his and kissed him hungrily. They were locked together, and when he wanted to move too quickly, she slowed him until their rhythm became one. And the best part was bringing her to that sweet, warm, satisfying place that she had taken him.

Afterward, they lay together quietly, and Michael felt a physical and emotional high beyond anything he could have imagined.

"I love you," he whispered.

Nancy kissed him on the lips. "I love you too." She hesitated, considering what she wanted to say while continuing to gaze at Michael affectionately. "I guess I've been afraid . . . of my feelings for you. Can we just make of this what it is? Take it as it comes? Can we?"

Michael wasn't sure what she meant and wasn't sure how to respond. "Sure," he said.

"Look, we don't know what's going to happen. I know that, eventually, I should get back to school, and . . . and I'm not sure what I'm saying. All I know is that I don't want to hurt you."

Michael felt a twinge deep inside and didn't know what to do with it. He'd fantasized often about being with Nancy. And thought he was willing to accept anything. He knew he was lucky just to be with her, should be happy to take whatever he could get.

But at the same time, he didn't think he could stop himself from giving her everything he had.

She held him close and, lifting her head to look at him, said with a sweet smile, "For future reference, I don't wear panties to bed."

"So I'm learning."

Twenty-Nine

THERE HAD BEEN TIMES IN HIS LIFE when Michael desired something to the point of obsessive distraction, only to find that when he finally arrived at the promise of his expectations, the satisfaction was fleeting and soon replaced with self-reproach—that his imagination had served him better than the actual, somewhat disappointing, outcome. Nancy was not one of those times.

He made no announcement, but the goofy smile that occasionally replaced his protective frown was enough for his parents to see that his relationship with Nancy had changed. His mother had expected this to happen and just hoped it would turn out well. She consoled herself with the thought that at least she knew where he was. Michael's father was more accepting of the time he spent with her; he thought that Nancy would, in some ways, be good for Michael. He gave Michael additional time off so he and Nancy could do things together, but made it clear that he still expected him to do his job. He also told him that as long as he continued to take care of his responsibilities, he'd buy him a car at the end of the summer.

Nancy was coming to the store more often now, and though Michael enjoyed having her close, sometimes it made him uncomfortable. They'd occasionally steal kisses behind the shelves or in the back. Nancy liked to tease him, but she was respectful of his parents and tried to show Michael that she understood his family dynamics. But Michael's lack of experience made him insecure, causing him to worry that she'd meet someone older, more interesting, smarter—and he'd become just a memory. She did nothing to make him believe that. In fact, she openly embraced Michael as her boyfriend and treated him with genuine affection when they were alone, like a lover. But he still couldn't rid himself of the feeling.

"I want to prepare a salad for you from the vegetables I grow in my garden, like my mother did when I was a little girl," Michael's mother said. Their new house was coming along, and she was looking forward to the move. Even Michael found it sort of exciting to watch it being built. If his mother had a concern, it was that the move would take her even farther away from her beloved church in Brooklyn. After they had settled into the apartment above the store, she'd either driven herself to church or arranged to have a cousin or sister take her, rarely missing a Sunday.

Even Michael's father was caught up in the anticipation and announced that their new home should have all new furniture. So Michael's parents started shopping, something Michael didn't remember them ever doing before. He couldn't recall a time when they had worked together on a project, something that was personal for them. His father sometimes took his mother to the fabric store to buy bolts of fabric, but that was different.

The first time Michael saw them leave together on one of their shopping excursions, he was caught off guard by his sentimental feelings.

Thirty

Billy's face was drawn, wizened, the outline of his skull visible through his pale, paper-thin skin. His blue eyes had sunk deep into the hollow of his head and were ringed by dark circles that accentuated his gaunt features. His dirty-blond hair was long overdue for a washing, and his hands shook noticeably. Michael had seen Billy beaten up before, but never so physically wasted.

Billy was sucking on a beer can that was sticking out of a crumpled paper bag and taking deep drags off his cigarette, just wasting time. Since he'd been fired from his job, he'd been hanging around the store. Michael's father was out. Otherwise, Billy wouldn't be welcome for very long—and he knew it.

"Billy, isn't it really hard to get fired from the Post Office?" Michael asked.

"Fuck you. I didn't get fired, I quit. It's a shitty job for fucking assholes." Billy dropped his cigarette butt on the floor and crushed it with his sneaker.

"Hey, I gotta sweep that up. Asshole."

Billy smirked. "It'll give you something to do."

"At least one of us has a job," Michael shot back.

"Hey, I got some things working."

Michael knew what *things* he was referring to. "Heard from Jelly?" he asked.

"He's coming home—"

But Michael had seen a police car cruising up to the curb across the street. "Billy. Give me the beer."

"Fuck it. No one's here," Billy said, pushing back.

Michael gestured to the window. Billy glanced over at the police car and immediately panicked. "Let me out the back door!"

Michael hesitated, not sure if he should. He didn't like this; it felt like trouble.

Billy scrambled to the back and ducked behind the counter "Get over here!" he said, his voice taut with urgency.

Michael rushed over and let Billy out the back door, locking it behind him. By the time he returned, two policemen were in the store. They ordered a roast beef hero and a ham-and-cheese on rye, picked out a Coke and a Seven Up, and then made a halfhearted gesture to pay, which Michael politely refused. They thanked him and left.

Michael had always thought of Billy as small-time—and maybe that's all this was—but he certainly looked like hell. Billy seemed possessed. Michael knew that Billy's family life wasn't the best, but still didn't understand how he got this bad. Roger and Freddie were both about Billy's age, but each one of them was so different, had traveled such divergent paths. Did they do what they believed they should? Or were they driven to do the things they did? *Are we in control of the choices we make, or is where we end up somehow predestined?*

Michael thought of Ben, with his steadfast conviction about what he saw as his place in this world. Michael wasn't sure he understood what made someone like Ben, or someone like Billy, act like they did. Or what drove Freddie or Roger, for that matter. He did, however, occasionally wonder what province in Canada Roger had ended up in. But what truly plagued Michael, what he'd silently anguish over, was where *he* would end up.

Thirty-One

MICHAEL AND NANCY WENT TO SEE *The Graduate,* and after the movie they settled into a booth at the diner waiting for their cheeseburgers to arrive. The waiter was the owner's nephew, recently arrived in this country from Greece, and would tell anyone who would listen, in his broken English, how happy he was to be here. He delivered their food with a wide grin, and after he placed the plates in front of them he waved his hand at Michael and asked excitedly, "You Greek, right?"

Michael suddenly felt trapped, as if he'd been caught cheating on a math exam by that teacher, Mrs. Wills. He hated being asked things like that, and if he couldn't blow off or sidestep the question, he'd give a defensive knee-jerk response—"What do you think?"—and just agree with any answer that was given. And then immediately feel guilty, as if he'd just betrayed his family. He rationalized that it was easier than being questioned about—or accosted for—being an Arab. So it was second nature for him to respond the way he did, not even thinking about Nancy sitting across from him.

Michael threw off a shrug and gave a slight nod, as if agreeing with the waiter.

"I knew, it's good," the waiter said, pleased with himself.

Nancy was taken aback by the exchange. "What the hell was that about?" she snapped after the waiter left.

"What? I didn't want to get into it."

"Get into what? Get into the fact that you're Arab, not Greek? I don't *believe* you," she said, turning away.

"Hey, it's just easier. He caught me off guard, okay?"

Nancy looked at Michael with obvious disappointment and neither of them touched their food.

"Look, I don't know why I did that, okay? You're right, it's stupid. It's just easier."

"You keep saying it's easier. What does that mean? It's easier to be someone other than who you are?"

"I don't know." Michael felt ashamed.

Nancy studied his face. "I guess I'd be a hypocrite if I said I didn't understand. I haven't always liked who I am either. But I finally realized that it's bullshit to feel that way."

"It's just that most people are clueless." Michael clenched up. "When I say I'm an Arab, they just look at me funny and don't know how to respond. They ask where my sheet is or where I parked my camel. It's no big deal being Italian. You're not called a sand nigger."

"I got my share of epithets hurled at me . . . *guinea, dago, wop*. But it's not just about that, is it?"

"It's different for Arabs. We're the outsiders. Italians, Jews, Irish—even Greeks—are more accepted here. On top of that, the only thing this country knows about Palestinians is that we got our asses kicked by Israel. And we're the bad guys."

"That's ignorant bullshit," Nancy said. "No, let me say it another way. It's the ignorant who *think* that bullshit. And by you not standing up as an example to them, they'll continue to think that way." She paused a moment and then added, "And that's what I hope you figure out. It's something that took me a while to understand."

He stared at his plate of food.

"Michael, I know you're proud of who you are, of your heritage, by the things you've told me about your family. The stories of the old country, the passion your people have for life. Hey, I know it's hard sometimes being raised in another culture. But believe it or not—that's what gives you the advantage." Nancy paused again to see if she was getting though to him and then continued in a loving tone. "I didn't get it either, until I had time to think. When I was taking care of my mom and away from everybody and all the bullshit that we're constantly bombarded with, I came to realize that it's not what other people think that matters, but how I respond."

"That's easy to say. And I do know better. That's what really digs at me," Michael said and sheepishly raised his eyes. Nancy reached across the table to take his hand.

"I didn't say it was easy."

"Hey, there's one benefit with the waiter thinking I'm Greek—I got more fries than you," Michael added in an effort to lighten the tone.

"Yeah well, maybe he likes you in a *special* way."

"Who's throwing around stereotypes now?"

Nancy laughed. "Okay, can we get back to discussing Mrs. Robinson's need to quell her boredom by having an affair with Ben?"

"I can understand why Ben was attracted to an older woman," Michael said as he grabbed the ketchup bottle.

"Ah, but was he attracted or seduced?" she shot back. "Besides, he ended up with the younger one," she added, raising her eyebrows.

"Well, who could argue with . . . that actress, what's her name?"

"Katharine Ross," Nancy said.

"She's very pretty."

"Yeah, if you like those sweet innocent types."

"What a bitch Mrs. Robinson was. He was good enough to sleep with *her*, but not good enough for her daughter." Michael thought about that for a moment. "It *would* be a little messy, I guess."

Nancy picked at her fries, then said, "It was too pat an ending for me."

"You just don't like happy endings."

She rolled her eyes at him and took a sip of her Coke.

Michael was biting into his cheeseburger when he saw Shelly, dressed in her white nurses' uniform, step up to the counter to place an order to go. Shelly never seemed to change: same platinum blond hair, cut in the same style. Her eyes landed on him, and he waved, hoping she wouldn't come over. But she immediately headed in their direction.

Michael hadn't seen that much of her recently. She still came in the store occasionally, but she was getting most of her groceries—and her cigarettes—personally delivered. Once he'd gotten past the humiliation of being beaten up, Michael always remembered her as an angel. It took a unique kindness to pick someone up off the street, take him home, and care for him the way she had. No matter what happened in the future, and no matter what might be going on now, Michael would always see her as a considerate and loving person. Besides, he wasn't sure what, if anything, was really happening between her and his father—even though the evidence was pretty damning. He decided it was better if he didn't think about it too much.

Shelly seemed a little hesitant, almost shy, as she approached them. "Michael, how are you? It's been a while."

"I'm good. Uh . . . this is my girlfriend, Nancy."

Shelly turned and briefly but warmly acknowledged Nancy. "I'm Shelly."

"Hi," Nancy replied. But Shelly couldn't seem to take her eyes off Michael. "It's *really* good to see you." When she was ready to leave, she turned to Nancy and added, "Nice to meet you."

"You too," Nancy said. Shelly went back to the front counter, picked up her order, and glanced back at them one last time before she stepped out the door.

Nancy watched Michael intently. "Okay, who is she *really*?"

"Just someone from the neighborhood." Michael struggled to meet Nancy's eyes. "She shops at the store. Sometimes I'd make deliveries to her. That's all."

"That's all, huh? And what do you deliver?" she asked with a smirk, eyes gleaming with mischief.

Michael could feel his face turning red.

"No wonder you liked the movie! You have your own 'blond' Mrs. Robinson."

"No! It's not like that and you know it."

"Ah, so let me guess, you deliver the usual bread, milk, and . . ." Nancy paused and then quickly added, "Virile young man!" She started laughing.

His face now registered full embarrassment. But her teasing made him happy—even if it was at his expense. It was nice to see Nancy being playful again.

"Let's go. I have a *delivery* to make."

"*Do* you? Well, you'd better not be late," she said as they got up to leave.

The basement room seemed smaller than Michael remembered. Nancy grabbed the white sheet with both hands and, like a Matador flinging his cape high, lifted it off the barber chair in one swooping motion.

"Sit," she said, patting the chair. He did and leaned back against the leather. She flipped open her father's straight razor and began gliding it up and down the leather strop that hung off the chair.

"What are you doing with that?" he asked, feigning panic.

"Well, it looks like you need a shave. But I'll have to get closer to that pretty face of yours to be sure." Nancy yanked the lever, causing the chair to recline. She loomed above Michael and smiled wickedly. "Let's see . . . No, this won't do, I still need to get closer." She climbed up on top of him, softly kissing his face as she unbuttoned his shirt. "I was mistaken. You don't need a shave here . . . but let's see if you might need one somewhere else," she whispered as she continued to kissing down his stomach, undoing the belt on his pants.

Michael kissed her passionately, then said, "I know what you need," as he pulled off her tie-dye T-shirt.

"And what's that?"

"One of my special deliveries," Michael said, trying not to groan after delivering such a corny line.

"Oh brother," she said softly. "We've created a monster." She kissed his bare chest, beginning to work her way down again. "A monster I happen to love."

Michael took note of the irony and secretly took extra pleasure from it: they were making love on the very chair that a little over a year ago had been the scene of serious adolescent angst.

Thirty-Two

Jelly was stoned when he boarded the plane that took him out of Vietnam. But it wasn't like he even needed to get high; in the last few days he'd been experiencing a strange numbness, feeling isolated, removed from everything around him. But that feeling didn't last.

On the flight home, Jelly was racked with an emotional mixture of gratitude and guilt. He'd met and spent time with some quality guys over here, guys who really had their shit together. Guys who had good lives back home, some with wives and kids waiting for them. Smart guys. Tough guys who fought hard. And just because they were in the wrong place at the wrong time, these guys were going home in boxes. What made him so lucky? Why was he given a ticket out? Jelly didn't want to think about that. He used to wrestle with those thoughts daily and had worked hard to expel them from his mind. It was just that—luck—and that's all there was to it. But like the memory of the bloody village, the thoughts appeared without warning. Something was said, a particular voice was heard, and the face of a dying soldier—or worse, that dead little girl—filled his head, the vivid image as stark and in focus as the Playboy centerfold that hung next to his bunk.

Jelly tried to stay focused on seeing his mother and brother and going out with the guys and having the freedom to do what he wanted. These kind of thoughts sometimes helped him to dispel the others. But unfortunately, his best efforts often failed him, and then he would have to resort to stepping outside of his mind—a place where he was growing more and more comfortable.

Jelly craved a decent meal, and began to fantasize about a cheeseburger and fries, his mother's greasy bacon and eggs, all the things he'd taken for granted before he was sent to that fucked-up country. But what he'd missed the most was the ability to run away, even for a day, like he and Billy used to do when they were in school. They'd ditch, ride the subway into the City, and visit one of the cheesy movie theaters that showed those bad skin flicks. They would screw around all day and at night walk up and down Broadway and Forty-Second Street hassling the hookers. Grab a slice of pizza. Score some dope and get high. Jelly felt indomitable when he was with Billy.

It was a carefree and careless time; they worried about very little. Their only concern was having enough money left over to buy a subway token home. And if they didn't, they'd just hop the turnstile.

Thirty-Three

THE END OF SUMMER WAS APPROACHING, and Michael continued to remind his father about his promise to get him a car. A customer told them about a used green Mustang for sale, a 1965, six cylinders, with a three-speed stick shift. And without even seeing it, Michael though it was perfect and begged his father to buy it. He would have to learn how to drive a stick, but he wanted to own that car so bad, he'd have learned to rebuild the carburetor if that's what it took. Of course, someone would have to point out to him which part was the carburetor.

Nancy had been doing some serious thinking about what she wanted—whether she should return to school in the fall or wait until the spring semester. She was entertaining another idea as well, but chose not to share it with Michael. Nancy was considering transferring to the University of California, Berkeley. She'd remained close with her roommate Susan, who often spoke of her home in Mill Valley as if it were some magical place.

Blond and buoyant, Susan possessed a warmth and openness that had at first made Nancy suspicious. But once Nancy let down her guard, she quickly learned that Susan was genuine. And that despite her airy optimism and free-spirited nature, she had a serious side. As different as they might seem, they both shared a desire to be independent and not conform to expectations. While Nancy had been consumed with her mother, Susan had been her one reliable connection to school. And now Susan had decided to stay in California and continue her education at Berkeley.

"The City's great. I proved to myself that I could do it—that I can make it on my own—but now I want to be closer to home," she told Nancy. Susan encouraged Nancy to consider joining her, to at least come out and visit. The idea of a major change, a new adventure, was beginning to appeal to Nancy. Maybe because it was a chance to *really* run away, but she quickly dismissed that idea. There was nothing to run away from anymore. But for some reason, she couldn't quite convince herself of that.

Nancy sent for a catalog and application. She needed to talk with someone, and though she very much wanted it to be Michael, she knew how he'd react. She hadn't even made up her mind yet, and she needed to think it through without that pressure. As it was, leaving Michael was one of the main reasons she struggled with the decision. She decided to run the idea by her brother the next time he stopped by to check on her.

Louie was sitting across from Nancy, clutching a mug of coffee, when she sprang it on him. "What the hell ya wanna go there for? Why would you do that?" he said, shaking his mug and spilling hot coffee on his hand—and the floor—as the words flew out his mouth.

Nancy was surprised by his response; it reminded her of her mother. But while she was still searching for how to answer him, he added in a softer tone, "Look. You wanna go, go. It's your life. The kids'll miss you, but do what you need to. Just know—I'll always be here for you."

"I know, Louie. And I love you for it."

"That's the point! Here—you get in a jam, we have friends that can help. There, it's like you're in a fuckin' foreign country! We don't have people there. *Our* people."

Nancy was touched by her brother's emotional outburst. She'd always known that he loved her and that she could count on him, but this was one of the few times he'd been so direct. It reminded her of high school. Even though her brother was so much older, everyone knew she was his little sister and treated her with respect. It was like Louie's reputation had created a protective shield for her that lingered long after he was gone, something that had always amused her.

She realized that she'd already made up her mind, and that the exercise of talking to Louie had been just that. Maybe she'd wanted to play it out with her brother as practice—because she had no idea how she was going to break it to Michael.

Michael's father had started asking him about colleges and which ones he was planning on applying to—a subject Michael would rather avoid. It just reminded him that his grades weren't high enough to be accepted at Columbia.

One night as Michael and Nancy sat watching the *Smothers Brothers Show*, she turned to him and joined his father's chorus. "Have you picked the schools you're applying to?"

"Not yet," Michael answered.

"What are you waiting for? You need to start. Your applications need to be in this fall. You want me to help?"

"No!" Michael said. What he didn't want to admit was that he hadn't requested any applications.

"It's important, Michael. And I know you—you'll put it off

until it's too late." Her voice rose as she became increasingly upset. "You want to end up wearing a green uniform? Do you!"

Michael turned away. She was right. He knew it. He needed to get moving, but even the idea of considering schools, filling out applications, made the inevitable feel too real.

"Besides, you look like shit in green," Nancy said in an attempt to lighten things up.

Michael shrugged. "I still don't know what I want to do."

"Lots of guys in school don't know what they want to do." And then added under her breath, "In fact most of them are clueless."

"I'm not as smart as you."

"Stop it! You might not have the grades, but don't think for a minute that you're not smart." She paused and then asked, "What's this about? You know what can happen if you don't go to school. You want to get drafted? And even if Vietnam *wasn't* looming, would you want to get stuck here? You're better than this place. You want more, even if you're not sure what more is. And the best thing you can do is get the hell out of here."

He turned his head to avoid looking at her. She reached out with both hands and gently turned his face toward hers. And then it hit him, he saw a glimmer of fear, the fear you feel for someone you love when you're uncertain of what might happen to them. The fear you feel when someone you love dons a uniform and travels to a dark unfamiliar part of the world and, despite the facade of valor, you no longer have the illusion of control.

"Did you hear me?" she asked in a firm but soft tone. "It's funny, but in a strange way my crazy old-world mother did me a favor. Because of the way she was, I wanted out of here in the worst way. And getting out was the best thing I ever did." Nancy moved her face closer to Michael's to emphasize her next statement. "You're the same. I know it, even though you're not sure of what you want right now. You know better, and you'll refuse to settle."

"But what about us?" Michael asked.

Nancy paused and then said lovingly, "I believe, if two people really love each other, then neither one will stand in the way of what's best for the other. That could mean different things. It could even mean not being together."

"Is that what it was about for you and Roger?"

"No. I cared a lot for Roger. But I'm not sure I really loved him. I think I loved the *idea* of him."

"I don't understand."

"I'm not sure I do either. All I know is sometimes people come into your life and they're just an experience, while others come into your life and make it richer. Like you have."

Michael didn't expect that. He welled up with emotion and struggled not to cry. She reached for him and held him.

"What about us?" he asked again, in shaky voice.

"It's *about* us and we're living it and we'll do what's right for each other, because that's what two people who love each other do." She moved closer and then kissed Michael tenderly, reassuring him that they were indeed together—at least for the moment. Michael welcomed her embrace, but it nagged at him that his question remained unanswered.

That night, Michael paid attention to every curve, crease, and birthmark on her responsive body. While he made love to her, he imagined it was the last time. And even though he was aware that it wasn't true, it spurred him to give her as much pleasure as he possibly could, tasting all of her, moving deep inside her. He gave himself over to their lovemaking and yearned—as a young child yearns on the night before Christmas for that special gift to be under the tree—for it not to end.

Thirty-Four

"It's great there. Unspoiled. And I can get twice the house for half what it costs here."

John Harris had just returned from a week long visit to Manassas, Virginia, where his brother lived, convinced that moving there was the right thing to do. This was what John was declaring to Michael and his father late one evening when Ben and Janet walked in.

Ben's wife was striking. She was tall and slender, with long black hair and chiseled cheekbones. But it was her infectious smile that assured everyone she met of her easygoing personality.

"Hey, there's my man," Ben said, walking around John and stretching his hand out across the counter to Michael. "Janet, remember when I told you about the young man that was going to build the next A&P? Well, here he is." John went silent, and Michael could see his face tighten up.

Michael's father looked amused at Ben's comment. Michael reached out and shook Ben's hand, and Ben nodded at Michael's father in acknowledgment.

"It's nice to meet you," Michael said to Janet.

"Nice to meet you too. Has my husband been giving you

grief?" she asked playfully.

"No, I like talking to him."

"Talk he can." She winked at Michael and then stepped away to pick up a few groceries.

John grabbed his bag and scurried out the door.

Ben couldn't resist. "Something I said?"

"I think he's in a hurry," Michael said, shrugging his shoulders.

Ben knew better, but dismissed it.

"Right," Ben said, nodding his head. "Can I have two packs of Pall Malls?" Michael's father pulled them out of the rack and laid them on the counter.

"Ben, you're supposed to be quitting," Janet said as she returned to the counter with a quart of milk and a bottle of orange juice.

"Not just yet, babe. Soon."

"You enjoying your summer?" Ben asked Michael.

"I am."

"Enjoy it, because pretty soon summer will mean a hot, sticky subway ride to your job."

Janet laughed and shook her head. "Ben, give the boy a break. He has plenty of time before he needs to worry about that." Ben paid, they said their good byes, and left.

"Nice people," Michael's father said.

"What's up with John?" Michael asked indignantly.

"I don't know . . . maybe he had to leave."

"You know what I mean. He's a complete asshole when it comes to Black people."

"What're you saying? You don't know what he's thinking."

"Yeah, I do." Michael said sharply. "The last time John ran into Ben here, he called him a nigger, said he was ruining the neighborhood."

"Maybe it's how they think where he's from, how he was raised."

"That's bullshit. It's no excuse—he's supposed to know better."

"Hey! You can watch your language," his father said, getting irritated.

"There's a lot of ignorant people in this neighborhood," Michael said. "I'm glad we're moving!"

"And what? What do you think? The new neighborhood will be different? People are people. They don't change. You can't move away from stupid. It's up to you to be smart."

"It's just *wrong*."

"Let's close," his father said, pulling the money out of the register to count. Michael slammed the candy boxes together as he stacked them up and began to restock the depleted rack.

"Things happen to people. You don't know what someone's been through," Michael's father said after he'd counted the piles of ones, fives, tens, and twenties twice and was sticking the wad of money into an envelope.

"There's no excuse for being a bigot," Michael said.

"You know why you never see John's son?"

"I did see him. Once. He was standing in their front window, just staring out."

Michael's father shook his head. "The boy's slow. Did you know that?"

"No! What does that have to do with John being a bigot?"

"Nothing. But it's something you didn't know about him."

A picture of the boy's sad face popped into Michael's head.

"He doesn't talk about his son," his father continued, "not a word. But he's told me many times how impressed he is with you." And then he said, "*Yallah*, sweep up, let's go," with a tone of finality that told Michael that the discussion was over.

Thirty-Five

THE BASEMENT WAS A MESS. Cases of beer, Coke, and other soft drinks had piled up precariously and required sorting and stacking so they'd be easier to retrieve for filling the refrigerators upstairs. There wasn't even a whisper of the slight coolness that usually made the basement a fleeting retreat for Michael—a result of the heat wave afflicting the city that summer. In the hour and a half that he'd been down there working, Michael had sweated through his clothes several times over. His fine cotton shirt stuck to him like fresh tar to the sole of a leather shoe. Nancy had said that she might stop by, and he was eager to get this chore over with so he'd be upstairs when she arrived. What he didn't know was that his father was gone and had asked his mother to work the store until Michael was finished in the basement.

Jamila was helping some customers when Nancy walked in. Nancy hung back, watching and waiting until the customers left. As Jamila bagged groceries and made change, she was also studying Nancy—her son's infatuation. She desperately wanted to understand what it was about this young woman that so appealed to him. And she needed to know what Nancy wanted with *him*. Why her son, a boy a couple years her junior? Other than that one discussion where she'd cautioned Michael, Jamila hadn't brought up the subject of Nancy. Not that she hadn't wanted to, but when she mentioned it to Aziz, he said, "Don't worry about it. The boy will be fine." But Jamila didn't believe that.

Sometimes she asked Michael how Nancy was doing. "Fine" was his stock answer. And if they were going out, she'd ask where, always hoping for more than his standard brief reply of the location or name of the event. But he wasn't forthcoming, so she stopped herself from pushing.

Jamila's shyness was painfully evident and so different from her husband's outgoing nature and enjoyment of people. Despite the odd contrast in their personalities, they'd learned how to share a life together. Jamila preferred to express her affection through the simple, everyday actions she performed: preparing a meal with care, crafting a suit with the best material she could find, and giving loving attention to every detail of these tasks. She remembered how much she used to look forward to Michael coming home after school. How she'd take a break from her sewing machine, fix him a snack, and sit listening intently to whatever adventures he'd had that day. She'd review his work with effusive pride, encouraging him and promoting his imagination. Like Aziz, she understood the educational value of experience, especially for a boy, and encouraged Michael to try different things. But this girl, this Nancy, was an experience that *she* wasn't ready for. He was too young. She was convinced he was going to end up hurt.

Nancy was still standing several feet from the counter when she addressed Jamila. With an easy smile and open manner Nancy said, "Hi, how are you? Has it been busy?"

As much as she tried, Jamila found it difficult to be put off by Nancy. Her directness—her habit of looking whoever she was talking to directly in the eyes with a genuine openness that said, "this is who I am, take it or leave it"—pleased Jamila, but still challenged her. She was both unnerved and intrigued by Nancy's boldness, and Jamila sometimes wished *she'd* been raised to be more intrepid. She felt her frown dissolve as she answered, "No. It's slow. Michael's in the basement, working."

"That's okay. I'll wait," Nancy said.

"Would you like something to drink?"

"No, I'm good, thanks." Nancy approached the counter. "He's a hard worker, isn't he?"

"He is," Jamila said, nodding.

"You must be proud of him."

The comment caused Jamila to pause; it aroused mixed feelings in her. Of course she was proud, but how strange it was hearing this from the young woman standing in front of her. The discussion felt awkward, out of place. She reminded herself that she did not approve of their relationship, but felt inclined to remain polite. Maybe this was a chance to understand.

"Yes, I am. As I'm sure your mother was very proud of you."

"I hope she was," Nancy responded.

"I'm *sure* she was. Michael told me how devoted you were to her, how you took good care of her." This caught Nancy off guard, but before she could respond, a customer walked in.

A slick, well-dressed man in his late forties approached the counter and ordered two packs of Tareytons. He gave Nancy the once-over and she shot back a contemptuous frown. He paid, picked up his cigarettes, and left.

"I'm not sure I realized how much Michael helped me get through it until it was over," Nancy said. Jamila was deep in her own thoughts and only heard a little of what Nancy said. "He's a good boy," she responded distractedly.

Nancy hesitated for several seconds, uncertain if her reaction was appropriate, but then let it out anyway.

"He's not a boy anymore." Then she quickly added, "I guess what I mean is, he's more mature and responsible than many guys his age. More mature than a lot of men I know."

"He's grown up fast," Jamila said, nodding.

"What was he like as a little boy?"

Jamila smiled at the thought. "Very shy, very quiet."

"I can see that. In some ways he's still shy, isn't he?"

"He tries hard to please the people he cares for."

Nancy instinctively reached out and touched Jamila's hand as it rested on the counter, and without thinking she just said what she felt. "I just want you to know that I care for him very much."

As Jamila looked at Nancy, a collection of confused emotions rushed through her. How quickly it had come to this: a young woman declaring her affection for her son, so different from the world she'd come from. She studied the woman who had become the focus of her young son's life and thought, *Yes she is too old for him, but he could have chosen worse. She is attractive in her own way, bold and smart.* But concern for his well-being kept Jamila reserved. She nodded, acknowledging Nancy's comment, not knowing how else to respond. But then a sly smile began to take shape as another thought came to her mind. "There's something I'll tell you. I probably shouldn't, but it's something that, when I think of him as a little boy, makes me smile."

After the last case of beer was piled high and the makeshift aisles were clear, Michael started up the stairs and heard voices, recognizing immediately that the two women he cared most for were collaborating. His stomach tightened. What information were they exchanging? What secrets might be revealed? He ran up the last few steps and through the back and said a loud, "Hi!" to Nancy, who faced away from him as she engaged his mother in conversation.

Nancy spun around with a mischievous smile and said, "Hi! We were just talking about you."

"Great!" he replied with false enthusiasm.

"You look like you've been working hard," Nancy said.

"Yeah, I'm going to wash up. I'll be right back. Mom, did you bring a fresh towel down from upstairs?"

"Funny you should mention towels . . ." Nancy said.

"What?"

"Superman."

"What are you . . . No!"

"Yeah, your mother was just telling me how you used to pin a large towel around your neck and run around jumping off furniture . . . faster than a speeding bullet, more powerful than a locomotive!" Nancy and his mother both started giggling.

"Ma! Really? That's great. That's just . . . great." Michael stomped into the back room flushed with embarrassment, mumbling under his breath, "Thanks a lot, Mom." And for the next few days he had to endure Superman references.

Thirty-Six

Michael's father finally relented and took Michael to "see" the Mustang, but he knew that this meant buying it for his son. Before they arrived, he instructed Michael not to say anything—not how much he wanted it, what a great deal it was, what great shape it was in, nothing. "Just listen, learn," he said. Michael's father negotiated hard. But not too hard. The owner came down another two hundred dollars, and they struck a deal.

Michael talked his father into giving him a day off, and he and Nancy took off for Jones Beach. As he drove his new car—Nancy next to him—an exhilarating sense of freedom came over him; as if with each mile he drove, he was leaving something behind, something from his past. Not something unpleasant, just something he didn't want to go back to. It was one of those moments in life when everything felt right.

It was a spectacular late-summer day, and the breeze from the ocean alleviated the heat and humidity that hung thick in the City. They laid a blanket and some towels down on the sand and stretched out, basking in the luxury of a languid, peaceful moment, listening to the crash of waves and feeling the sun warm their bodies.

Michael reached for Nancy's hand and leaned in and kissed her. She responded by first becoming playful, then kissing him back passionately.

For a weekday, the beach was relatively busy. They'd set up as far away from the crowd as possible, and the old blanket and bath towels that Michael's mother had given them came in handy. Covering themselves up as best they could, they quietly made love. When they had finished, but were still enjoying their closeness under the blanket, a little boy about five years old ambled up to them. With a quizzical look he pointed at Michael, who was still on top of Nancy, and said, "What're you doing?"

"Resting," Michael shot back.

"You're hurting her," the boy said in a loud, squeaky voice.

Nancy started to giggle.

"Willie, leave those people alone!" the boy's mother called from some distance away.

"But Ma, he's hurting her, I saw it. He was jumping on her, Ma!"

"Willie," Michael said calmly. "Go play. Let us rest. Come back later. Okay?"

"You better get off her!" Willie said, pointing a reprimanding finger.

"Willie, get over here now!" his mother yelled.

The little boy shook his head in adult-like disapproval and then turned and ran toward his mother, saying, "Ma . . . Ma, he's hurting her!"

Michael laughed. "Kid's gonna grow up to be a policeman."

"Vice squad," Nancy added, still tickled.

"He's definitely going to work for the government."

After they managed to slip back into their bathing suits, they lay quietly listening to the soothing sound of the ocean. Michael closed his eyes and was starting to doze off when Nancy, who'd been watching the water's edge as each wave lapped the shoreline, asked, "How can anyone who's growing up now work for the government?"

"Somebody has to," Michael murmured.

"No, seriously. Think about what's going on, how we're being lied to, how many lives are being lost because of it."

Giving up his last hope of catching a cat nap, Michael engaged. "Should I go get Willie and straighten him out before it's too late?"

"I'm being serious, Michael. Look at us, how lucky we are. We're here, smelling the clean ocean air. And you, enjoying that great car your dad got you, don't you feel a little spoiled, a little indulged?"

"Grateful . . . I feel grateful, I can tell you that."

"I know you are, I didn't mean it that way. It's just, I can't stop thinking about the kids that don't have a chance, that are brainwashed into thinking they're doing what's right—what's patriotic—and end up in uniform killing other kids somewhere we shouldn't be, while the politicians sit in Washington and stir up the fear necessary to convince everyone that if we don't go—the bad guys, the *communists*—will be attacking our shores."

"On top of that, look at the South. Our own country still hasn't figured out how to treat each other equally," Michael said.

"Exactly," she said, sitting up straight.

"But, what can we do? Look what happened on campus. If we'd ended up in jail, I don't know how I would've explained it to my dad."

"You would've told him the truth, and that's just what we need to force the government to do. We need to speak truth to power, otherwise it grows corrupt and runs roughshod over the people."

"No one tells the truth. You taught me that."

"Yeah, well, it's costing all of us."

"I think I should go get Willie and straighten his ass out right now so he doesn't end up working for the CIA," Michael said.

Nancy laughed, appreciating his effort to lighten things up. "Save the world one kid at a time?"

Michael thought back to earlier that week. His father had taken his mother to see how the house was progressing and had asked him if he wanted to come along. Michael had declined because they were expecting a dry goods delivery and he needed to help Jimmy stock the shelves when it arrived. As soon as his parents returned, his mother began packing the household belongings that they wouldn't need until after they settled into their new home.

Remembering his mother's excitement over the move made Michael realize that there was something he wanted to do. He stood up and stretched out his hand to Nancy. "Come on, let's go. I wanna show you something."

"What?"

"You'll see."

They dusted off as much sand as possible from their legs and feet, and then walked back to the Mustang, feeling the slight sting and glow of sun on their skin.

"I think I'll probably go back in the spring instead of the fall," Nancy announced matter-of-factly. "It'll give me a little more time to decide what to do."

Michael didn't like the sound of that. "What to do?"

Nancy turned and looked out the passenger side window at the apartment buildings and businesses that shuttled by. "I don't know,

I'm thinking about changing some classes, maybe my major."

"Oh." Michael wasn't relieved of his concern, but whatever was going on, she clearly wasn't ready to tell him. He didn't want to press her, so he pushed it out of his mind and focused on driving, watching as the tree-lined streets passed by, thinking about how this would soon be his new neighborhood and wondering if he'd ever get used to it. They rode quietly for the remainder of the short trip.

Nancy figured out where they were headed and felt a little rush of enthusiasm knowing that Michael wanted to take her to see his new house. It was an odd feeling, like going to see the progress somehow made her part of their family. But it seemed silly when she thought about it.

When Michael and Nancy arrived, there was a contractor's truck parked outside. Michael parked next to it, and as they started up the driveway, Nancy turned in front of him and took his hand, as if to reassure him. "Do you know when I first wanted to make love to you?"

There was a sweet tenderness in the way she asked him the question.

"No," Michael said, searching her face for the answer.

"Remember the night of my mother's funeral, after Louie and his family left?"

"Yeah," he said, thinking back.

"We were lying together on the sofa, and you held me tight. I felt watched over, safe . . . loved. I'd never felt that close to anyone before. I wanted to make love to you right then, but I was afraid. I didn't want to risk changing those feelings. I know now that if we'd made love, it would've only brought us closer sooner."

Michael stood there, filled with warmth at her revelation but unprepared with a response. He opened his mouth, but what came out was an uncertain stammer.

Nancy covered his mouth with her hand. "You don't need to say anything. I was just thinking about that night, and wanted to share it with you." Then she lifted her hand from his mouth and kissed him.

The house was a single-story ranch on a block where most of the other homes were two-story colonials, and it had a spacious back yard, a feature that Michael's mother commented on frequently. She was pleased that she'd finally have the space to grow the large garden she'd always envisioned. The house had three bedrooms, a formal dining room, and a sizable living room that appeared even larger because of the bay window that opened up the room. Michael's mother had first noticed this type of window traveling through New England and liked the look. Michael's father had initially resisted, but came around when she pointedly reminded him that she was the one who would be spending the most time in the house since he was hardly ever home—and that his absences had been including more and more evenings.

The house still required more work; the plumbing and fixtures had only just been installed, and the interior needed to be painted. When Michael and Nancy walked through, two men were still working in one of the back bedrooms. While the house prompted a sense of pride for Michael, it also felt strange, abstract, and he thought that it would probably feel that way for a while, even after they moved in. Somehow he had grown comfortable in his cramped little bedroom above the store.

On the way back, Michael drove by Freddie and Yvonne's store. He'd been hoping to visit all along, but threw it out to Nancy in a casual manner, saying that since they were so close, he wanted to make a quick stop. "They're my cousins. You know, I've mentioned them to you before. You'll like them." He'd told Nancy about how Freddie had decided to go into the grocery business despite having graduated with an engineering degree. He'd even mentioned Yvonne and how she wasn't given much choice about school. That had started a giant discussion between them about the choices people make.

For some reason, he really wanted Yvonne to meet Nancy. Michael wasn't looking for Yvonne's approval or anything like that, but he still wanted her to like his girlfriend. In some ways they were similar. They both had a natural intellectual curiosity, a strong desire to learn as much as they could about life and the world around them. But there was a conspicuous difference between them. Nancy rebelled—challenged and questioned everything—while Yvonne acquiesced, quietly following a traditional role.

"Sure, happy to meet your cousins," Nancy said.

Freddie and Yvonne's deli was designed well. The front door opened onto an aisle that led straight to the checkout counter, which was spacious enough to bag groceries and make change. Adjacent to the counter on the left was a deli case about five feet high and eight feet wide that was full of cold cuts, salads, and cheeses. Behind that was the Hobart slicing machine and counter space for making sandwiches, which did good business at lunchtime, because of the number of office buildings nearby. There were two openings, one where the counter ended and another at the other end where the deli case left off, which made it easy for Freddie or Yvonne to slip out if they needed to assist a customer. Several well-stocked shelves formed additional aisles across the length of the store. The tall refrigerator that held the milk, beer, and soda was up against the far-left wall.

Yvonne and Freddie were both behind the counter. Freddie, head down at the Hobart machine, right hand positioned high, glided it back and forth in careful rhythm, slicing bologna for one customer while Yvonne bagged groceries for another. Yvonne lit up when she saw Michael walk in. He reached for Nancy's hand, and Yvonne waved at them as if acknowledging his gesture. They stayed back, waiting for Freddie and Yvonne to finish with their customers.

"What are their names again?" Nancy asked.

"Freddie and Yvonne."

"Cool."

"Want a Coke?" Michael asked.

"Sure."

He slid open the soda cooler, popped the caps off two bottles of Coke, and handed one to Nancy.

Freddie turned with wrapped cold cuts in hand, and when he saw them standing by the entrance shouted out, "Hey stranger, you lost? Need directions?" before handing the cold cuts to the customer, who paid and left.

Michael and Nancy approached the counter. Yvonne didn't rush to greet him as she had the last time he'd stopped in. But she did smile warmly at him before fixing a curious gaze on Nancy, and then shifting her focus back and forth between Nancy and Michael.

"*Walak*, where've you been?" Freddie asked.

"Working."

"Yeah, working, with no time for family," Freddie nagged.

"You're starting to sound like one of my aunts. I'm here now. And I brought my girlfriend to meet you. This is Nancy." Michael turned to Nancy and then pointed to Yvonne and Freddie. "This is Yvonne and my 'aunt' Freddie."

"It's nice to meet you, Nancy," Yvonne said with a polite smile.

"Would you like something to eat?" Freddie asked.

"Thanks, we're fine," Michael said. "We were passing by. We went to see the house, and I wanted to stop in and say hi."

"Are you going to school?" Yvonne asked Nancy.

"Yes," Nancy said.

"What school?"

"Columbia,"

"Oh!" Yvonne's smile waned.

"Good for you," Freddie said, and then asked, "Were you there when they had those riots on campus?"

Nancy and Michael glanced at each other, holding back grins. Nancy shook her head a little too vigorously. "No!"

"It's too bad that a few have to disrupt things for the rest," Freddie said.

Nancy shrugged. Michael could tell that she was restraining herself.

"Did you come in your new car?" Yvonne asked.

Michael held up his car key. "Yeah!"

"I want to see it."

"Go." Freddie said, waving Yvonne on. "I saw it yesterday when I was over there. It's very nice. *Mabrouk ya*, Michael."

"Come on," Michael said to Nancy as Yvonne rounded the counter.

"Nancy, stay. Talk to me while he shows off his car," Freddie said, and Nancy gave Michael a slight nod to let him know that she was okay.

Michael and Yvonne walked quietly until they reached his car. When Michael opened the door to show her the interior, Yvonne stared at it for several moments and then turned to Michael and said, "She's very nice."

"My dad got a great deal."

Yvonne shook her head. "I'm talking about *Nancy*."

"Oh . . . Yeah, she is."

Yvonne barely even looked at the car, instead searching Michael's face as though examining him for changes she fully expected to see. As she moved closer to him, he caught a whiff of the familiar fragrance of her perfume. She leaned into him as she gave the interior of the car a cursory glance over his shoulder, then she turned, her face now less than an inch from his and said, "Is she good to you? You deserve someone who's good to you."

"Yes," he said softly.

As Yvonne stepped back, her breasts brushed against his shoulder.

"The car's very nice," she said, and then added, "Now you can stop by more often."

Inside the store again, Michael took a dollar bill out of his pocket and held it out to Freddie. "Let me pay for the Cokes."

"Stop. Is that how you act? You don't come around, you don't visit, and now you insult me? Stay for a while. Have something to eat."

"No, we have to get back. Thanks for the Cokes, Freddie."

"It was nice to meet you," Yvonne said to Nancy.

"You too," Nancy replied.

"Don't be a stranger," Freddie called out to him as they left.

On their way home, Nancy was quiet for the first couple of miles and then blurted out, "They seem nice. And you called it on all three."

"Three?"

"Yeah, you said they wouldn't take money for the Cokes. That they'd ask if we wanted something to eat, and . . ."

"And, yeah, what's the third?" Michael asked.

"Yvonne is very pretty."

"I never said anything about her being pretty."

"I know." Nancy shrugged. "It's not that you said it specifically. It's just the things you've said *about* her."

Michael glanced at her quizzically and she gave him a knowing look. "You know she likes you, right?"

That night, Nancy took Michael to see *One Flew Over the Cuckoo's Nest*. It was playing off-off Broadway, and one of her friends from Columbia had a part in it. After Nancy had read the book, she'd passed it along to Michael, and even though it wasn't how he'd imagined when he'd read the book, Michael enjoyed the play. The actor that played the chief did a great job filling the stage with his presence and quiet strength.

On the way home, fluorescent lights blinked on and off as the subway car rattled and rocked on its tracks, speeding by stations it had no intention of stopping at. Michael stared out the window; the flashing lights were creating asymmetrical shadows and reflections inside the subway car as the train rushed forward, and the patterns had a lulling, hypnotic effect. Like an apparition, the reflection of John's son suddenly appeared in the window, staring at Michael with the same cheerless longing in his eyes that Michael remembered from that day. Michael couldn't fathom not having the mental capacity to function normally. Would you be happier because you didn't know any better? Or more desperate and pained for the lack? As he studied the phantom face staring back at him, Michael was struck by a profound sadness.

When they arrived at their subway stop, Nancy took hand his and stood up. She had to tug at him to get his attention. "Hey, this is us. You okay?"

"Yeah, I'm fine. I was just thinking," Michael said.

"Thinking!" Nancy laughed. "You were in another world!"

Thirty-Seven

JELLY LOOKED GROWN UP. Muscle had hardened his previously soft frame, and his face was less round, having lost the last of its baby fat. He also looked tired, drawn, with dark circles under his eyes, which could be explained away by the long trip home if there hadn't been something else about him: he now had a jaded, haunted expression permanently imprinted on his face. He wore it like a mask over the adolescent innocence that had once resided there.

Billy and Jelly came into the store together and bought beer, soda, assorted cold cuts, Wise potato chips, Fritos, and pretzels for the welcome home party their mother was giving him. Jelly was wearing a new pair of jeans and a clean white T-shirt. He refused to wear his uniform when not required, although if the air cooled down at night, he'd be forced to wear his Army jacket since it was all he had. Given that it was August, that wasn't likely.

Michael wished he could pull Jelly aside and ask him what being in Vietnam was like—he wanted to know if Jelly had killed anyone and what that felt like.

Instead he said, "Welcome home."

Jelly acknowledged Michael with a brief nod.

"Yeah, some fucking welcome," Billy said. "Ya wanna know what kinda welcome he got? Some fucking hippie bitch at the airport spit on him as he was getting off the plane. You believe that shit?"

Michael didn't know how to respond, just shook his head in disbelief. Billy and Jelly scooped up their grocery bags and scuttled out.

Jelly's mother had invited a few relatives and neighborhood friends to his welcome home party, and even Bernard was on his best behavior. Jelly was polite, but withdrawn. It seemed strange to him to be welcomed by people that previously hadn't acknowledged his existence. While he'd never felt like he fit in—everyone around him was so loud, so over the top, while he was taciturn, preferring to stay in the background—he understood now just how different he was. This was his home, but today he felt like someone visiting from Mars.

It was good to see his mom and brother, but his father repelled him. The vivid, disturbing memories of his father's violence had unconsciously helped Jelly sustain the rage he'd needed for combat—and they were not easily dismissed. Even now, with his father sitting there looking small and weak, Jelly had to suppress the urge to hit him.

That night, in a rundown tenement shooting gallery in the South Bronx, Billy and Jelly had their own private party, shooting the heroin that Billy had scored for the occasion. They spent the next three days getting wasted until their money ran out.

Thirty-Eight

Nancy drove to New Jersey to spend a few days with Louie and his family. Louie wanted to discuss the details of their parents' estate and whether they should sell the house. She loved her brother's kids and was impressed by the fact that her brother had managed to create a relatively normal household for them, despite having been raised by their mother. But Nancy also thought that getting away for a little bit might be good—it would give her time to think. She had a decision to make.

Michael told his father that he was going out to shop for school supplies—and he intended to do just that—but found himself pulled in the direction of Freddie and Yvonne's store. He'd been trying not to think too much about it, but there was something about the way Yvonne had acted the last time he was there, something left unsaid. He told himself that stopping by was no big deal, he'd just check in and see how they were doing. And he really did want to ask Yvonne what she thought about Nancy. Her approval was important to him. He did wonder whether he should be asking one woman's opinion about another, but decided that since Yvonne was a good friend, why not?

As Michael drove around to the back of the store, he noticed that Freddie's station wagon wasn't there. *That's right*, he thought, *this is the day he usually makes a run to Farmingdale to get produce.* Michael sat in his car for a few minutes, collecting himself. He felt a little unnerved, as if he were doing something wrong. But he wasn't. Then his father's standard refrain popped into his head. *Be careful.*

When Michael walked in, Yvonne was assisting a customer, a tall woman who had some groceries on the counter. He knew Yvonne had seen him, but she didn't say anything. He slipped around the other end of the counter and waited behind the deli-case, a few feet away from her, watching as she bagged the woman's groceries. Through the sliding glass door he could feel the cool air drying the light sweat off his back. Yvonne didn't turn his way or acknowledge his presence until the woman, hugging her grocery bag, walked through the aisle and out the door.

And then, without saying a word, Yvonne was next to him, her eyes searching his as if she were trying to find an answer to a complex question. She reached up and ran her fingers through his hair, and then she kissed him. Michael felt a surge of excitement and yearning—coupled with fear—run through him.

They paused to catch their breath, still holding onto each other, both charged with guilty energy. Michael glanced around, fearful someone was watching them. A vulnerable expression washed over Yvonne's delicate features. She held Michael tight, wanting to feel him, wanting the physical reassurance of his response to her, and then reached down and touched his erection. Her stroke sent shivers through him.

A Wonder Bread delivery truck rolled up in front of the store, and through the window Michael could see the delivery man lifting a tray of bread out of the back. He forced himself to release Yvonne, and she took a step back. Michael needed to steady himself; his head was spinning with a combination of lustful elation and abject terror. *What the fuck is happening?* he thought.

"What are we doing?" Michael whispered. Yvonne didn't say anything, but she reached for his hand and squeezed it reassuringly. The bell above the door rang as the delivery man entered and began to quickly but methodically organize the bread on the shelf, swapping out the few loaves that were past the sell date and filling in the gaps with fresh loaves. Yvonne released Michael's hand and stepped out from behind the deli case. Michael felt his blood leave the surface of his skin and begin to circulate again, and his breathing settled back into a steady rhythm.

"Hey Yvonne, how's it going?" The delivery man smiled at her as he handed her the receipt to sign.

"Fine Jeff, how 'bout you?"

That was the first time Michael had heard her voice since he'd arrived, and he was surprised at how calm she sounded. He needed to leave. Needed to step away and make sense of this.

Jeff picked up his tray, which had the few loaves of old bread on it, and left. As soon as the Wonder Bread truck pulled away from the curb, Yvonne rushed back into his arms.

"What're we doing?" Michael asked again, in an anxious tone, this time.

"I don't know," she whispered against his ear. After a brief pause, she added, "That's not true." Her warm breath tickled his neck, sending fresh shivers down his body. His nerve endings seemed hypersensitive. He took a deep breath and let it out slowly.

"I have to go. I'll try to come back soon. We can talk or something."

He gave her a soft kiss and reluctantly eased himself away. He could feel Yvonne's gaze following him out the door. He turned to glance at her one more time before he left, and as her melancholy expression retreated, Michael wondered if she regretted what just happened.

He took his time driving back, and at two separate intersections the drivers behind him had to honk their horns to get his attention. He was too distracted, too befuddled to notice that the stoplights had turned green. Guilt and apprehension collided with delicious lust. The thought of being with Yvonne made his blood pressure rise, but the thought of betraying Freddie—not to mention Nancy—made his mouth so dry and his throat so tight that it was becoming impossible to swallow. He needed to get his head straight and not allow any residue to linger, because each time he'd glance in the rearview mirror, he saw himself wearing his feelings like a bad case of chicken pox, where your face breaks out in pus-ridden boils, ready to burst. All anyone needed to do was look at him, and his face would betray all.

He worked to control his breathing, consciously pushing each breath in and out. *Nothing more needs to happen; it was all a mistake.* There was some comfort in this mantra, so he repeated it again and again, managing to calm himself down considerably. The drive gave him the time he needed to tuck what happened with Yvonne away in some hidden compartment, allowing him a respite—for now.

Thirty-Nine

NANCY WAS LOOKING FORWARD to leaving her brother's house and heading back. It had only been a few days, but she was surprised by how much she missed Michael. Maybe it was because they spent so much time together. Away from him, she felt like something was missing, something was a bit off balance. She had called him several times a day since she'd left. Queens was only about a two-hour drive from her brother's place, and she planned on having an early dinner with the kids and leaving right after. This should get her back to the house around seven tonight.

After what happened with Yvonne, Michael was eager to see Nancy. He couldn't wait to be with her, make love to her, hold her—and get further distance between him and that afternoon behind Yvonne's deli case. Since summer was running out, Nancy had suggested that they spend this weekend in the City, go to a museum and maybe see a show.

At around six thirty, Michael saw his father filling a grocery bag with a few items—including a six-pack of Miller and a carton of Salems.

"Are you leaving?" Michael said abruptly. "I wanted to leave early. Nancy's coming home tonight."

"If it's slow, close early."

"Yeah, right," Michael said. He took a deep breath, paused a moment, and just before his father was about to pick up his grocery bag and leave, he asked, "Can I have the weekend off? Nancy invited me to go visit her brother in Jersey tomorrow."

Michael's father eyed him suspiciously, but then his attention shifted back to the grocery bag, with the carton of Salems sticking out.

"School's starting in a couple of weeks. Next weekend is Labor Day."

"Can Jimmy work?" his father asked.

"He can."

"I'll think about it."

"I need to let her know," Michael said, whining a bit more than he wanted to.

His father picked up the bag of groceries and said, "Okay, you can go," and continued out the front door.

"I'll tell Mom you won't be home for dinner," Michael called after him, but his father was already out the door. Michael had only said it to satisfy himself. Of course, with what had just happened with Yvonne, he wasn't sure he had any right to be judgmental.

The store wasn't busy. Families had probably skipped town for last minute vacations before school resumed. As the day wound down, so did the trickle of customers. It didn't matter to Michael that his father had suggested closing early; he wouldn't close any earlier than nine. But he did decide to get a jump on things by getting all the closing tasks done ahead of time. He swept the floor, restocked the soda and beer, and even totaled the cash register and counted out the money. Then he put the money in an envelope, wrote the date and time on it, and locked it away in a drawer in the back room. His father could retrieve the envelope when he returned tonight, or in the morning when he prepared tomorrow's deposit.

At seven thirty the phone rang. "I'm back, and I need a really, really big favor," Nancy said. "Something showed up unexpectedly on my drive home and I need to ask you . . ."

"What? What is it, are you okay?"

"I'm fine, a little messy. I got my period and I'm out of tampons. Could you please—pretty please?—bring them over now?"

"I'm closing in an hour. Can you wait?"

She moaned, then said, "*Please* don't make me wait. I'll make it worth your while."

"Okay, let me see what I can do." After they hung up, Michael took a box of Tampax from the shelf and stuck it in a bag. Then he called his mother on the phone—she hated him opening the back door and yelling up the stairs—and asked her if she'd come down and cover the store for a half hour. Michael could hear her stirring a pot of food as she was listening to him. After several minutes, his mother came through the back door. Michael thought that she seemed okay with him asking her to watch the store, but he still felt guilty calling on her. *She'll probably be happier when we move and can't do this to her anymore.*

"It's been really slow," he said, picking up the bag. "I just need to bring this over to Nancy's—she can't wait. Everything's taken care of, and I'll come back and close up. I'll hurry."

"It's okay. Go."

"Thanks, Mom." He rushed out the front door.

Michael would have jumped in his car, but in his eagerness to see Nancy he decided to go on foot. It was just a couple of blocks, and he could make it just as fast if he didn't have to pull his car out of the garage. It was closing in on eight o'clock and the last of the sunlight had begun to recede, cooling down the late-summer heat. Michael could tell it was going to be a clear, moonlit night. He took long strides, walking swiftly but not running.

As Michael reached for the door, Nancy opened it wide, wearing a T-shirt and a towel wrapped around her waist. She gave Michael a quick peck on the mouth and reached into the bag.

"Thanks, you're a life saver. I knew there was a reason I love you," she said as she grabbed the box of Tampax. She left Michael holding the empty bag and ran up the stairs, her bare feet on the wooden steps making a rhythmic, galloping sound.

"Tampax? *That's* the reason you love me?" he called after her.

She yelled from the top of the stairs, "Sit! I'll be right down."

"I don't have time, I need to get back!"

"Sit!"

Michael ambled over to the sofa and plopped down. He called out to her again, "I really gotta go!" The television was playing a rerun of *Bewitched.* He couldn't relax; he hated having the store closing hanging over him. It was like he was in one of those Laurel and Hardy routines where a piano hangs from a frayed rope high over some dupe, waiting to crash down.

After about ten minutes—but what felt for Michael like ten days—Nancy came bouncing down the stairs in her T-shirt and underwear. "Better," she said, and jumped onto the sofa and into his arms. She gave him a long passionate kiss and reached down and unbuckled his belt, then eased his zipper down and reached in. "I . . . I . . . need to—" Michael started to say. She shushed him and eased his penis out of his pants. Then her mouth was on him.

After he came, Nancy glowed as if she were the one that had

just experienced the physical rush. Michael lay there for a moment, savoring the pleasure of her generosity.

"I have another surprise," she said, smugly.

"Nothing could top that."

"I got tickets to *Hair* for Saturday night."

"That's so cool! I forgot to tell you—I got it off. The whole weekend." He stood up reluctantly. "I really need to go. I shouldn't leave my mom hanging. I'll be right back—I just need to close." He tucked his shirt in and buckled his pants, then hugged Nancy and added, "I can't wait for the weekend."

"Go. I still have to unpack and do some laundry. I have lots to tell you."

Twirling red lights projected crimson ripples into the darkness, cascading their fractured light through the store's windows and onto its brick walls, lending an eerie, surreal quality to the night. Michael was a block away when he saw those lights, and an instinctive, visceral fear stole his breath and propelled him forward as fast as he could go.

The store was crowded with blue uniforms. His mother was on the floor, covered in blood, being worked on by two paramedics. "Mom!" he yelled, pushing his way toward her. Two policemen grabbed Michael and held him back—he struggled to break free. "Let me go!" he shouted.

"Let them help her," one of the policemen said in a firm but gentle voice. They eased their grip on Michael, and he tried again to elbow his way closer to his mother. The paramedics were moving her onto a gurney.

"Mom, I'm here!" he called out. She didn't turn her head his way. Her eyes stared with a blank darkness, and then she closed them. Michael's head spun, his heart pounded in his throat. Fear vibrated through his whole body and tears rolled down his cheeks. "Mom!" he called out again, his voice breaking.

The paramedics worked diligently, their movements precise with a focused urgency. Ben and several policemen, including Sergeant McClusky and Officer Bosco, were in the inner circle crouched around Michael's mother. Ben looked up at Michael. His face was etched with despair. There was blood on his shirt and hands.

The paramedics lifted the gurney up and over the counter, and Michael immediately rushed to his mother's side as they carried her outside to the ambulance. He took her hand, desperate to hold onto it, to hold onto her. "Mom, I'm here," he said again. She opened her eyes slightly but didn't turn her head his way—then she closed them again, and her head sank back into the gurney.

He had to release her hand when they lifted her into the ambulance. One of the paramedics climbed in with her, and the other paramedic closed the door, turned to Michael, and said, "We'll take care of her."

Sergeant McClusky came up to Michael. "Come on, I'll take you to the hospital."

A small crowd of people had gathered outside the store and were being held back by policemen. Dazed, Michael followed McClusky to his patrol car, where McClusky radioed dispatch with his intentions. The crackling and clipped jargon that came back was garbled, and Michael wondered how anyone could understand what came across those radios. And then he wondered how such an irrelevant thought could cross his mind at a moment like this.

"Do you have any idea who'd do something like this?" McClusky asked.

Michael shook his head. "No." His voice was barely audible.

McClusky slammed the shifter into gear and made a swift U-turn. Then he gunned his engine to catch up with the ambulance and trailed it as closely as he could without hitting it.

"Where were you?"

The picture of where he was—and what he was doing—flashed in his head like a grainy eight-millimeter homemade porno movie.

"I was making a delivery," he heard himself say.

"Do you know where your father is?" McClusky asked.

"No—yeah—maybe."

"Can you try and reach him when we get to the hospital?"

"Yeah."

After a few moments of listening to the grind of the police car's engine, Michael turned his head toward McClusky. "Why?"

"Robbery. Looks like they went for the cash. Do you know how much was in the register?"

"Thirty dollars." Michael shook his head in disbelief. "Someone shot my mom for *thirty dollars*?"

"It's hard to know what they were thinking. They may have thought she was holding out."

Sergeant McClusky pulled up to the hospital. Michael was glad; he didn't want to talk about this anymore. He didn't want to think about his mother being shot because he'd cleared the money out early. He wanted to reach his father.

McClusky escorted Michael to an inside waiting room where he could be alone, away from the emergency room crowd. There was an old black phone sitting there. It was worn and beat-up and the numbers around the dial were nearly rubbed off. McClusky left to check on Michael's mother.

Michael never thought that remembering Shelly's last name would be important. But he'd cashed a check for her once, and when he'd seen her name was Wilson, he'd thought about Mr. Wilson from the *Dennis the Menace* show. How dumb was that? Whatever the reason, he knew it—and when he called information, she was listed as "S. Wilson." As he dialed her number, he wondered how many times bad news had been handed out to anxiously waiting family members in this ugly, bleak little room with cheap vinyl furniture. A shudder ran down his spine.

"Hello," he heard Shelly's voice answer.

"Shelly, can I talk to my dad?"

"Michael? Yes, of course."

"Hello?" His father sounded cautious, tentative.

"Dad, Mom's been shot. We're at Queens Hospital . . . Please come," was all he was able to get out before his voice cracked.

"What!"

"Someone tried to rob the store, and they shot Mom," Michael said, shaking. He was amazed at his ability to translate this information somewhat coherently.

"I'll be right there," his dad said, and hung up.

Michael pressed the receiver button to get another dial tone and then dialed Nancy's number. He let it ring at least ten times, but there was no answer.

McClusky came back into the room. "There's some girl out there named Nancy making a big fuss about seeing you. You want her back here?"

"Yes. Please."

"I'll get her. Did you reach your father?"

"He's on his way."

"Okay," McClusky said as he left the room.

Nancy came in and wrapped her arms around Michael, holding him tight as he cried.

When Michael's tears slowed, he took a deep breath and said,

"Heard you were giving them hell out there."

"You bet," she said. "How is she? Have you heard anything?"

"No, but I think they're just waiting for my father to get here, to tell us she's dead."

Nancy just looked at Michael, neither challenging nor supporting his theory. She knew that in times like this, instinct—that knowing internal voice that sends signals of impending doom—speaks more truth than a dozen witnesses.

When Michael's father arrived, Michael couldn't look him in the eyes. But before they could exchange any uncomfortable words, a young doctor stepped into the room, his light blue eyes darting back and forth between Michael and his father. And then, in a tone soft with compassion and strong with authority, he spoke nine words: "I'm sorry. She died. We did everything we could."

Michael's father, stunned, turned to Michael and searched his face as if answers might be written there. Michael stared blankly back at him. Nancy held Michael's hand tight and waited for him, saying nothing. Michael's tears dried up; he was emotionally and physically numb. Questions formed in his mind, some he was afraid to ask, and some that he already knew the answers to.

Michael didn't want to go home. He felt torn between his need to run and hide and his responsibility to his father—it would be wrong to leave him to cope with this alone. In the end, Nancy took charge and went home with them. At first they all sat together in a heavy quiet, unable to say or do anything, but then Nancy got up and wrapped up the food Michael's mother had been preparing for their dinner and stuck it in the refrigerator. And while she did this, Michael told his father as much as he knew about what happened.

Aziz tried making a few phone calls but found it was too difficult, so he decided to wait until morning to make the rest. He knew that even with the few relatives he'd managed to contact, everyone else would know by morning, and his phone would start ringing. After a while, he decided to retreat to his bedroom and encouraged Michael and Nancy to get some rest. "There'll be a lot to do tomorrow," he said in a flat, defeated tone.

Michael's body would not allow sleep, and he was sure that his father lay sleepless in his room as well, that he'd just wanted the sanctuary of a closed door to process his shock and grief. Michael and Nancy both lay awake through the night. Michael's mind raced, questioning everything. He was not tired or hungry or thirsty. It was as if all his senses had been suspended by the ultimate anesthetic. Long stretches of time would escape him as he listened to the quiet, neither one of them uttering a sound.

When morning approached, Michael nudged Nancy and asked her if she'd like some coffee. But as they entered the kitchen, the sight of his mother's coffee pot stopped him cold. He just stood there for several seconds, staring. "You know what?—I've never made coffee." He picked up the pot and held it out to her. "I don't even know how to use this," he said, feeling pathetic at his incompetence.

Nancy took the coffee pot from him and said, "It's okay. I'll show you."

Forty

Michael's mother hadn't created controversy in her life, instead fulfilling a private role of caring for her family in a quiet, loving manner. But her murder did. The day after she died, a malicious rumor spread throughout the neighborhood: "The nigger killed her!"

The wake, that ritual viewing of a dead person's body, of the hollow remains of what was once a living person, repulsed Michael. This lifeless, stiff presentation of cold human flesh lying in its overpriced box bore no resemblance to his mother, and he refused to acknowledge otherwise. And he didn't care if this attitude made him appear cold and unfeeling.

The room had a used but sterile feel even with every effort made to dress it up. The lighting was muted. A dozen stands of ornate flowers crowded around the casket. The aroma of mixed bouquets wafted through the air with a pungent bite. There were a couple of sofas off to the side, one of which Michael and Nancy sat on, and rows of chairs set up several feet from the side of the casket. At first Michael's father sat with them, but he soon grew uncomfortable just sitting. He needed the distraction of walking around, mingling with the relatives and friends that had come to pay their respects. The director of the funeral home gently reminded Michael's father several times that smoking wasn't allowed, but eventually gave up and handed him an ashtray.

The members of Michael's extended family were gifted with high emotion and prone to dramatic displays, and the grief of the older Arab women often took the form of wailing as an expression of their sorrow. It was their ritual of mourning the dead. Out of respect to the others, when one of these women became too loud or hysterical, a couple of the men would intervene and escort her to another room. To Michael, it seemed a parade of the sincere, the dutiful, and the curious, and he sat there dutifully, Nancy next to him, as the evening viewing droned on.

Michael's relatives scrutinized Nancy with both suspicion and curiosity. They were rarely pleased to see one of their own involved with an outsider and, despite the occasion, were unable to hide their disapproval. At the very least they viewed whoever the young man was involved with as a whore, and at the worst they believed she threatened the cultural doctrine that stated you should only marry "one of your own kind" and reduced the list of possibilities for their own daughters and nieces, or other distant relations. Nancy was familiar with this attitude and knew better than to play into it; if anything, her indifference was cause for more gossip. Nancy made an effort to hold on close to Michael, for both their sakes.

Michael's mother's parents and sisters were in attendance, but while they came up to him, too grief stricken to say much, they stayed clear of his father. Michael suspected that they somehow blamed his father for what happened.

Michael and his father hadn't spoken very much. Neither one knew how to articulate emotions that had yet to form into anything more then a surreal, abstract haze. His father was overwhelmed by grief, and Michael was glad that his family was there for him in full support. They approached Michael as well, expressing their heartfelt sorrow and offering to help in any way they could. Despite his emotional detachment, he appreciated their earnest concern; it gave him a new understanding of what it meant to be a part of a community. Michael, in turn, thanked them politely and introduced them to his girlfriend, Nancy.

John took a break from packing up his house to stop by and pay his respects. He appeared upset, and Michael could imagine John fostering the rumor that "the nigger did it," and suspected that his mother's murder had further solidified John's decision to move.

Jeannie and her husband Steve also came. She remained steadfast in her support of the family she enjoyed working for. Jamila used to come downstairs with a container of the food she'd just prepared for dinner and insist that Jeannie take some home for her family. Jeannie took her death personally—it bothered her on many levels. She suspected that the killer was someone from the neighborhood and wondered what would have happened if she'd been there that night. Steve wanted her to quit, but she'd refused. She wouldn't abandon the Haddad family when they needed her the most.

Many other people from the neighborhood came by to pay their respects. These were the faces Michael had grown accustomed to seeing weekly, sometimes even daily, and they seemed out of place viewed anywhere except across the counter or through a screen door.

Michael noticed Angela immediately when she came in with her mother. Angela looked taller and her face and body had the maturity of a young woman now. Michael was surprised that seeing her didn't stir him more. His memories of wanting her had become faint and distant, like a sweet, innocent dream. Though that dream would sour, like the putrid taste of spoiled milk, if he couldn't separate his memories of Angela from the memory of that hateful, ignorant man shoving him against a tree.

"Who's that girl?" Nancy asked him.

"She used to come to the store. We were sort of friends for a while."

"Well, she can't take her eyes off you."

When Angela came over to extend her condolences, Michael could see how uncomfortable she was. He was distant but polite and thanked her for coming. He knew it really wasn't her fault. After all, she didn't choose her father.

Much to his shock and to her credit, Shelly showed up. It amazed Michael that he felt no ill will toward her, though at this point he wasn't sure what he felt about anyone involved, including himself. Shelly had rescued him when he was vulnerable, exposed. She'd swept in and tended to him with an unselfish compassion that had convinced him of her decency. It would be easier for Michael to direct blame elsewhere: on the person he thought had been absent from much of what he should have been responsible for. But if he did that, he might also have to look in a mirror.

When Michael spotted Ben and his wife Janet entering the crowded room, he was struck by both the sharp pain of a visual replay and the strong desire to talk to him. But as eager as he was, Michael knew it wasn't the right place to engage him in that conversation. Ben came over and extended his hand, his face wearing the same sorrowful expression Michael remembered from that night, and said in a warm, consoling tone, "I'm very sorry about your mother."

"Thanks. Um . . . can we talk? Sometime?" Michael was surprised by how unnerved he got asking such a simple question.

"Of course," Ben said, "I'd like that. Anytime you want." Ben handed Michael a business card. "Call me. I put our home number on the back. We'll set something up."

Freddie and Yvonne, after greeting Michael's father and paying respects to a few of the older relatives, came over to Michael and Nancy. The four of them exchanged warm hugs. Both Freddie and Yvonne were grief stricken: their faces were red and swollen from crying, and they would occasionally dab wadded-up tissues to the corners of their inflamed eyes, catching the tears before they rolled down their cheeks. Michael remembered how Freddie was his mother's favorite house guest, how she used him as an example, making sure Michael knew that, if he should ever stay at someone's home, Freddie's was the behavior to emulate.

Freddie and Yvonne were among the handful of relatives who stayed the entire evening to help Michael and his father throughout the ordeal.

When Nancy stepped away to use the ladies' room and Freddie was outside having a cigarette, Yvonne took the opportunity to embrace Michael again. As she held him tight, she whispered to him in a hoarse voice ready to crack, "Oh, Michael, it's so terrible . . . so . . . sad. If you need anything, anything at all, please, please let me know. You know I love you."

"I love you too," he heard himself whisper back.

"She's not family. It's not appropriate!" Aziz was incensed. He couldn't believe he needed to have an argument about Nancy riding in the limo with them.

But Michael remained adamant, reminding him that Nancy had insisted he ride with her when she'd buried her mother.

"It makes no difference. It's still not right!"

"If she can't be with us, then I'll drive myself," Michael said.

Aziz unhappily relented. He was worn out. He reminded himself that he really didn't care what other people might think. Well, maybe he did a little. He had never buried a wife before, and he felt like Michael was taking advantage. Still, maybe he was overreacting. In any case, he didn't have much fight in him.

Before the funeral, Michael went over to Nancy's. She was already dressed and ready. She pulled out a small joint and asked him if he thought they should. It had become a morbid ritual—they'd also smoked prior to her mother's funeral. He figured a couple of tokes couldn't hurt, and might take the edge off.

The funeral progressed like a dream, as if Michael were outside looking in, not really a part of it. After the service he moved to the side of his mother's casket, following the directions that had been given to him and the other pallbearers, and reached for the brass bar that ran alongside it. This was the last time his mother's body would occupy her beloved church.

His hand, along with the rest of his body, was wet with sweat, but he clenched his fist tightly around the handle. The mahogany box felt heavy, even for the short distance to the hearse. As Michael was walking to the limousine, where Nancy and his father were waiting, a few people came up to him and attempted to console him—"She was a wonderful woman . . . so loving, gentle, so giving." But Michael didn't want to hear anything about his mother from them, and resented the words they used to sum her up. What did these people know about her? And yet, he was so overwhelmed by a consuming emptiness, he couldn't bring himself to talk about his mother with anyone. Because if he thought too deeply about her, if he forced himself to articulate her qualities to others, he would have to admit that she was gone forever.

Uncle Elias and Aunt Sue hosted the after-funeral gathering. Many of Michael's relatives had cooked, and there were platters and trays full of delicious food. Michael was starving. His appetite had returned thanks to a wonderful side effect of one of nature's finest contributions to the plant family—cannabis.

Among the many dishes was a large plate of *warak dawali,* stuffed grape leaves. Since Michael had brought his mother's food over to Nancy's house on many occasions, she was familiar with many of the dishes being served. And after Nancy sampled one of the *warak dawali,* she made one of those offhanded comments you make without thinking: "Your mother's are much better."

Forty-One

NOTHING COULD HAVE PREPARED MICHAEL for the swollen emptiness and deafening silence of his ineffable loss. Like a sudden earthquake that shifts the ground beneath you, the violent death of the person who brought you life robs you of your solid foundation and leaves you hobbled and emotionally naked. Michael found himself immersed in a thick fog, which allowed him to see only as far as his next step, but also provided him with a comforting shroud of denial.

On the night that he'd arranged to meet with Michael, Ben left his office early even though it wasn't necessary. Ben had originally invited him and Nancy to join them for dinner, but Michael had to work late and didn't want to leave his father alone in the store just yet. So they'd set it up for around nine.

Nancy ran out and bought a bottle of wine to bring but wondered if it was enough to walk in with. Then she met Michael at the store and helped him close. His father had already left to have a late dinner with Freddie and Yvonne.

Ben and Janet greeted Michael and Nancy warmly and seemed pleased over Nancy's wine selection. The house was decorated well, not overstuffed like many others in the neighborhood. Ben and Janet's furniture was sleek and angular and suited them, including a modern white leather sofa with six-inch legs and two matching chairs, one white and one black. Over the sofa hung a Picasso print in a black lacquer frame. The room also had a 25-inch color TV and a reel-to-reel tape player, and a turntable was spinning the warm jazz tunes of Coltrane's *My Favorite Things*.

Janet had put out bowls of chips, pretzels, and a sour cream dip which didn't look appealing to Michael. "Nancy, would you like a glass of white wine?" Janet asked. "Or would you prefer I open up the bottle you brought?"

"No, the white is fine. Save the red for a steak dinner with Ben."

Ben poured some Johnnie Walker Black into an ice-filled crystal glass and asked if Michael would like to join him. "Sure," Michael said, even though he'd tasted hard liquor only once before. Ben handed him the glass and asked if he'd like to see his den. Michael nodded. "Would you excuse us for a few minutes?" Ben said to the women.

Michael sipped his scotch as he followed Ben into the small bedroom that he was using as a den. The first sip gave Michael the willies, but by the second he started to like the smooth, sweet bite and the warm feeling that traveled over his tongue and down his throat. And as the ice melted, the water blending with the scotch cut the edge and made it taste even better.

In the center of the room was a small desk, and behind it a rich-looking, high-backed cordovan leather office chair that was way too big for the space. A couple of side chairs, similar but obviously not the same quality as the high-backed one, sat in front of the desk. Two walls were covered with stuffed bookshelves, and the others were covered with framed pictures of Ben and Janet and people Michael assumed to be family.

"My dad bought me this chair," Ben said with pride as he stood behind it, "right after I graduated law school. Go ahead, sit in it," he insisted. "He wanted me to go into private practice. He said he looked high and low for a chair that could hold my big butt and my equally big head."

Michael sat in the chair and immediately appreciated the craftsmanship as he sank into the smooth, comfortable leather. "Very nice."

Ben sat across from him in one of the smaller chairs. "Now these two chairs," he said, tapping the arm of the chair he was sitting in. "Not good enough."

Michael looked at him, puzzled.

"You see, Michael, lawyers charge by the hour, so the idea is to have big comfortable chairs for your clients to sit in. So comfortable, they never want to get up. Because the longer they sit, the more you can bill." Ben grinned broadly, flashing a row of perfect teeth.

"Is that what they teach you in law school?"

"No. You learn that one when you hit the streets." He paused and then asked in a more solemn tone, "How've you been?"

"I'm okay."

Ben sighed. "I can't imagine how you're feeling."

"Thanks for being there. With my mom."

"I wish I'd been there sooner. You okay with me telling you what happened? It's not much."

"Yeah . . . I am."

Ben lit a cigarette and took a long drag. Smoke streamed from his mouth and nose. "I was coming home from work, and of course I needed cigarettes." He gestured with the one that he was holding. "As I was starting to cross the street to your store, this guy in an Army jacket comes charging out, his head bent down, racing out of there like the place was on fire."

"What did he look like?"

"That's the problem. I didn't get a good enough look at him. I gave the best description I could to the police. What stuck out was he had light brown or blondish-colored hair."

Blond hair? Army jacket? Michael tried to imagine Jelly running out of the store the way Ben had described, but the picture wouldn't come into focus. Michael thought back to the last time he saw Jelly, the day of his party . . . Jelly hadn't been wearing an Army jacket.

"I rushed into the store and found your mom . . ." Ben paused. "You okay?"

"Yeah." Michael said, taking another sip of scotch, trying to relax. Listening to Ben had ignited a conflict within him. Did he really want to know? If he stopped Ben now, then his sole memory of that night would be him running into the store to find his mother surrounded by uniforms. Was that enough? Was he willing to be deprived of the picture Ben was about to share, the picture that would be burned into his mind forever? No. He needed to hear more.

"Your mom was on the floor . . ." Again Ben hesitated, trying to get a read on Michael. "She was bleeding from the chest, pretty badly. I called an ambulance and tried to make her comfortable. I took her hand . . . let her know she wasn't alone. She struggled to say something, but it came out in whispers. I told her to save her strength. I kept telling her she'd be okay and to hang on." Ben turned his head and stared at his bookshelves for a minute, weighing what he was about to say. Then he turned back. "She *did* say something, but I could barely make it out. What I heard was, "my son." That was all I could understand, and I don't know if she was asking for you, telling me to tell you something, or what, but I know she was thinking of you at that moment."

Michael added Ben's description of what happened to his own mental motion picture. He wasn't sure whether to feel grateful for this new information or not. But it didn't change the one dominating thought that kept gnawing at him, replaying in his mind on a perpetual loop. *I should have been there. If I had, she wouldn't have been on that floor.* Like all Michael had taken in since that night, he swallowed it into the tight ball of suppressed emotion he'd become, like the hard core of a golf ball, compressed and sealed deep inside.

And then Michael remembered something, a minor detail in the enormity of that night. "Ben, your suit jacket," he said.

"What?"

"Your suit jacket."

Ben shook his head, not sure what Michael was getting at.

"You took your suit jacket, folded it into a pillow, and put it under my mom's head."

Ben was taken aback by Michael's description. He nodded slowly.

Michael only knew this because when the ambulance technicians lifted his mother onto the gurney, he remembered catching a glimpse of Ben's jacket on the floor where her head had rested. He probably only saw it there for a second. Why would he remember such an obscure detail? But now, it was as if Michael had actually seen Ben taking off his jacket, folding it, and tucking it under his mother's head—his attempt to make her comfortable. Ben's act of kindness struck Michael, and he was grateful that she'd spent her last moments with someone thoughtful and caring. When that night flashed into his consciousness, that's the memory he would prefer to replay. "Thank you for that," Michael said with a lump in his throat. He took a long drink of scotch, hoping it would melt the tightness and allow him to swallow.

Ben pointed to a picture that was hanging on the wall. "That's my dad." Michael thought he looked like an older version of Ben. Under his gray hair he had the strong, handsome features that Ben had inherited. "Michael . . . I know you probably haven't been thinking much about this lately with all that's happened, but I've been meaning to tell you. If you're interested, I know a few people at NYU, and I'd be pleased to write a letter or even talk to some of them if it would help."

Michael thanked him and told Ben that he'd think about it. They rejoined the women, and Michael could tell that Nancy was enjoying herself with Janet. Before Michael and Nancy left, they talked about getting together again for dinner, or maybe a movie.

Billy's house was dark—and not just because there were no lights on. The worn structure appeared hollow, empty, just as Michael's life felt now. Michael fixed his gaze on it and clutched the switchblade tucked deep in his jeans pocket. Billy had sold him that knife. At the time, Michael wanted it for protection, but now the idea of plunging it into someone who deserved it was a satisfying fantasy that he allowed to play out in his head.

Ever since that conversation with Ben, Michael's suspicions had grown, reinforcing his desire to *do* something. But he also felt an equal sense of impotence at his inability to follow through.

Driven by a mix of desperate feelings, Michael approached the house from the side and entered the backyard. Adrenaline coursed through his body, heightening his senses and causing his skin to tingle. The dirt yard was cluttered with weathered yard tools and an old rusty bike, but there was enough moonlight that Michael avoided tripping over these hazards. He leaned against the side of the garage, under an oak tree. He had a clear line of vision into their kitchen, which was as black as the rest of the house. Through his shirt he could feel the cool aluminum siding against his spine—a sudden shiver ran through him.

He picked up a rock, weighed it in his hand, eyed the window. He cocked his arm back, prepared to hurl the rock through the window—but a light came on, startling him. Someone was home. He dropped his arm to his side, still clutching the rock. Michael could see Lucy O'Neil outlined by the kitchen light. Hair unkempt, haggard, she stood at the sink and stared out the window, right at Michael. He knew he had the cover of darkness, but it was still unnerving. His body tensed. To leave he would have to move past her line of sight. He pressed himself against the garage, trying to make himself invisible. As he did this he heard a noise from inside the garage—a thud—and then the vague sound of movement, something sliding across the garage floor. He held his breath, then glanced at Lucy. She hadn't moved. The kitchen light went out and she was gone. Seconds later, Michael slipped out of the yard and into the street.

As Michael crossed the street, he paused under a streetlight to look back at the house. An unmarked police car was parked a few yards down on the same side of the street, staking out Billy's house.

"Who's that? . . . And what's he up to?" the homicide detective seated in the passenger's seat said, pointing at Michael through the windshield.

Garrett King, the senior detective, looked where his partner was pointing. "I know exactly who that is."

Two days later, Phillip Bosco came into the store looking for Michael. Aziz was out, and Jeannie was working behind the counter with Michael. Phillip was off duty and wanted to talk to Michael alone.

As he stepped up to the tall cooler that held the sodas, Phillip caught his reflection in the sliding glass door and tried to relax his serious expression. It had developed over the past year and now seemed permanently fixed on his face. Wanting to counteract his benign baby face, needing to be taken seriously, he'd worked hard to cultivate an air of professional authority. His mother had even commented that he'd forgotten how to smile. Phillip grabbed a Seven Up and stepped back, waiting for the customers to leave.

When Phillip approached Michael, Jeannie, sensing something was up, organized and carried the loose delivery receipts into the back room.

"Got a minute?" Phillip asked.

"Sure."

"Can we step out?" Phillip tilted his head in the direction of the street.

Michael nodded. His mouth was dry. And his stomach rumbled from not having put anything in it all day except coffee. He stepped around the counter and on his way out grabbed a Yoo-hoo, calling to Jeannie, "I'm going out for a minute. I'll be right back."

She emerged from the back room. "Okay."

Outside, Michael pulled the bottle opener from his pocket and opened Phillip's Seven Up and his Yoo-hoo, then stuck the opener and bottle caps into his pocket. Michael took a long drink, freeing up the tightness in his throat.

They walked side by side, heading east on 112th Avenue. Phillip wanted to tell Michael that if someone had shot *his* mother, he'd do whatever it took to find that person and put a bullet in his head. And the day before, when Phillip had arrested the scumbag that he *knew*—but at that moment couldn't prove—had done it, he'd wanted to do just that for Michael.

"How you holding up?" Phillip asked.

"Fine."

"When I was a kid in this neighborhood I couldn't jaywalk without some neighbor ratting me out . . . It's changed."

"How?"

"I'm not sure, but it seems like people are so afraid of who might move in next door that they've shut their blinds tight. Stopped watching out for each other." Phillip leaned in and lowered his voice to make sure he had Michael's attention. "I *know* what you want to do. Don't! We've got it."

"You're a cop *and* a mind reader."

"Listen to me. I'm telling you this as a friend and a neighbor—and as someone who still lives with his mother. We've made progress. I arrested one of the guys that we believe was involved. We're holding him on drug charges, for now. We're searching for one other suspect. He's missing. But he'll show up."

"Are they brothers?"

"You're smart. I promise you, we'll put them away. Just stay clear. So you know where I'm coming from, the guy I brought in, he got a little roughed up resisting arrest."

Michael studied Phillip, measuring his sincerity, absorbing what he was hearing.

"I'm really not supposed to be here," Phillip said. "You

understand?"

"I got it."

The sugar from Michael's drink was making him light-headed, but also helping him digest Phillip's words. Michael stopped walking, but Phillip continued until he rounded a corner and was out of sight.

Forty-Two

"I DON'T GIVE A SHIT. FUCK SCHOOL!"

"Don't talk to me like that!" Aziz snapped, his face hot with anger. Michael hadn't returned to school, and Aziz was furious. There was no need for a discussion. He was staying at his current high school. They'd postponed moving into the new house until the thick fog that had swept over their lives cleared a little.

"You have to go to school, and that's it! This is your future. It's over—we can't change what happened And I need you to stay at home more." He paused, and then added, "I need you back at the store."

"It's not *my* store!" Michael spat out. Aziz sighed. This had become his son's favorite retort. Aziz tried not to bring up the store to avoid being assaulted by the caustic refrain.

"Give me your car keys," he demanded, his disappointment and frustration heavy in his voice.

"You want the fucking keys? Here, take them!" Michael's key ring—with his car, apartment, and store key—flew past Aziz's head and hit the apartment wall with such force they left a deep gash.

Michael slammed the door, ran down the stairs, and hurried back to Nancy's. It had been close to midnight when he'd left her. She told him that if he came back, she'd meet him in bed.

Michael had spent the last week hiding out at Nancy's. He found solace in her bed—making love or just holding her close. He would also get stoned to deepen the numbness he already felt and to shove the tragedy out of his mind. Even Nancy tried to tell him that he needed to go back to school. But Michael didn't want to hear it.

When he got to Nancy's, he hopped in the shower. The hot water should have felt soothing, but it didn't calm his mind, which was racing from thought to thought. He wanted to kill the people that had murdered his mother. And while the legal repercussions would normally have scared him off the idea, he had a burning desire to hurt them, to make them suffer. This obsession evaporated fear or logic from his system as readily as a steam iron evaporates water off a cotton shirt.

The water rained down on him from the shower head, and he watched as it rinsed off the soap he had vigorously lathered onto his tired body. Thoughts of Yvonne provoked him, and he grew hard remembering the delicious sensations of their illicit encounter, and in that moment he wanted to fuck her. Fuck the consequences. Fuck the store too. It loomed as this big burden, and he no longer felt compelled to take care of it as he once had. Sleep was fragile and intermittent, and he was weary of the conflict that churned inside him, painting his face sullen, deepening the dark circles under his dull eyes.

Naked, his hair still damp, he climbed into bed, careful not to wake Nancy. He lay on his side, his back to her, trying to let go, to settle in and get some needed rest. Nancy rolled over and hugged him, wrapping her arm around his chest, her face up against the crook of his neck and breasts pressing against his back. Michael could feel the motion of each of her breaths. This usually brought him great comfort, but tonight comfort eluded him. Tears flooded his eyes, and he started to cry. Despite every effort to stop himself, his body, the colliding emotions—the overwhelming grief took charge. It was not the crying of a man, but of a little boy, erupting, sobbing uncontrollably as his body shook and tears poured out of him.

Nancy held him tight as he cried like a baby in her arms. She whispered to him over and over, "It's okay, let it out." He cried for what felt like an eternity before he could even begin to compose himself, and it took even longer before he could string a coherent thought together. Throughout, Nancy held him.

When he could finally form words, he asked the same question over and over, one of the many that had plagued him since his mother's murder. "Why didn't I hear the fucking sirens that night? Maybe I'd have gotten there sooner! Why?—Why didn't I hear them?"

Nancy brought his head to rest against her breasts as if she were cradling a young child. "I don't know," she whispered.

Even after Michael stopped crying, he felt raw and exposed. He sat up in bed and shared with Nancy what an asshole he had been to his father, how he'd like to kill someone, and how his head rattled around—sometimes in a fog and sometimes so full of rage and nonsense that it felt like it was going to explode.

She reminded him that she fell apart not that long after her mother died. "I never felt so helpless in my life until I tried to take care of her," she said. "I remember the night I couldn't stop crying and tried chasing it away with a bottle of vodka." She paused for a few moments. "And then some guy came along, picked me up off the floor and gave me a bath, tucked me into bed."

Nancy told Michael not to worry about his father, that he could make things right with him in the morning. And that it would never really feel the same, ever, but in time the ache would fade a little. They made love. Michael wanted to be inside her, as close as he could, to feel her build with anticipation and then shudder and tremble with pleasure. He wanted to let himself go in her warm, welcoming body.

After Michael fell asleep, Nancy slipped out of bed and called his father. She assured him Michael was okay and that he had told her about the fight and how sorry he was. And that in the morning he'd come home and talk to him.

Aziz was annoyed. He had expected the call to be his son and wanted to blame Nancy for Michael's behavior. But before he could respond, she asked him in a sincere tone how he was.

At first Aziz had believed that Nancy would be good for Michael, give him some experience. She reminded him of an exciting and spirited woman with whom he'd had an affair while traveling in Italy, some years before arriving in New York and marrying Jamila. But recently he'd come to resent Nancy, and he believed she had too much influence over his son. He wished he had listened to his wife, because even though he hadn't let her say what she'd been thinking about Michael's relationship with this girl, he'd known how she felt. And remembering this upset him even more.

But Aziz was tired and lacked the energy to sustain his animosity. And Nancy *had* made the effort to call him. He decided it would be better to deal with everything tomorrow. So Aziz calmly said, "I'm fine," and ended the call.

Forty-Three

JELLY WOKE TO FIND HIMSELF LYING on top of a filthy mattress that smelled of stale puke. For all he knew, it could have been his vomit. He vaguely remembered getting sick on the shit that he and Billy had been using for the last few days. It was pretty nasty—not like the stuff he was used to. He had to plunge more of this shit through his veins than he usually did to get to the place he needed to be, and it made him puke.

He hadn't left this rat-infested, abandoned tenement for three days, not since he and Billy had crashed here the night of his mother's party, and his face was beaded with sweat from the stale, humid air that suffocated the room. His lips were parched, and they cracked and bled when he opened his mouth to yawn. His tongue felt swollen and stuck to the roof of his mouth. He couldn't work up enough spit to swallow, and when he did move his tongue around his mouth, he could feel the grit that had built up on his teeth. He lifted his head up and surveyed the room, wondering where Billy was.

Billy jumped the turnstiles, hopped on the subway, and made his way home. The shit he and Jelly had been using ran out early last night, and he was starting to get sick. The nausea was coming in waves. Billy was surprised by how bad he was feeling; he was accustomed to handling the time in between better. Maybe they'd just partied too hard. But it had been easy, his brother had come home flush. But now they had burned through all of Jelly's cash. Billy convinced himself that he just needed to get right, and then he'd back off a little. When he could focus, he'd help his brother get well too before his leave was over and he had to head out. But in order for Billy to get well again, he needed to raise some cash—so he'd left Jelly a note telling him to sit tight and he'd be back.

Billy peeked through the back window to be sure that his mother wasn't home. He was in no condition to see anyone, and if he ran into her, she'd call him out. He went right for her bedroom, pulled open the dresser drawer that neatly held her bras and panties. She somehow believed that her money was safe there. Billy, hands shaking, rooted through her undergarments to no avail. The envelope that typically held the five or sometimes six twenty-dollar bills she kept for emergencies was missing. Didn't she know this was an emergency? Maybe his drunk fuck of a father got to it. *Fuck*. What now? He'd have to resort to his old standby.

Billy went to his room and bent down deep in his closet and, from under a pile of old clothing and shoes, pulled out his old, beat-up leather mailbag, which he hadn't returned after he'd been fired. They never could prove he stole those checks from his route. He sat down on his bed, opened the bag, and pulled out his gun, which he'd wrapped in an old kitchen towel. He peeled off the towel and held the Smith & Wesson six-inch .357 Magnum. He tried aiming it out the window at a squirrel that was sniffing around their backyard, but his hand was shaking so bad he couldn't get a bead on the animal. Holding the gun reminded him of how heavy it was. When he bought it, he liked the fact that it was big, thought it added to the scare value. It was clear to anyone he pointed it at that it wasn't a toy. But it hadn't taken long for him to realize that it was hard to conceal on his skinny body.

The nausea was getting worse, and the shaking from his hands seemed to travel through his whole body. He stumbled into the kitchen, grabbed a beer out of the refrigerator, and went back to sit on his bed. He stuck a Marlboro in his mouth and, despite his shaky hand, successfully lit it. He eyed the gun and figured that after dark he'd scare a few tourists hanging around the theater district and pick up a few dollars. That had worked before. A few times he'd even been able to take advantage of some dumb hookers—he'd lure them into an alley and grab their cash. But with the way he looked now, he knew that any hooker who'd been on the street for more than ten minutes wouldn't fall for it. Besides, it worked best later in the night, after they'd made a few dollars. Same with the tourists. It was better to catch them after they'd gone to the theater and were walking off a late dinner, sight-seeing in places they shouldn't be. The later it was, the better Billy made out. But the way he was feeling, he knew he couldn't hold off too long.

Billy was getting twitchy. He needed to wait out the day but knew his mother would be home soon. He stood up and stuck the gun in his pants. It immediately fell out. "Shit." Billy dug through his closet again and pulled out a worn belt. He threaded it though his belt loops, missing a couple, and again shoved the gun down the front of his pants. This time it held. He realized he still couldn't go around like that, so he grabbed his brother's Army jacket off the other bed, figuring he had no choice but to wear it when he went out. Then Billy wrapped the gun in the jacket, took a few beers out of the fridge, and headed out the back door.

He cracked opened the garage door and slid under it, leaving it open just a little to allow some air to flow through. It did nothing to alleviate the oppressive heat and humidity that lingered inside like a thick wool blanket. The air in the garage was stale and smelled of gas from a broken lawn mower and old tires. The garage was filled with junk: old furniture, tools scattered about, and boxes of crap his father kept. Toward the back, Billy had arranged several boxes and an old blanket into a haven he could safely creep into and use, unmolested by the outside world. He settled himself in and swilled his beer in between the waves of nausea, trying to kill time.

Jelly found his way out of the hole he was in and went into the next room where he ran into the skanky waif who had offered to suck him and his brother off if they gave her a hit of their stuff. Jelly had declined the sexual favor but helped her out anyway, over the protests of his brother. He wondered how long she'd been there. If he hadn't walked in on her, he wouldn't even have known she was there. That's how quiet she was, and it gave him the creeps. She was all eyes and blinked at him wildly as he walked over to where she was sitting on the floor.

"You know where my brother went?" he asked. Jelly had found Billy's note, but couldn't make out his scribble on the torn piece of grocery bag. He planned on going outside and trying to read it in better light, although he was pretty sure the sunlight wouldn't change the illegible scrawl.

"He didn't check in with me," she said. "You scoring again?"

Jelly needed a fix. He thought of the two twenties he'd folded and tucked in his shoe, a habit he'd picked up from his mother.

"Never be without a little something in case of an emergency," she used to tell him.

Jelly was feeling it. "You got a reliable source?"

"Better than the crap ya had last night," she said.

Jelly thought about it for a second. He wanted to know his brother's intentions before deciding to use the last of his money. "Where can I find a phone in this shit hole?"

"The corner. Outside the store."

"Sit tight," he told her.

"Ain't no place for me to go."

Jelly let the phone ring twenty times, as if the first ten were just enough to wake up whoever was sleeping and the next ten were to give whoever woke up enough time to get to the phone. Billy's note didn't read much better in the sunlight, although Jelly thought he could make out something about Billy coming back. He hung up, then stepped into the store and bought a carton of orange juice, a six-pack of beer, a pack of cigarettes, and asked for extra matches. As he walked back to the tenement, Jelly pulled the juice out of the bag and drank from the carton. He decided he'd wait a little longer but would probably need to trust the skank to score for him. He wasn't sure when Billy would be back, and if he didn't come back soon, before Jelly had to make his way home, he'd need to get right.

Billy was in pain. The beer had run out and his shakes had returned worse than before, seizing his body. He was pissed about how long the day was. He needed it dark. A little before eight he decided to leave. Most of the light had been squeezed out of the day, and the gray haze that was left was steadily turning darker, as if someone were slowly turning the dial of the sky's color palette. He figured by the time he made it to the City, it would be dark.

Billy snuck out, stood in the shadows next to his garage, and took a piss. When he was done, he zipped up and tightened his belt, then stuck the gun in the front of his pants and threw on Jelly's Army jacket. The gun's handle still stuck out a little, but at this point he wasn't thinking about anything other than getting to where he was going. He pulled out his last cigarette and crumpled the empty pack, throwing it on the ground. He checked his pockets for matches, but no luck. He eyed his house, but there was no way he was going in there, so he headed in the direction of the subway.

As he passed the grocery, he peered in. There were no customers in the store and he needed a beer and cigarettes. Michael's mother was behind the counter, straightening out the candy rack when he went in, and her back was to Billy as he grabbed a can of beer out of the case and placed it on the counter. That and a pack of cigarettes were all the seventy-three cents in his pocket would buy him. Before she could turn around, he called out, "Pack of Marlboro!" She bent down to get the cigarettes out of the rack, and Billy was overtaken by a wave of shakes. And as she swung around to place the Marlboros on the counter, Billy's shaking caused the Army jacket to open, revealing the gun.

She gasped and stepped back from him in fear. Billy hadn't planned to hold up the store, but it was too late to worry about that now, and in a surprisingly swift motion he drew his gun out and thumbed back the hammer—a skill he'd developed during his muggings. The sound of the hammer being cocked added to the intimidation factor. He stretched out his arm and pointed the gun at her. The gun barrel made little circles as he did his best to keep his shaking hand steady. "Gimme the money and no one gets hurt. Okay?"

She didn't move. Her eyes grew wide. She was frozen with fear.

"Come on, lady, just give me the fucking money and I'm outta here! I don't wanna hurt you!" Billy knew her and she knew him. But at that moment—he didn't want to know anybody.

Her eyes fixed on the barrel of the gun, she finally, slowly, started to move toward the cash register.

Billy was losing his shit, wondered why he even pulled the stupid gun. But he was on automatic now and couldn't turn back. He needed to remember to get matches. He wanted a cigarette in the worst way and this stupid bitch wasn't moving fast enough. "Fuck! Come on, lady!" The stress was taking a toll on him.

Jamila pulled out what few bills were in the register and knew immediately that her son had already prepared the deposit. This only added to her panic, but what could she do about it? She stepped to the counter, getting only as close as she needed to hand Billy the money, then took a deep breath and stuck out her hand.

As Billy extended his free hand for the bills, he started shaking. And at that same moment, the headlights from a car making a wide turn flashed through the window and a dog started barking somewhere nearby. Billy's gun went off, and the bullet hit Jamila in the center of her chest, knocking her to the floor. The money floated onto the counter.

"Fuck, oh fuck. What the fuck happened . . . ?"

Hyperventilating, panicked, Billy scooped up the money, shoved the gun back in his pants, and ran out the door, head down.

He saw a tall figure crossing the street toward the store, so he veered right, heading in the other direction. Good, someone will call an ambulance. She'll be okay. He circled around the block and then headed for the subway. *Fuck! The matches!* What an asshole. He didn't even grab the pack of cigarettes off the counter.

Jamila lay bleeding under the open cash register drawer. She felt like she'd been hit by a speeding car. Her chest burned. It was hard for her to breathe. She could hear an alarming rattle deep inside each time she took a breath. She stared at the plaster ceiling, her thoughts muddled . . . how did she end up on the floor? The back of her head throbbed, and she remembered hearing a loud pop . . . *Is Michael okay? Where is he? Is he hurt?*

Jelly waited as patiently as he could for the rest of the day. He didn't know why, but late evening, when darkness fell, was always worse for him. He'd learned that the skank's name was Jill. She came from Raleigh, North Carolina and moved here to live with her older sister—who was a secretary at some large insurance company—until her sister caught her fucking her boyfriend and threw Jill out. She was explaining to Jelly that she really didn't fuck him as much as he forced himself on her. And that her sister was always a bitch and jealous of her anyway, because growing up, her sister was the one with a weight problem.

Jill's prattling was in equal parts distracting and adding to his headache. He could see how maybe when she cleaned up she could be pretty, but as it was now, she blended into the city like any other emaciated junkie he'd pass in the street. Jelly suspected that his brother had fucked Jill, which could have been one of the reasons Billy had such contempt for her. That's how he was with women. He had a talent for talking the best-looking of them into bed and afterward treating them like shit. Jelly didn't understand it.

Night was falling, and Jelly couldn't wait any longer; he needed to get high and would have to trust Jill to score for them. But he didn't trust her *that* much, so he followed closely behind her when she went to find the dealer. It took her longer than expected to ferret him out, and Jelly didn't like the neighborhood where she was knocking on doors, trying to locate this guy. It put him on heightened alert, like he was back in-country. When Jill finally made the deal, Jelly stayed back and watched, and as soon as she took a step away from the dealer, he ran up and grabbed her and made her hand over the dope.

Back in the tenement, Jelly needed to use Jill's works since Billy had taken his with him. He sat down on the floor with his back against the wall, tapped the white powder onto a bent spoon, and added a few drops of water. Then he heated the spoon over a flickering candle. After filling the syringe, he wrapped the belt around his bare arm, pulled it tight, and searched for a willing vein. He took a deep breath and released it slowly, trying to still himself. Then, with practiced ease, he stuck the needle into his exposed vein, plunging the cloudy fluid into his blood stream, setting himself free once again. Jill was right, it *was* good shit—he could feel the warmth rush through him. He rolled onto the mattress and nodded off.

Jill took the needle out of his limp hand and followed him. She lay down close to him on the mattress. She liked Jelly more than she had let herself like anyone in a long time. He was a decent guy. He let her get high on his supply and didn't expect anything back. She wasn't used to that. If she didn't have to degrade herself sexually in some way, she'd have to beg to the point of humiliation before she'd get thrown a taste, if she were lucky. It felt good having the warm body of a decent guy up against her.

Billy climbed the steps of the Forty-Second Street subway exit, rounded a few street corners, and scoured faces and movements, looking for likely targets. Despite how much pain he was in, he needed to score some additional money. He owed his dealer more than the few dollars he picked up off the counter. Billy stuck his gun in the face of two unsuspecting victims and scored another $186, and a few pieces of jewelry. He sure gave those tourists from Kansas something to tell the family back home. Why couldn't it have happened that easily in the store? It was her fucking fault for hesitating the way she did.

Billy jumped back on the subway and headed for the Bronx, where he got even and hit up his dealer. "Hey, how 'bout better crap than the last shit ya' handed me?" he snapped.

After pocketing the money Billy owed him, the dealer eyeballed him and then nodded. Billy watched as he moved to where he kept the primo stuff and grabbed several wax paper bags. "Here, go easy with this, it's the real shit."

Billy was jonesing too much to wait until he walked the couple of blocks to where Jelly was holed up. His dealer didn't let anyone he didn't know real well use in his apartment, but he let Billy step into his back room and get right. Billy sat for a few moments, allowing the rush to clear his head of the shit that had gone down earlier that day. Despite his euphoric fog he somehow managed to remember his brother. He knew he had to be hurting, so Billy carefully refilled his spike.

When Billy saw Jill lying next to his sleeping brother, he got incensed. Enough was enough! He stepped up to the mattress and kicked her hard. "Get the fuck out of here!"

"Shit! That fucking hurt, asshole. What did you do that for? I just helped your—"

"Shut the fuck up." Billy pulled out his gun and pointed it at her. "I'll shove this up your fucking pussy and pull the trigger if you don't get the fuck out of here *now*."

Jill knew better than to mess with a mean junkie pointing a gun at her. She crawled on all fours until she scooted past him, then stood up and ran out. Billy heard her hiss, "Fucking asshole," as she cleared the room.

Jelly had opened his eyes during the ruckus, but looked confused.

"Jell, I got something sweet for you." Billy got down on his knees and took Jelly's left arm. He wrapped the belt tightly and searched for a vein.

"Hey bro, I'm cool," Jelly said, just above a whisper.

"You will be." Billy found a good vein and stuck in the needle he'd prepared, slowly releasing the good stuff into Jelly's arm.

Jill poked her head back in. "Hey! Hey, don't—" But before she could finish what she was trying to say, Billy jumped up and shouted, "Shut the fuck up!" and chased her out of the tenement.

"I'll take care of you now, you ugly cunt!" He didn't need her ruining his high. Aggravated by the events of the day, Billy was determined to get rid of her, and he chased her for two blocks before he gave up. When he got back to the tenement, Jelly was dead.

Forty-Four

Garrett King, the detective in charge of Jamila Haddad's murder case, was a stocky man with a heavy Brooklyn accent. When he sat, his shirt stretched tight over his stomach, buttons straining like they were ready to pop off. His face still bore faded acne scars left over from his adolescence some twenty years earlier, and gray had begun to creep past his temples and pepper his light brown hair.

"Billy O'Neil killed your wife. He's going to prison for a very long time." This is how Detective King presented the news to Michael and his father. It was a little after 8:00 pm, but they'd decided to close early in order to meet with him in their upstairs apartment.

Garrett paused a moment to check the reactions on their faces as he sat across from them in their living room, then lifted the small, ornately designed coffee cup with his stubby fingers and took a sip. Garrett's tone wasn't cold, but retained an undertone of official distance.

"Anyway, Billy tried to pin it on his brother."

Michael just watched and listened; he wanted to know every detail but was also guarded against allowing any of the news to strike too deeply.

"Andy's dead. He overdosed. We actually have a witness that has accused Billy of killing him. It's the same witness that gave Andy his alibi. He was with her when your wife was killed."

Michael was caught off guard by someone calling Jelly by his real name. No one ever called him Andy. It was like Garrett was talking about someone else. He was also sad to hear that Jelly was dead, but that feeling was immediately followed by a rush of guilt because it felt like a betrayal of his mother—and then *another* rush of guilt because he'd wanted Jelly dead. He'd thought retribution was his to mete out—and of course he hadn't, he couldn't—but it wasn't Jelly who killed his mother. It was Billy.

"The gun was on Andy's body, Billy's attempt at trying to stick his brother with the killing. He's a real scumbag. He'll fit in *real well* where he's going."

"Did he confess?" Michael asked. Detective King turned to him.

"Officer Bosco arrested Billy on a drug charge a few days after the shooting. So we already had him in custody. When Andy turned up dead, we charged Billy with both murders, knowing that his brother's would be hard to prove. The witness is a junkie and . . . well, who knows where she'd be when trial time rolls around. We used his brother's death as leverage to get him to admit what happened. We offered to cut a deal: If he copped to your mom's murder, we'd drop the charges on his brother's."

Garrett paused and took one last sip of his coffee.

"In Billy's statement, he claims that he didn't mean to kill your wife. The gun went off accidentally. It's the kind of bullshit we hear a lot. But . . . he really didn't have anything to gain by killing her. So who knows? Anyway, it's over."

Over. Aziz filled with sudden despair. No longer would the face of the man that killed his wife be blank, a mere silhouette—as it had been those many sleepless nights when he'd imagined what the last moments of his wife's life had been like. This stark news filled in the shadows, added vivid color to an otherwise abstract black-and-white picture. Not knowing had allowed him to *keep* it abstract. These facts, this news, made it all too real.

Michael was overwhelmed. Maybe it hadn't completely sunk in . . . but why did hearing this news feel so anticlimactic? Hadn't he been desperate to know what happened? Wasn't this what they'd been waiting for? The phone rang. The sound startled Michael and he jumped up to answer it with every intention of telling whoever it was that they couldn't talk. It was Freddie.

"Dad, it's for you. It's Freddie. He says it's important."

Detective King stood up. "Take the call," he urged Michael's father. "I need to get going anyway."

Forty-Five

SCHOOL WAS A DRAG, BUT MICHAEL SETTLED into doing what he knew was expected of him. He and his father fell into a routine, a schedule where they passed each other coming and going, implicitly acknowledging each other's separate worlds. Michael informed his father of his plans to attend college. This was all Aziz wanted now, for his son to be educated, something he himself was not. Michael had requested applications for various schools, including NYU, and he'd also made it clear that Nancy was helping him with the process. Aziz wasn't fooled; he knew Michael was using this excuse to spend more time with Nancy. But it still worked, allowing him to dismiss his son's behavior.

There was one significant change between father and son. They let each other know where they were at all times, regardless of where that might be. Now when his father visited Shelly, he told Michael. He still refused to allow Michael to spend the night at Nancy's during the week, but weekends were acceptable as long as he showed up for work. And Aziz ultimately came to terms with Michael working a reduced schedule. Jimmy had become a good employee, and it had been Jimmy and Jeannie who'd come in early the day after the police were done and cleaned up the bloody floor.

Aziz never discussed that night with Michael, preferring to grieve in private.

Aziz immersed himself in his new business venture, spending more and more time with Freddie now that their partnership was sealed. Freddie had heard about an A&P in Bethpage whose lease was up, and that A&P had no intentions of renewing. This was a real supermarket, fourteen thousand square feet with six registers—and a hefty payroll to meet. It was a great opportunity for both of them, and they'd begun negotiations with the owners of the building.

Because of the oppressive Israeli military occupation in Palestine, and to be close to Freddie and Yvonne, Freddie's parents moved to New York. Samir helped Yvonne at their store while Freddie was off doing business with Michael's father. Michael knew there were times when she was alone, and he sometimes considered visiting her, but decided that it probably wasn't a good idea. He'd gone over to their house with his father several times, though. His dad wanted him to hear what they were working on, wanted his son to be a part of it, wanted his input. But Michael couldn't have been less interested. In fact, the thought of grocery stores left him a little nauseated.

Yvonne had welcomed Michael warmly, as usual, but when Freddie and his father were engrossed in their conversation and too distracted to notice, she would gaze at Michael with a yearning that he hoped was only obvious to him. He could feel her loneliness, but he didn't know what to do with it. He still thought about being with her, but he was conflicted. His desire for Yvonne was still very real, but that desire collided with his fear of betraying Freddie and

Nancy. On their last visit, when his father and Freddie had been comfortably out of earshot, Yvonne had reminded Michael that the men got together on Tuesdays to play poker. "You should come over and keep me company. We can go for coffee like we used to." The thought of being alone with her sent an excited shudder through Michael, and he told her that he'd like that and said he'd try to stop by on an upcoming Tuesday.

He wasn't just being polite either, because as wrong as it may have been—and as guilty as even the *idea* of spending time with her made him feel—being with Yvonne continued to tug at him. Maybe this was a test of his love for Nancy. He resolved to spend as much time as he could with her. She was headed back to school soon, and he had a disconcerting feeling that once she left, he'd lose her to someone who was worthy of her.

Forty-Six

THE LEAVES SPLASHED DIFFERENT SHADES OF ORANGE, red, and yellow. Summer's humidity had long since suspended, and the temperature was comfortably cool, a sweet, clean crispness to the air. Fall was Michael's favorite season—and they were in the middle of it—and yet time couldn't pass fast enough for him. Even though he was worried about losing Nancy to school, he was beginning to think that getting out of this place wasn't such a bad idea.

When Michael arrived at Nancy's, there was a white truck parked in front of her house with "Conte's Construction" painted in dull, black flat lettering on the doors. Two guys, one burly and the other short and squat, were there to pick up the barber chair, some furniture that Louie wanted, and some other things that Nancy had no use for. Michael watched as they loaded the heavy chair onto the truck, sorry to see it go.

Nancy wanted to carve jack-o'-lanterns, so she'd bought two pumpkins from Bianci's vegetable stand in the Village. She covered her living room floor with pages from the Daily News, and she and Michael sat down on them and drank from a jug of Gallo Chablis to help them get in the mood.

"Why can't we just buy them already cut?" Michael said.

Nancy's face contorted into a sourpuss expression. "That's no fun! My mother never let me do this because she didn't like the mess it made. So be sure to make a *big* mess."

"That'll be easy." Ignoring the knives Nancy laid out, Michael slid his switchblade out of his pocket and hit the button, releasing the blade.

"I wish you'd throw that thing away," Nancy said.

"Now? I finally found a good use for it."

Nancy shook her head, but was in too good a mood to get into it with him like she had when she first found the knife. It had scared her, and they'd had one of their first big arguments. She understood why he felt comforted by it, but didn't care for the violence it represented—plus, it was illegal for him to carry, and she didn't want him to get in trouble if he was stopped and searched by the pigs.

Michael turned the large orange squash in circles. "I don't even know where to start."

"Looks like we found another important skill for you to learn before you leave home," Nancy said, and then told him she had a new album she wanted to play for him and one other surprise: two tabs of acid for later. She said she tried dropping a tab once with Roger, but didn't like it, and he had kept pressuring her to try it again, but she had refused.

"I had this friend at school, she'd drop acid and go to class," she told Michael. "But the first time you drop acid, it's important to be with someone you trust."

Michael watched her work on her pumpkin with a delicate, creative touch and a childlike enthusiasm. He hacked away at his like a new cub scout given his first hatchet. Nancy's pumpkin turned out like something displayed in a Macy's window (that is if they displayed pumpkins in Macy's windows—Michael wasn't sure) while his looked like something from *Night of the Living Dead.*

Nancy put her new album on the phonograph and lifted the arm so it would repeat. They sat on the sofa and swallowed the two tabs of acid. That night Michael fell in love with Janis Joplin; her throaty, soul-rendering, bluesy voice took hold of him, touched him like no other vocalist ever had before. She filled the air with raw emotion and pure feeling. When she sang "Summertime," it vibrated, tingled deep inside him, making falling in love with her easy.

As the album played, the sound of the music became heightened, lights grew brighter, items in the room appeared in vibrant color, smeared into stretched oblong and bloated shapes, as if he were looking into one of those trick mirrors at a carnival. Things took on different shapes and sizes, billowing out of proportion and then blending together. The pumpkins glowed without candles, and at one point it looked like their orange faces were throbbing. Michael and Nancy made love with heightened pleasure and intensity. Their senses were electric, and it seemed like they could make love all night.

At some point they went upstairs and continued their lovemaking until, exhausted, they finally fell asleep some time in the early morning. At least Michael thought he was asleep. Until he found himself outside the store, watching blood seep from every crack and pore of the building's brick exterior. He ran inside and—as if the flood gates of a dam had been let open, releasing thousands of gallons of water—thick, bright red blood was pouring in, filling the store, rising faster and faster. It covered the counters, the displays; it rose quickly over his head. Michael held his breath as the blood filled his nostrils, and he was pulled down by a strong undertow. The suffocating, drowning sensation frightened him awake, and he sat up abruptly, breathless, shaking, soaked in sweat. His heart was beating as fast as a racehorse crossing the finish line at Belmont. Nancy was sleeping peacefully next to him.

Michael took a few deep breaths and slid out of bed. He splashed cold water on his face in the bathroom and shuffled down the stairs—*Cheap Thrills* and Janis were still playing. He turned them off. The cold air felt refreshing on his naked body.

He sank into the sofa and suddenly flashed back to a night when he had occupied that same seat. While his mother was being killed. The memory constricted the muscles in his throat, in his chest, choking him. Each breath became shorter, allowing him only small gasps of air. He felt like he was having an asthma attack. He flushed, hot, all over. *What if I'd left sooner? What if I'd told Nancy no? What if I'd handed her the bag and gone right back—my mother would be alive!*

Michael continued to take slow, shallow breaths until his breathing developed a normal rhythm. He looked around the room, trying to distract himself from his claustrophobic thoughts. It was a mess: sticky pumpkin pulp and seeds all over the place, their crumpled and scattered clothes lying on the floor. He smiled slightly at the sight of it, at how they'd played like little kids. Then he noticed his pumpkin—his switchblade was plunged into it. He tried to remember sticking the knife in it like that and leaving it there, but couldn't. He stood up and pulled the switchblade out of the pumpkin, then sat back down on the sofa, studying the knife in the palm of his hand for a few moments. He tightened his grip on it and leaned over, and—touching the point to the floor at a 45-degree angle with the blade away from him—he stomped on it with the bare heel of his foot until it snapped it in two.

Frankie's Italian Cafe was a small restaurant with red-and-white checkered tablecloths, fresh Italian bread with a sharp crust, and a small menu of rich, homemade food that tasted like you were eating in an Italian grandmother's kitchen. Frankie's was famous for their pizza, but when you saw what was being served to the other customers, you forgot about the pizza and ordered from the other side of the menu. Tucked away in a nondescript brick building between a hardware store and a barber shop (that Michael had been successfully avoiding), the cafe had only a dozen tables but was always packed and did a brisk takeout business. It was Michael and Nancy's favorite restaurant. They had a special corner table and if it was occupied, they'd often wait. The family that ran the business had come to know them, and the wait staff didn't hesitate to serve Michael a glass of Chianti, even though he wasn't eighteen yet.

Michael was a little surprised they were going again so soon, since they'd been there last Saturday with Ben and Janet. Michael could eat there every night; it was Nancy who liked to pace their visits because the food was rich and fattening. Since going over to their house that first time, they'd been out with Ben and Janet on several occasions and enjoyed their company. Ben continued to encourage Michael to consider NYU and offered to do whatever he could to help him. Michael was beginning to feel a little like

Ben's project, but he was still flattered by his interest and allowed him to write a letter and contact a few people on his behalf. With Michael's GPA he could use all the help he could get.

Since it was a Tuesday, they were able to get their favorite table without a wait. Winter was still a few weeks away, but it was already cold, which made the restaurant's warmth even more inviting. Michael already knew what he was going to order, the linguine with clam sauce. It was an impressive combination of clams, garlic, white wine, and extra virgin olive oil served over long, flat pasta. Added to that was a dash of red pepper flakes for kick, and parsley and a squeeze of lemon to finish it off. Nancy liked to give Michael a hard time for not venturing beyond his beloved linguine dish. Michael's revenge was introducing it to Ben, who couldn't stop raving about it.

When their food arrived, Michael dug in. Nancy seemed distracted, but Michael dismissed it. She'd grown more introspective lately, and Michael knew from experience it was better to back off when she got that way—on a couple of occasions he had questioned her relentlessly, close to the point of exasperating her. She insisted that these moods didn't have anything to do with him, so he tried to give her space when it seemed like that's what she wanted, as difficult as that sometimes was.

So he was completely relaxed, savoring each rich bite of his pasta, when she blurted out, "I've never lied to you, but now I feel like I am."

Michael stopped eating mid-bite, swallowed, and held his breath. His mind raced with the possibilities, he braced himself, here it was—she was seeing another guy or she'd finally realized he was too young for her. His appetite vanished as his insides clenched.

"I'm not going back to Columbia in the spring."

That's it.

"I was accepted at the University of California, Berkeley, and I'm leaving in January."

He was still holding his fork and spoon. He let both drop into the bowl of pasta.

"How long have you known this?"

"I've been thinking about it for a while," she said.

"How long?" he snapped at her.

"I started thinking about it late summer and applied for the spring semester. I should've told you sooner. I'm sorry."

He felt a surge of anger, but knew it was mostly hurt, a sense of betrayal. His eyes stung, readying to cry, but he successfully held back his tears. Nancy reached for his hand, which was resting on the table, but he pulled it away and tucked it under crossed arms.

"Please, let me explain, Michael. I was going to tell you, but then, with what happened—you were going through so much, it just wasn't a good time. And then as time passed it became harder, more and more difficult for me to tell you." Her eyes grew wide and wet, and she tentatively touched one of his arms, but he folded them even tighter. "I feel so bad because I never meant to hide this or to hurt you. I know that regardless of what I say about how this won't change what we mean to each other, you're going to take this on as if it's about us. It's not. It's about what's right for me, and I need your support."

"How can you say it won't change? You're moving three-fucking-thousand miles away!" he shouted, causing a few heads to turn at the tables closest to them. "I need some air." He stood up abruptly and walked out.

Outside, the slap of cold air tempered his shock. His need to cry passed, but a heaviness was settling inside him. After a couple of minutes, Nancy followed him out of the restaurant, carrying the leftovers in a bag. They walked to his car without exchanging a word.

When they arrived in front of her house, Nancy said in a quiet voice, "The other night when we were with Ben and Janet, talking about all the plans we have for the future, I realized I hadn't shared mine with you, and I want—no, I *need*—you to be excited about them for me, just like I get excited for you when we talk about *your* life and what you want to do with it."

Michael turned to look at her; a tear was running down her cheek. She opened the door but paused before getting out. "Are you coming in?" she asked.

"No."

"If you decide to come back, I'll be here."

For now. He wanted to say out loud, but didn't.

She stepped out of the car, closed the door, and stood there as he drove off.

Michael drove out of the neighborhood and onto the Belt Parkway and then merged onto the Southern State Parkway, not sure how far he'd drive or where he was going. He thought about taking a ride to the new house, maybe passing by Freddie and Yvonne's. It was poker night. But he kept pushing forward, the power of his car vibrating under him. He was closing in on ninety miles an hour and the rush felt invigorating. Signs flashed by for Meadowbrook Parkway and then Jones Beach. He could smell the salty ocean air. He took the exit and eased off the parkway, then slipped the car into one of the parking spots.

The cloud cover allowed only some smoky moonlight to peek through. The streetlights that lined the walkway cast beige semicircles onto the dark sand, and not far beyond that was the water's edge. Michael ventured several yards onto the sand, wanting to be close enough to hear the ebb and flow of the ocean as it lapped on the shore. The cold stung his ears and nose, and a damp mist blanketed him. He sat on the soft, clammy sand, listening to the sound of the waves while he filled his lungs with the chilly air, and tried to hear a rhythm, if one existed, in the back and forth rush of the seawater.

Michael replayed the events of the evening, pictured Nancy's sad face and pleading eyes as she made her appeal. He thought about Yvonne and how tempted he was and how close he had come, if he wasn't there already, to his own private betrayal. He shifted a bit on the sand as his thoughts muddled on, but no magic answer manifested for his congested emotions, no real clarity. His mother was right—he cared too much. But she was dead. He couldn't tell her she was right, he couldn't tell her he was sorry, he couldn't tell her anything at all. He had absolutely no control over what happened around him.

After a while Michael began to feel silly sitting there, like he was acting out some melodramatic scene in a bad movie. He felt suddenly eager to head back and see Nancy, to not waste any more time now that it was limited.

As he got to his car and was about to climb in, he looked back at the beach, and Steinbeck's *The Winter of Our Discontent* came into his mind. He had just finished reading it. The beach was where the protagonist, Ethan Hawley, ended up after his own moral decline, and it was where Steinbeck chose to end his story. As Michael drove back carefully, Richard Harris's "MacArthur Park" played on the radio, and the long melancholic ballad, with its odd lyrics, suited his mood perfectly.

Nancy was in bed, unable to sleep—hoping, straining to hear the sound of Michael's footsteps climbing the stairs. Now that she'd let him know she was leaving, she was flooded with feelings, and was questioning whether going to Berkeley was the right decision. She cared for Michael more than she ever expected to. She remembered the first time she saw him as more than just the store clerk across the counter: he'd knocked on their front door, and as brief an encounter as it was, Nancy had been struck by his face. Young, kind, not yet hardened . . . but beyond that there'd been a connection. He had seemed like a kindred spirit, someone like her.

She was relieved when she heard Michael finally enter her bedroom. He undressed quietly in the dark and slid into bed next to her, pulling her close. "Promise one thing?"

"What's that?" she asked.

"Promise me you won't join any communes."

"Promise."

Nancy took a deep breath and let it out gradually, and with it the anxiety she was holding onto. Their bodies settled into the bed. She rested her head on Michael's chest as he held her, and they both fell asleep.

The next day Michael skipped school and spent the day with Nancy. His father gave him shit for sleeping over on a school night and not taking his education seriously. "Don't be foolish," he reminded Michael. "It's your future." Michael told him what was going on, and while his dad said he understood, Michael suspected that he was glad Nancy was leaving.

The time after Nancy's announcement flew by, and on New Year's Eve, they decided to brave the Times Square crowd and watch as the ball dropped, ushering in 1969. They wanted to share something that neither of them had ever done before, something that might be fun and might bring them better luck for the coming year.

Louie and Nancy had discussed the idea of putting their parents' house up for sale in the summer. Louie wanted to wait until then in case this school thing in California didn't work out and Nancy wanted to come back, so he found a family he trusted who wanted to rent it.

On Saturday, January 18th, Michael drove Nancy to Kennedy Airport and waited with her at the gate.

"I got you a small gift," she said.

"You already got me something." She'd bought him Tom Wolfe's *The Electric Kool-Aid Acid Test,* which—after he'd read it—had made him worry even more about her decision to go to California.

"No, this is something small." She pulled a black-and-white composition book out of her carry-on, the kind he remembered using in elementary school.

"Here," she said as she handed it to him. His confusion over her gift was a nice distraction from his sadness.

"Thanks, I guess," he said, trying to sound grateful.

"I wanted to get you a journal, something you could write in, but I couldn't find anything. They were all girly, you know, diaries—like little girls keep."

Michael just stared at the black-and-white splattered cover.

"Write in it. You know, your feelings, dreams, stories, whatever you want," she instructed.

"I know what a journal is."

"Good. Use it."

They kissed goodbye, holding each other tight, and as their faces touched, Michael felt her tears mingle with his. And then he watched Nancy until she entered the jet bridge and the door closed behind her.

Forty-Seven

For Michael life had gone flat. Like January 2 after the holidays and parties were over, when all the preparation, thought, and energy put into those few days with loved ones, surrounded by life and joy, had become just a memory. Now it was back to the dull routine of everyday living. He felt empty; an undeniable energy was missing from his life now that Nancy had left.

His father's negotiations with Freddie over their new grocery store were coming to a close, which meant that his father would have to sell their store. And he was talking about finally moving into the new house, which had been ready for months now.

Nancy wrote often and Michael wrote back not as often, but they spoke on the phone at least once a week. Before she left, Nancy had made Michael promise that he would visit her in the summer. She wasn't planning to return home since she'd lost a year of school caring for her mother and wanted to attend summer classes to catch up. Michael had agreed, and though he'd meant it at the time, somehow he felt it wouldn't happen. When he imagined visiting Nancy—picturing himself as the little boyfriend from back home surrounded by her new college friends—it made him feel small, and like he would be out of place in her new life.

Beyond his insecurity about being the younger boyfriend, Michael didn't want to meet her new friends. He didn't want to wonder who she might be with, because before Nancy had left, they'd had *that discussion*, the one where they'd agreed that they should be open to new relationships.

Michael held out until the fifth Tuesday after Nancy left to make his first visit to Yvonne. Earlier that day Michael casually brought up poker night with his father. "Why can't I play?" he asked.

"It's not for you," was the response.

Michael continued to question his father, asking him who goes to those games. His father provided Michael with a few names of uncles and cousins, including Freddie.

"Is Freddie any good?"

"Not bad." And then after thinking about it, his father added, "He's too careful sometimes."

Since Michael's father always told Michael where he'd be, Michael knew the game was not at Yvonne's and Freddie's that night. He also knew that these games could last until two or three in the morning. Satisfied, he changed the subject and asked when his father wanted them to move. His father said, "Start packing," and that they'd be moving within the month. He also told Michael that he'd found someone who was serious about buying their store.

Driving out to Yvonne's, Michael convinced himself that all he wanted to do was talk to a friend, someone he enjoyed being with and could trust. Freddie and Yvonne's house was an older two-story three-bedroom with a finished basement, and was only a few blocks from Michael's new house. Yvonne had decorated it simply, and Michael thought it had a homey, comfortable feel.

Michael stopped at a 7-Eleven and sat in his car, having second thoughts. But then he jumped out and called Yvonne. He told himself that he wanted to make sure she was there, forgetting that he'd spoken with her a few days ago and mentioned that he might stop by.

"Where are you?" she asked as soon as she heard his voice.

"Oh. I'm on my way. I just wanted to see if you needed anything."

"No, just you. Come. I'm waiting."

Michael swallowed hard. "Okay, bye."

Michael drove the last few blocks with nervous anticipation. And despite taking pride in his ability to always park evenly against the curb, he scraped his car's tire. In his head he kept repeating, *She's just a close friend, that's all. She's a great friend. A close friend.*

Whatever he was trying to talk himself into on the way over was gone in a flash of heat the minute she dead bolted the lock and hooked the chain across the door behind them. They reached for each other and kissed with a feral hunger, and then without saying a word, they were on her living room sofa. The only light came from a small table lamp, which created flickering shadows on the floor that mirrored their every movement. "White Room" by Cream was playing softly from a small radio in the corner.

Yvonne undid the buttons on Michael's shirt, kissing down his chest. He eased Yvonne's blouse up over her head and unhooked her bra, releasing her soft, full breasts. Michael kissed and cradled them. She was even more exquisite than his imagination had painted her. Yvonne unzipped his jeans, reaching in to touch him, to hold him. They made love without speaking, the only sounds their moans and sighs of sexual satisfaction.

After their lovemaking they lay holding each other, still saying nothing, their clothing littering the floor next to them. Yvonne's head was buried in Michael's chest, and he could feel the rhythm of her warm breath against his damp skin. Michael kept expecting to wake up from this dream he imagined he was having. The quiet progressed into an awkward silence, and he was unsure of what to do or say next. There was no going back now.

"Are you okay?" Michael asked in an almost whisper. He wanted to ask her if she was sorry it happened. He wanted her to be sorry, so he could say he was.

She let out a sigh and whispered, "Yes."

Michael began to get anxious about them entangled together, naked, on her sofa. "We should get dressed." They both sat up. Yvonne's face glowed pink from the heat they'd generated, and her eyes were shiny with tears. A couple broke loose and rolled down her cheek.

"Are you okay?" he asked again. Then it dawned on him that if she'd been okay, this wouldn't have happened. He pulled her close and kissed her lightly on the lips and cheek, tasting her salty tears.

"Crazy, huh?" she whispered.

"Yeah."

Michael was at a loss. He moved his lips in an attempt to say something, but nothing came out. Yvonne put her fingers on his lips, letting him know nothing else needed be said at that moment. Feeling her fingers linger there stirred him.

Yvonne stood up and began to dress. Michael watched as she put each item of clothing back on, wanting to stop her, to make love to her again. But he was coming to his senses, waking up to the magnitude of what they'd just done. When Yvonne went upstairs to the bathroom to freshen up, Michael quickly got dressed.

She was gone for what seemed like a long time, and Michael sat nervously, the radio playing in the background. Alone with his thoughts, he imagined what a fucking disaster it would be if anyone found out. He felt both ashamed and amazed—and when he thought of Yvonne naked, aroused.

While he waited, he took inventory of each piece of furniture and all the decorative items in the small living room. This room was seldom used. The basement with its large family room was where they entertained guests, and Michael couldn't recall ever sitting on this sofa before. As his eyes darted around the room, Freddie and Yvonne's wedding picture, which was sitting on top of a small table, jumped out at him.

Michael stood up suddenly and moved to the bottom of the stairs. "Yvonne, are you okay?" he called, then started up.

"I'm fine," he heard her say, but he continued climbing. Yvonne met him at the top of the stairs. She had brushed her hair and touched up her makeup, and there was a relaxed glow about her. They came back together and kissed intensely, reigniting their passion.

Yvonne broke away, took some deep breaths, then wiped the fresh lipstick off Michael's mouth and said, "Let's go downstairs."

Yvonne was in the process of making coffee when she suddenly stopped what she was doing and went to the front door—where she undid the dead bolt and unhooked the chain. Then she put out some homemade *ma'amoul*, Arabic cookies filled with dates or walnuts and finished with a sprinkle of powdered sugar, and sat down at the small Formica kitchen table with Michael. They sipped coffee and nibbled at the cookies.

Michael glanced at the big round black-and-white clock on the wall. 12:20 am. If Freddie arrived home now he wouldn't think twice about Michael being there. Freddie knew that Nancy had just left for school and that Michael had been missing her. Freddie also knew that Yvonne had always been close friends with Michael, long before their marriage. That was the tough part, the part Michael tried not to think about. Freddie's trust was a given.

As they sat across from each other, there was a new, awkward, closeness. Neither of them knew what to expect or how to handle what happened. Michael extended his hand across the table and caressed Yvonne's. She had long slender fingers that she kept perfectly manicured, and her hands were soft. The grind of her daily work hadn't caught up with them yet.

Yvonne's expression grew soft and tender, and she said quietly, "It's important—really important—not to hurt anyone."

A discomfiting thought struck Michael: hadn't they already? Then he remembered something Nancy had gone on about . . . *if a tree falls in the forest and no one's there, does it still make a sound?* It was something like that anyway. But it dawned on him that Yvonne was the one most at risk of getting hurt, the one who had the most to lose. And that thought scared him. He felt responsible.

"Maybe we should stop. Not let it happen again."

Yvonne squeezed his hand and shook her head, then gave him a reassuring smile. "We'll be careful."

Michael nodded but wasn't convinced.

"I always seem to want what men have," she said.

"What do you mean?"

"Freedom."

"But things are changing."

"No. The outside world might be, but not the one I'm in."

As Michael drove home, filled with a guilty energy, he relived the intimate moments he'd shared with Yvonne and tried to understand what she was feeling. Yvonne was more vulnerable than he'd ever realized. And then a thought smacked him like the swift crack of a policeman's nightstick—*What the fuck am I doing?* He desperately wished he could talk to Nancy about this.

Forty-Eight

BEN GOT A PROMOTION INTO A NEW DEPARTMENT that was putting a high-tech stock fund together, one with high expectations. Given the rumors after Michael's mother had been killed, and that it was hard for Ben to walk by the store without remembering that night, the promotion was all Ben needed to put his house up for sale. He and Janet planned to move into the City. During Michael's Easter holiday break, Ben invited him to his downtown Manhattan office for lunch. He wanted to show Michael what life could be like if he decided on the world of finance.

Michael was impressed by Ben's large corner office on the thirty-sixth floor—it had a great view of the skyline—and by all the polished-looking professionals. Ben took Michael around the different departments of the firm and introduced him to more people than he could possibly remember, treating Michael like a brother. The trading department, where the stockbrokers sat, caught Michael's attention; it buzzed with energy, and as he watched the manic swirl of work, Michael understood how someone could get swept up by this world.

For lunch, Ben took Michael to a French bistro and suggested he try the eggs Benedict. This was Ben's way of returning the favor for the linguine and clams dish. Ben ordered a Cobb salad for himself; the egg dish was a little too heavy for him since he was going back to work. It was Michael's first experience with eggs Benedict, and he was amazed at what could be done with an egg, Canadian bacon, and an English muffin. The tangy, buttery, golden-yellow sauce melted in his mouth. The businessmen's chatter, the restaurant's fastidious setting, and the expensive menu all added up to an appealing display of refinement.

"Congrats on NYU," Ben said. "They'll be lucky to have you. You figured out what you want to do? What you want to study?"

"No. But I figured out a few more things I *don't* want to do."

This elicited a wry smile from Ben. "You know, Wall Street is a lot like what you've been doing in that grocery of yours. Selling stuff."

"With all that's happening in the world, it seems out of touch. Like I'd be selling out."

"Is that you or Nancy talking?"

Being called out like that caught Michael off guard. But he had to admit, these ideas did come from discussions with Nancy, and sometimes the four of them—Ben and Janet, Nancy and Michael—had gotten into heated debates about them.

"This one's me, Ben. I'm still not sure what it is I want to do, but I'm hoping that whatever it is, I don't know . . . makes a difference." Michael was surprised by his confession. He hadn't said this out loud to anyone before.

"A worthy ideal, Michael. But in business, you create jobs that employ thousands of people, which keeps the economy going. And that makes a difference."

"I hear you," Michael said, "but I was thinking more along the lines of how your wife makes a difference. I actually had a couple of teachers that I paid attention to, who had something to say that I cared about. They got me thinking, even when I didn't want to be there. Now that I think about it, that was pretty cool."

"You have plenty of time, so don't feel rushed into making a decision. And when you're ready, I'll have a desk waiting for you."

Hanging out with Ben must be what it was like to have a big brother, one that rescued you from bad situations, one that protected you from yourself.

Ben's expression brightened. "And you never know, I might run into you at school. I've decided to go back at night and get my MBA."

Aziz was consumed with the activity of his business. He continued to see Shelly, but the tragedy that made him available also placed a new and unexpected pressure on what they shared. One night Aziz, holding a bag of groceries, tapped lightly on Shelly's door. But there was no answer. Shelly sat inside in the dark, sipping her third vodka and fighting her desire to open the door. Aziz tapped again. Still no answer. He placed the grocery bag down in front of her door and left.

Aziz sold the store, which was timely since he was committed to purchasing the new supermarket with Freddie. They were scheduled to take over the new store on July 1.

It amazed and scared Michael how comfortable he was around Freddie. Was he one of those people who don't have a conscience? Was that why he was so at ease? His handling of the affair was nothing like he had originally imagined it would be: his face wasn't a flashing neon sign saying, "Hey, I'm fucking your wife!"

Maybe it simply had to do with protecting Yvonne, ensuring that she didn't get hurt. A good liar is someone who believes his own truth.

The new owners were eager to take possession of the store, and the Haddads needed to be completely moved out by the first of May. Michael's father had already given away most of the old furniture from the upstairs apartment, having purchased the furniture Michael's mother picked out for the new house—including a new full-size bed for Michael. But even though they'd been living in the new house for a while now, Michael kept his small bed at the apartment, along with a few other belongings. He'd stay there sometimes during the week to avoid the long commute to school.

Michael could still feel his mother's calm, warm presence in the small apartment, but especially in the kitchen where he'd become proficient at making coffee in her old pot. He had even woken up one night to something that sounded like his mother's sewing machine stitching away. Once the new owners moved in, he'd only have five weeks of high school left before graduation.

"It's lame. I don't want to do it," Michael said.

"Stop being foolish. You worked hard, and I'm proud of you. You have to do it," his father insisted.

"You just want me to go through that ridiculous, pompous ceremony so you can invite some of our boring relatives to stare at me. And then they can tweak my cheek and say how proud of me they are!"

"What the hell's the matter with you? What's the big deal? This is an important day," Michael's father snapped back.

"I don't want to. Can't you understand?"

"Why? Just tell me *why*."

"I don't know, okay? I just don't want to." Michael did know, but couldn't say. Yes, a part of him thought the whole ceremony was bullshit, but the truth was, the only person he'd have endured such nonsense for was his mother. He couldn't bring himself to think about her not being there.

His father, sensing that there was more to it, suddenly changed tactics. He told Michael that he'd given a lot of money to all the graduating relatives over the years, and if they had a small gathering, he'd have a chance to get some of that money back for Michael. It was a return on investment for him. So Michael struck a deal with his father: he would go through with the ceremony and his father could invite one family to it, and then Michael would show up at the house for a family gathering where his father could invite a handful of relatives.

His father told Michael he was going to invite Freddie and Yvonne. But at the last minute Freddie's father, who was going to mind the store, couldn't make it. So it was only Yvonne. Michael felt like a little kid during the procession. But after the ceremony, when his father was off having a cigarette, Yvonne gave Michael a tight hug and whispered in his ear the sexual things she'd thought about doing to him while she watched him walk up to the podium to receive his diploma.

With the help of some aunts and Yvonne, his father had arranged a small party at their new house. Michael was relieved that the whole pomp and circumstance thing was over, but as he stood there surrounded by extended family, watching their proud, boisterous behavior, he came to the realization that he felt at home with them, that they were his people. He also realized how much they all had been there for him and his parents.

Michael had a couple of beers, which helped him relax. His aunts had prepared platters of traditional Arabic foods, but Nancy was right—none of it was as good as his mother's.

Forty-Nine

MICHAEL AND YVONNE HAD MOVED their lovemaking to her guest bedroom, where they would escape together and indulge in their private world. Their illicit romance filled different needs for each of them, and their desire for each other required compartmentalizing their lives. They learned and enjoyed each other's bodies, deepening the physical and emotional connection they had skirted around for years. (Though, given their circumstances, if it had remained unfulfilled, time probably would have facilitated its passing.) Their newfound intimacy was more satisfying than Michael expected, especially considering his long-standing yearning for Yvonne. And he came to understand one thing with certainty: some boundaries get tested and broken regardless of good judgment and the best intentions.

Michael and Yvonne had only been in the kitchen for few minutes when they heard the sound of the front door opening and Freddie's keys being tossed on the table in the hallway. Freddie wasn't having much luck at cards that night and had decided to call it quits. He was pleased to see Michael, glad that his wife had company when he was out for the evening. Michael stood up to leave, but Freddie insisted he stay a while longer. "Have you heard from Nancy?" Freddie asked him.

"I talked to her yesterday."

"You should stop by the new store. We just hired a cute cashier. *Helwi eketeer,*" Freddie said, raising his eyebrows.

"I'll do that. I'll stop by."

Yvonne, who was standing behind Freddie, rolled her eyes at Michael.

"Yes, Michael, you should go and meet her," she said.

"Um, another thing," Freddy said, hesitant. "Your father and I talked about you . . . about you coming back to work."

Michael immediately pulled back—his father had agreed that he could have a few weeks off before he had to work. Michael had finally taken out the journal Nancy gave him and was planning to write down some of the thoughts rattling around in his head. He'd pictured lazy days reading at the beach, seeing Yvonne whenever he could, catching up with Ben and a few of his cousins—and in general, at least for a short while, not being run by a clock. He'd even entertained the idea of visiting Nancy, although as time went on, that prospect grew more dim. And not because of Yvonne. In fact, he was surprised by his ability to separate his feelings for each of them. When he and Nancy had discussed the idea of seeing other people back in January, Michael couldn't even conceive of the idea. And yet here he was.

"I don't know . . . I was sort of looking forward to some time off." Michael tried not to sound too irritated.

"Here's the thing," Freddie said. "I need to be at the new store, and I don't like to leave Yvonne alone. My father is getting too old. We wanted to ask you to work with her, just a few hours a day. You know, during the busy time, maybe help her close."

Okay, now, take a deep breath. Don't seem too eager. But before Michael could respond, Yvonne jumped to his defense.

"Freddie! Michael has things he wants to do. He spent years in his father's store. Let him have a break."

Michael was surprised by her sharp response.

"I know, I know, we just wanted to ask him. It's up to him," Freddie said defensively, and then added, "You know I don't like you being there alone, especially at night."

"It's okay," Michael said. "I understand. I do. Let me think about it, okay?"

"It's up to you. It's your decision," Freddie said.

"Don't do it," Yvonne countered.

"It's okay, I'll think about it. Really, it's okay."

The next day Michael called Yvonne at her store, careful to pick a time when he knew Freddie would be out. When Yvonne picked up, he mimicked her words from the night before: "Don't do it!"

"You're going to, aren't you?" she asked, sounding concerned.

"Yes, boss."

Working together was fun, playful, and felt like the natural next step for them. Michael couldn't believe how comfortable he felt with her considering the whole shameful arrangement. They flirted, but they also had some serious discussions. Yvonne opened up, sharing her unfulfilled dreams, her growing acceptance and appreciation for what she had. She talked about what a kind and gentle person Freddie was and how much she'd grown to love him. How she would rather die than hurt him. She asked Michael if that made sense to him, and he said it did. It raised questions he didn't dare ask, but he certainly understood her not wanting to hurt Freddie.

She made Michael's head swell with her whispers: how handsome he was, what a wonderful lover, and how he made her feel like a woman. If all that were true, she had Nancy to thank. Nancy was the one who taught him to appreciate a woman's body, to be gentle, to take his time, and when Yvonne would say those things, he'd miss Nancy even more.

Fifty

MICHAEL'S FATHER CALLED TO TELL HIM he was planning to stay at Yvonne's parents' house for the night. They lived in Bethpage, close to the new store. He and Freddie were working late, and then everyone was going over there to watch the big event. Yvonne was planning on joining them after she and Michael closed, but he didn't feel like being with family and told his father that he planned to meet some of his cousins for a drink, since it was a Saturday night. Yvonne tried to encourage him to come along, but Michael assured her that he was fine and drove home.

Since the move to their new house, Michael had been making an effort to be more social and occasionally got together with his cousins for a drink or to go to a club. His cousins were decent guys, focused on doing well in business or school, and hanging out with them helped distract Michael from thinking about how much he missed Nancy—or what the hell he was doing with Yvonne. But tonight he just wanted some time alone.

Michael picked up the mail and went in the house. The smell of fresh paint and new carpet had faded away, but there was still something stiff and unused about the place, like a baseball mitt before it had been worked and softened. The furnishings were sparse, and Michael and his father still hadn't hung any pictures. The new furniture wasn't nearly as comfortable as the old. There was too much wood trim on the sofa, and Michael missed the overstuffed softness of the old, broken-in one.

There was a letter from Nancy. In it she reiterated how disappointed she was that he wasn't coming to visit her, but that she'd try to understand, with him having to work in the new store and all. She quipped that selling the store was one way of getting out of the neighborhood. She wrote that she was excited for him starting school, and that she'd be coming home for winter break—staying with Louie in Jersey—and couldn't wait for them to be together. She loved San Francisco and had met a lot of really cool and interesting people that she thought Michael would like.

She had generously peppered the line, "I miss you," throughout the letter. Michael counted nine times, and each time he came across one, he felt like even more of a loser for lying to her. She had also enclosed a picture of herself standing next to the Volkswagen Bug she bought shortly after moving there. It was a stick, and it had taken her a few road trips before she finally stopped grinding the gears. Michael focused on her radiant smile as she stood next to her light blue bug, wondering who took the picture.

Hungry, Michael laid the picture down on the coffee table and went into the kitchen. He opened the refrigerator. The only time it had been full was right after his graduation party, and when he closed the door, he could hear the echo of the interior light shutting off. He should have stopped to get something to eat on the way home. A cheeseburger deluxe sounded perfect, so he drove to the diner several blocks away and ordered one to go. As he was standing there waiting, he noticed two couples sitting in a booth who seemed to be having fun. Facing him was a gorgeous blonde with big blue eyes and a short haircut like Joey Heatherton's. Michael couldn't take his eyes off her. She noticed him staring at her, and when her date slipped out of the booth and headed to the restroom, she gave Michael a big flirty smile. She was very sexy, and he was both embarrassed and flattered. *Maybe she's with her brother.* But that idea was dispelled the minute the guy came back and kissed her. Michael paid for his food, and as he was leaving he saw her glance at him one last time.

Back at home, Michael turned on the television. He laid out some old newspapers to make sure grease wouldn't drip on the new, expensive coffee table, and then sat and slowly ate his cheeseburger and fries, chasing them down with a bottle of Coke, while he watched the news. It was all about tonight's big event, which was still an hour away. And the network was planning on covering it live: the first manned moon landing.

After he ate, he felt like having some coffee. His father had bought—or been given—an electric percolator, but Michael preferred his mother's old coffee pot. He planned to pack it when he left for school. He now drank his coffee black, mainly because they never had fresh milk around. There was still an hour to wait, so he lowered the volume on the television, placed his full pot of coffee on the coffee table, and took out the journal Nancy gave him. He felt like writing, sorting his thoughts by committing them to paper, but wasn't sure where to start.

Michael's first attempt at unfettering his thoughts only resulted in him recognizing how clogged they really were, and like liquid pouring into a funnel much too fast, his feelings overflowed, flooding and splashing everywhere. He needed to sort his thoughts out a little at a time. He kicked off his shoes and stretched out his legs on the coffee table and sank into the sofa. With his BIC pen in hand, he wrote down some names: Mom, Nancy, Yvonne,

Dad. And then he added, in big bold letters, "STORE" and "NEIGHBORHOOD." *Hey, that's pretty good; I remember how to write,* he thought. But he knew Hemingway's ghost wouldn't be visiting him any time soon with words of encouragement.

The first anniversary of his mother's death was a month away. Shortly after that he would be leaving for school, still uncertain what he'd do when he got there. If he listened to Ben, he'd end up another suit in his office. Michael's life had felt uneven ever since they'd sold the store. Maybe he missed the daily routine; maybe he still hadn't adjusted to the change. His gaze landed on *"Mom,"* and he felt a wave of deep shame. If she were alive, maybe he wouldn't have let himself go as far as he had with Yvonne.

Despite the coffee, Michael's eyes grew heavy and the sofa underneath him more comfortable. Michael wasn't sure exactly when he fell asleep, but he'd never had a more vivid dream. He was back in the apartment over their store, and his mother was making him breakfast. His father wasn't there. His mother finished preparing the eggs and put them in front of him and then sat down next to him, as she'd done his entire life. He began to eat.

"Hey, Mom, they're landing a man on the moon tonight, you want to watch it with me?"

She looked at him with her soft, warm eyes, and as she did he could see the corners of her eyes crease ever so slightly, the way they always did when she smiled at him. "I've already seen it."

"You have?" Michael said, feeling disappointed.

"Yes. This time you'll need to watch it alone."

"Okay, Mom. I will."

She smiled at him, apparently pleased with his response. And what struck Michael, what filled him with a comforting, warm feeling, was that she looked truly happy.

Michael's eyes opened and the television was fluttering with a snowy picture of Apollo 11 on the moon. He glanced at the clock. 10:55 pm. A minute later, Neil Armstrong became the first man to set foot on the moon. Like millions of others, Michael sat there and watched in amazement as Neil took that first step, saying, "one small step for a man, one giant leap for mankind."

When the phone rang a few minutes later, Michael stood up and his still unused journal dropped to the floor. Maybe he could cut out the first page and return it, get back the thirty-nine cents Nancy paid for it. It was probably his father, checking to see if he was watching.

"Hello?"

Nancy's voice rang clear. "Did you see it?" she asked with her trademark enthusiasm. Michael could hear a buzz of people in the background.

"I did!" He was excited to hear her voice.

"I'm here watching this corny stuff with a bunch of people and all I keep thinking about is you. I know if I were home we'd be watching it together. I miss you so much!"

"I miss you too. More than you know," Michael said.

"Hey, did you ever find the note I wrote you? It was in the journal I gave you at the airport."

"Note?" he asked, embarrassed.

"You probably didn't even open it."

"I did! In fact I was writing in it tonight."

"Yeah, sure, I believe that like I believe a man walked on the moon." She laughed and added, "I don't want to go, but I have to," and then shouted through the phone. "I love you!"

"I love you too!" he shouted back.

Michael sat back down and picked up the composition book. He flipped through it.

On the second to last page, Nancy had written:

> *While there have been others, you were truly my first. The first I trusted my heart with. The first who was worthy of it. I feel fortunate to have you in my life. And no amount of distance or time can separate me from my love for you. You allowed me the naïve indulgence of loving without prejudice or qualification. You are a tender and loving soul, and I now know how fortunate I am to share in something so rare and beautiful. You will always remain a part of me. Love, Nancy*

Her words filled Michael with a reassuring warmth and a poignant sadness. What a night. It seemed like one big dream. And the best part was seeing his mother happy, truly happy. He felt stupid for not finding Nancy's note sooner, but somehow wasn't surprised that it had been there all along, waiting for him. And the night started out with that really cute girl smiling at him; he wondered if she went to that diner often. And oh yeah, those guys landed on the moon. That was pretty cool, too.

Fifty-One

MICHAEL WAS STARTING TO REALIZE THAT BEING with Yvonne was selfish, and he knew he couldn't continue with the affair. As much as he desired Yvonne, he cared about her more. If they were caught, the whole thing would blow up into a big ugly disaster. And he'd be off at school, while she'd be stuck dealing with the fallout alone.

A week after the moon landing, Freddie and Michael's father were working late finishing up inventory, so after he and Yvonne closed, they went to their old diner.

"Remember how we'd come here and talk for hours?" Michael said. "We had to keep ordering food we didn't eat, so the waitress wouldn't get mad at us."

"Of course, that's when I fell in love with you."

Yvonne wasn't going to make this easy. Michael wanted to tell her about that night at the party when he had desperately wanted to follow her into ladies' room, but decided not to.

"Yvonne, you know I love you very much."

A wistful expression crossed her face. She was ahead of him.

"It's because I love you, I think we should stop."

"But I don't want to stop," Yvonne shot back.

"Yvonne, it's not that I don't want you. You're all I think about, but I'm afraid—afraid if we get caught you'll be put through hell. I don't want that to happen to you."

"Please, let me worry about that. What you don't understand—what you probably *can't* understand—is that I never believed I could do something like this. But it's what I want. You make me happy. You help me feel . . . well, like I'm stealing something, taking something I deserve." She paused briefly, lightened her tone a bit, and added, "Please don't worry, Michael. I'm not some naïve little girl. I know what this is—and it's what I want. Can you understand?"

"I think so. And when I'm with you, it feels right. But when I'm away from you and I think about the *other* people involved, I feel guilty. It feels wrong. And as much as I love you, we should stop."

She reached across the table and held his hand, something they never did in public—for obvious reasons. Michael's automatic response was to glance around and see if there were any diners that might know them.

"*Habibi*, I know. But this has nothing to do with other people. It has to do with me. It's what I want. I know I'm going to lose you soon, to school and whatever lucky girl you find out there. Until then, I don't want to stop being with you."

Michael squeezed her hand a little tighter.

Fifty-Two

MICHAEL AND YVONNE AGREED TO BE MORE CAREFUL, and they both accepted that their affair would end when Michael left for school. But when he was away from her, he felt haunted, and he questioned what he was doing . . . until the next time he was in her arms.

One early September afternoon, Michael went out for one of his occasional drives—the kind where you go by an old girlfriend's home to see if she's still there, hoping you'll get lucky, that she'll come out just as you're driving by and you'll get a glimpse of her. Or perhaps the kind where you go by a house you once lived in to see if it still looks like it does in your memories. For Michael, these drives were to a grocery store. The one where he'd left his mother.

This time, Michael parked the car across the street and went into the store. It looked different but smelled the same, like home—like how he imagined it would have been for Anthony if he'd come home from Vietnam and opened the door to the smell of his mother's cooking. When Michael headed over to the cooler to grab a Coke, the new owner recognized him and shouted, "Hi!" Michael waved to him and was about to reach in for the Coke, when he spotted a hole where the milk cartons lined up. Michael slid open the door and re-stacked the quart cartons, moving them from the back of the refrigerator to the front for easy customer access. He stopped and smiled to himself, wondering what the hell he was doing. Michael moved to the other side to grab his Coke, but stopped when a bottle of Yoo-hoo caught his eye. It had been a long time since he'd had one, and on impulse he grabbed the bottle.

After playing a game of reverse tug-of-war with the dollar bill he tried to pay the new owners with (he should have known better than to try and pay for something in the home of a fellow Arab), he took a sip of the Yoo-hoo and grimaced—much too sweet, sweeter than he remembered.

"Michael, is that you?"

He recognized that voice. Michael turned to see Officer Phillip Bosco out of uniform.

"Phil! Hey, how's it going?"

"What are you doing here?" Phillip asked.

"Good question."

"Got time for a beer or do you want to keep sipping on that?" Phillip asked, pointing to the Yoo-hoo.

Michael tossed the bottle into the trash bin.

"You're legal, right?" Phillip added.

"Does it matter?"

"No . . . not often I get time with a friend from the neighborhood."

"Turned eighteen a few weeks back."

"I'm just down the street. But I'm sure you remember, with all the times you delivered groceries to my mom."

Phillip opened two bottles of beer, handed one to Michael, and sat down across from him at the kitchen table. There were boxes stacked everywhere, some still open and waiting to be packed with the years of belongings that made up this household.

"How's your mom?" Michael asked.

"She's not doing well. Got sick. I couldn't take care of her anymore. I didn't want to, but I had to put her in a home."

"Sorry to hear that."

"Your dad?"

"He's good. Busy," Michael said, letting it hang out there for some moments before adding, "Hey Phil, I don't know if I ever said thanks for what you did."

"Just doing my job, Michael."

This caused Michael to smile.

Phillip pointed to the boxes, and said, "My turn to leave the neighborhood."

"Where're you going?"

"Transferred to Manhattan. Moving to the City with my girlfriend. Never thought I'd leave. Growing up here, and then on the job, it always felt like a refuge from the chaos, someplace solid, predictable . . . But I guess things change."

Michael was driving away from the store, Cream's *Disraeli Gears* playing in his eight-track, when he spotted a familiar figure walking toward him, head down as if he were counting the loose pebbles on the sidewalk. Same greasy brown hair. Same peacoat. The coat was a lot dirtier, but Michael would never forget it—even though the first time he'd seen it he'd been lying on the ground, taking a beating.

Joey looked fatter, softer, worn out. Michael pulled over and took the cartridge out of the player, then rolled the window down and shouted, "Hey Joey, you're back—you made it alive!"

Joey stopped and gave Michael a suspicious glare. "What's it to you?"

Michael stepped out of his car and went up to him. "You don't remember me?"

"Why the fuck should I?"

"That's true, why should you?" Not only was Michael taller, he'd let his hair grow out almost to his shoulders, and was now sporting a goatee and a pair of dark wire-rim sunglasses.

Joey studied the stranger's face that now blocked his path.

"Yeah . . . yeah, you're the grocer's kid," he said, looking pleased with himself now that he'd solved the mystery. He looked Michael up and down. "You look different."

"You don't." Michael said, and turned and walked back to his car. Michael wasn't sure why he'd stopped to talk to Joey. Maybe he'd wanted to say something ugly to him, maybe even hit him. But the need for revenge hadn't materialized like he'd imagined it would. Surprisingly, he no longer felt the anger and hate toward Joey that had been a part of him for so long. Something had happened to it. But what really surprised Michael was that he no longer felt fear of what Joey used to represent, as if that too had been excised. So what was left to be said? Michael shoved *Disraeli Gears* back into his player and drove away, "Sunshine of Your Love" blaring out of his speakers.

Michael, like thousands of other freshmen across the country, began to prepare for college. He moved his clothes, some books, and his mother's coffee pot to the dorm at NYU—even though there wasn't a burner he could use it on. When he was checking his room to see if there was anything he'd missed, he came across an old cardboard box full of his books. As he shuffled through them to see which titles he might want to take with him, he saw it. The childish keepsake embarrassed him, and he remembered stacking the books over it in an effort to hide it. Michael lifted the dirty, crusty old brick out of the box. He sat there for a moment, just feeling the cold weight of it in his hand. Then he stood up, carried it outside to the back of the house where the trash cans were, lifted a steel lid, and dropped it in.

Acknowledgements

THIS BOOK IS DEDICATED TO LEILA, my Palestinian immigrant mother. She died at eighty-six on Labor Day, September 4, 2017. She raised three children and had eleven grandchildren, and left us a legacy of love and generosity, a determined work ethic, and pride in our heritage.

I would like to thank my wife, Terra, and son, Paul, for their continued love and support. I'd also like to thank Joanna Barakat and Dave Datz for their friendship and early feedback on my novel, and Kristen Chavez of Articulate Editing for her brilliant editorial help. I also want to thank Sahar Mustafah and Safa Suleiman, two wonderful writers, for their generous friendship and encouragement. Last, thank you, Michel Moushabeck for including me in the Interlink publishing family.

About the Author

PAUL AZIZ ZAROU is an Arab American writer born and raised in New York by Christian Palestinian immigrants. Paul moved to Los Angeles early in his professional life, where he raised his family and now lives with his wife. Paul has had a thirty-five-plus-year career in technology sales and leadership and writes fiction and screenplays in his spare time. His love of literature, history, and politics is what motivates him to tell stories. As a writer, Paul enjoys exploring both the social and political landscapes of the past and the timeless complexities of family dynamics. *Arab American Blues* is his first novel.